May the Light of the
infant Savior guide you
always God Bless,

Dennis Hart

THE
PRINCIPALITY
A NOVEL BY DENNIS HOLT

The Principality

Published by Cornelius' House Ministries
3115 Pyburn Extended, Pocahontas, Arkansas 72455

ISBN 1- 892031- 25 – 6

For more information write: Cornelius' House Ministries
3115 Pyburn Extended
Pocahontas, Arkansas 72455

Or go online at: www.corneliushouse.com

To Brent, Denise, Mark and Luke

The Principality

Foreword

After I had finished writing a book, *Strategies of Spiritual Warfare*, I realized that most of the people who really needed the information would never bother to read a book of that type.

I prayed and asked the Lord to help me find a way that people in every day life could become more exposed to the knowledge of the reality of the spiritual realm and the impact it was having on all our lives.

As the evil continues to grow in our world, I am amazed at how few people, even Christians, understand that evil has a source. The killing of children by other children with guns is not by accident but by design. Each awful occurrence touched my heart and caused my anger to flare at the evil one who comes to steal, kill, and destroy everything, even little children.

As horrible as the news reports were that were coming into living rooms, most people failed to understand that Satan is determined to destroy as many souls as he can before the return of the Lord. He shows no mercy.

It was during a time of prayer that I heard the idea of exposing people to the truth by using the format of a novel. In my prayer closet, Father Rex Macon was born.

Every person in this novel is fictitious and if any similarities are assumed, it is only by accident.

This novel was written not to just entertain but to teach. Every incidence of spiritual warfare in the story is the result of eighteen years of fighting the tactics of the evil one. As bizarre as they seem, it is the truth. Satan is real and as you read this novel realize that he desires the destruction of every person on this earth, including you.

This novel is NOT fantasy. It is words of truth set to the rhythm of a make-believe tune. Evil is on the increase and we watch callously as its tentacles wrap themselves around us more and more in nearly every avenue of our lives. We cannot run. We have turned our heads far too long. We must understand the severity of the situation and come together to fight this evil predator.

There is no real Father Rex Macon, but there can be. In each one of us there is s small "sensor" that responds to truth, but only for a while. If that sensor solicits no response from the person, it will, over time, grow hard and stop responding.

As you read this novel, open your "sensor" and allow it to stimulate your heart. The eternal destiny of so many souls depends on their hearing the truth. Parts of this novel are happening close to us every day and yet we refuse to believe that the source of "our" problem could be spiritual in nature.

Every area of this world has a dark warlord assigned to it and his only mission is destruction. Unfortunately it is the sins of the people that give it strength and make it an evil tyrant over any area. NO location is unaffected.

Know that as long as these horrible spiritual creatures are left in place in the spiritual realm above our cities and towns, only a few are safe. Only those who have washed their robes in the Blood of the Lamb are exempt, but they, too, must know how to use the exemption. That is the purpose of Father Rex Macon. He knows and if we will listen, he will teach us. In Jesus' Name, we will come to understand how to defeat, The Principality.

CHAPTER ONE

THE SIGNATURE

"Father! Hey, Father Macon!"

Father Macon turned his head toward the direction of the voices and saw a couple of boys approaching from the direction of the highway. As they drew closer he recognized them as two of his parishioners, Billy Geller and Eddie Long. He waited on the steps of the rectory until they came within speaking range.

"Hey, fellows, what's going on?"

The two boys stopped as they came to the steps where the priest stood, and paused momentarily to catch their breath.

"Father," said Eddie, "we just came from Mr. Bowman's farm. There's a whole crowd of people over there. Something really strange happened to one of his prize bulls last night."

Father Macon came down the steps closer to the two boys. "Did someone shoot it, thinking it was a deer?"

"I don't think so, Father. The sheriff and everyone else were pretty closed-up about the whole thing, but one thing that we know is there were no bullet holes found anywhere in the bull. They have the whole area barricaded off. Seems some big shot from out of Little Rock is coming up to take a look at the area and they don't want people in there gawking around and stirring things up. The sheriff told everyone to go home and he would keep everyone informed of the details."

"Are they sure it happened last night?"

"Mr. Bowman says he checked all his herd yesterday evening and everything was in order, so Sheriff Martin said it had to have happened last night."

Billy nervously reached over and tapped Eddie on the shoulder and mumbled, "Come on."

"Father, we've got to run," Eddie explained. "Billy's got to be at work in an hour, so we'd better hit the road."

With that the two boys turned and headed back toward the highway. Father Macon watched them as far as the bend in the road as he pondered the information. As he stared down the road, the boys now out of sight, his thoughts went back to a year before his ordination. He had been home for a month's break when suddenly cattle in the local area began turning up mutilated. It never was talked about publicly, and people seemed bent on keeping it quiet. His younger brother had discussed the matter with him at some length before his death in the car wreck changed the focus for everyone, and after about three months the whole thing faded and nothing more was said or done. Helping the family deal with the grief from the accident and with the preparation for his ordination, he had not had the time to pursue the matter. He had not even thought anymore about it until today. His concentration was broken by the sound of the phone ringing in the rectory. He again climbed the stairs and unlocked the side door to the rectory.

"St. Mark's parish. Father Macon speaking. May I help you?" He spoke into the mouthpiece, as he quickly pulled it from the desktop.

"Father Macon?" the deep voice asked on the other end.

"Yes."

"Father Macon, this is Sheriff Martin and I'm here at Carl

Bowman's farm. It seems we've had something happen over here that we thought you might assist us in."

"Does it involve the dead bull?"

There was silence on the other end for a few seconds then the sheriff replied, "Uh, yes it does, but how did you know?"

"Billy Geller and Eddie Long were just by here and they told me about the strange goings-on at Carl's farm."

The sheriff, somewhat relieved, spoke again, "News sure travels fast in this small community. I don't think we could keep anything quiet if we wanted to."

"That's very true. How can I assist you?"

"Well," the sheriff stammered, "there are some strange markings on the ground in the area and it's nothing like we have ever seen before. Mrs. Bowman says you speak Hebrew, Greek, Latin, and a few other languages and we thought maybe you might have seen something like them before. It's really weird and we thought that you might add something to this."

The desperation in the sheriff's voice was more than enough to convince Father Macon that he could at least take a look. "I'll be there in about thirty minutes, sheriff."

"Thanks, Father," the sheriff replied, obviously relieved, "we'll expect you."

Father Macon walked to his bedroom, removed his clerics, and put on his work shirt and blue jeans. He called them his "knock-a-bouts". He rarely wore them in public because he knew the people preferred him in his clerics. Tradition was a powerful force and in this Catholic community it was everything.

As he climbed into his jeep and started the engine, the words of the sheriff echoed in his mind. Engleton was definitely a close knit community. It had been settled by German Catholics around the turn of the century and in some ways time had stood still for the people who lived there now. They were very strong in the tradition of their faith, but it seemed to make no difference in their day to day life. In the year he had been there he had not grown close to any family and the more he learned about the community, the more he realized how dysfunctional they were. He had learned of the abundant alcoholism in the area when he closed down the Holy Name Society which was nothing more than a front for Monday night beer drinking. Many of the men had become angry over the closure but had very few grounds to argue the case.

Spousal abuse, incest, thievery, and destruction of property were only a few of the problems that seemed to be associated with the small community, but for some reason the bishop had seen fit to place him in this parish. The first year had been a definite struggle, full of frustration and even questioning of his vocation. How could people profess to be followers of Christ and still choose to do so much evil?

Mr. Bowman's farm was only a couple miles from the church so the drive was relatively short and as Father Macon pulled his jeep into the Bowman's driveway he could see the sheriff talking with a man and a woman and Carl Bowman, the owner of the farm.

Father Macon pulled his jeep along side the sheriff's Bronco and turned off the key. As he opened the door the sheriff had already made his way over to Father's jeep.

"I really want to thank you for coming, Father. This is a strange one," he said as he extended his hand.

Father shook his hand. "I'll be glad to do whatever I can but this is not my usual house call."

The sheriff laughed and motioned for him to follow him, "I'd like for you to meet Miss McClain and Mr. Bellows. They're from the State investigation bureau in Little Rock."

The couple looked as if they were deep in discussion until they saw the sheriff and Father Macon approaching. They stopped their conversation and turned to face the approaching duo. Mrs. Bowman had called Mr. Bowman to the house for a phone call.

"Mr. Bellows," said the sheriff, "this is Father Rex Macon, our local parish priest."

Bellows extended his hand. "Phil Bellows, Father. It's nice to meet you. This is my partner, Jamie McClain."

"Hello, Father," she said, smiling as she too extended her hand.

"Very nice to meet both of you," Father replied. "What type of investigative bureau do you belong to?"

Jamie looked at Phil as if to see who should answer the priest's question, then with a sense of affirmation she said, "We deal mainly in areas of investigation that do not fit what you would call mainline. We're not in homicide or property destruction unless it shows some aspect of abnormality."

Father laughed. "This sounds almost spooky."

Jamie again looked at Phil, who now decided to comment. "As you are well aware, Father, things are sometimes not what they appear, and as public servants we have an obligation to give the public at least an attempt at an explanation."

"Like the reason for a dead bull in a rural town in Arkansas?" replied Father, halfway laughing again.

"Well," laughed Phil, lightening up a bit, "like they say, it's a dirty job, but somebody's got to do it. We have no idea what's going on here. Sheriff Martin called headquarters this morning and the chief thought we should come up and take a look."

That caused the sheriff to perk up and enter the conversation, "Which is what we really need to be doing folks. Father, neither Phil nor Jamie have been out at the site yet. Let's all go to the field and take a look. Father, why don't you take your jeep and follow us because you may not want to stay as long as we do."

"Sounds good," Father replied.

"May I ride with you, Father?" Jamie asked as Father Macon turned toward his jeep.

"I would be honored with your company," Father nodded as she hurriedly walked to catch up.

Father climbed into his jeep and hit the automatic door locks to open the lock for Jamie. She then opened the door and climbed into the passenger seat. They both fastened their seat belts and watched as the sheriff's Bronco pulled out in front of them and started back down the drive.

"What do you think we have here, Jamie?" asked Father, mainly wanting to get her to talk.

"I don't know, but cattle mutilation is definitely nothing new. We have probably two to five cases reported every year. We have never been successful, however, in finding an etiology or purpose. Some areas have seen two or three but, in most areas, it has been only a single occurrence."

"Has there been no speculation?" Father Macon asked as he turned his jeep into the field behind the sheriff's Bronco.

"Oh my, yes," Jamie exclaimed, "UFOs is a big one. Little gray men. Occult activity. Kids playing pranks."

"Which one of those do you subscribe to?"

"None really, but we've never been able to come up with a good solid answer that satisfies every aspect of every mutilation."

"Well, let's see if we can find a good one for this one," he breathed as he pulled the jeep along side the sheriff's Bronco and shut off the engine.

They could see the carcass of the bull ahead of them with the yellow boundary tape circumscribing an area about thirty feet in diameter. The bull was huge and obviously a very high quality animal. Its form lay in a heap on the field of Bermuda grass that had recently been cut for hay, so the grass was fairly short. Each of the four seemed to approach the animal from different points of view as if surrounding the scene.

"Father," the sheriff called, causing Father Macon to look in his direction. "Don't touch anything, please, unless we say it's all right. Evidence, you know."

Father raised his hand to show that he heard and that he understood, then moved closer to the animal. No one said anything as each one intently surveyed both the animal and the surrounding area.

Father Macon was the first one to break the silence. "Where's the blood? This animal has been gutted like a deer and yet there is no blood anywhere on the ground."

"There is none," Sheriff Martin replied. "Our preliminary team found no blood anywhere around here. There are no tire tracks which would indicate the animal was slain somewhere else and dumped here. Besides, Carl Bowman said this is the field the bull was in when he checked on him before nightfall yesterday. Our team also found that besides the blood, the penis, testicles, and heart are the only parts of the animal missing. 'Doc' Tanner, on the team, also said that whoever did this was no amateur but very skilled in butchery, or as he called it, animal surgery."

"What else did your team find, sheriff?" Jamie asked as she surveyed the head of the animal.

"Not much except for those two marks on the left side of the bull's head and what appears to be some type of markings there on the ground." He pointed to an area six to seven feet in front of the bull.

The area was about three feet in diameter and the grass had been burned until the bare earth was exposed. A circle was discernible just inside the dirt area with two distinct upside-down triangles at the top of the circle. The rest of the inner circle had been obliterated.

The sheriff turned to Father. "Aren't these Greek symbols of some kind pointing to the two triangles?"

"Yes, but double triangles are not anything of any significance in the Greek language."

As Father said that, his mind began to think back to his pre-priest days when he worked in archeology with Dr. Bremlar Michaelson. He had seen those double triangles before, but where? As hard as he tried, he could not remember.

"How about this, Father?" Jamie interrupted as she motioned for the priest to come over to the head of the bull.

Father Macon approached where Jamie was kneeling and looked over her shoulder at the two marks which had been cut into the flesh of the bull. They resembled two small snakes or SS's or two backward ZZ's. As Father Macon's eyes hit the two marks he remembered. His face grew pale and his head began to spin.

"Father, are you okay?" Phil yelled as he noticed the priest's pale complexion and countenance.

Phil's voice shocked the priest enough to allow him to catch himself and keep from falling.

"Father, what's wrong?" asked Jamie as she stood up and grabbed his arm, helping him to steady himself.

"I'm all right, thank you," he stammered as he grinned in embarrassment. "It's just been a long time since I have seen those marks."

"You know what language they are?" asked the sheriff.

"Oh, it's no language. It's more like a signature."

"What do you mean, Father?" Jamie asked. "Whose signature?"

"Have you ever seen a dog urinate on every tree in a certain area, or a deer during rut scrape the bark off of trees with their horns?"

All three shook their heads yes as they waited for further explanation.

"Well, those animals were marking their territory or their boundaries with their signatures. This may sound off the wall but these marks are the signature of a Babylonian principality."

"A what?" asked Phil.

"Every one of you have seen these marks before if you will just think," said Father Macon, excitedly.

Father Macon could tell by their blank looks that nothing was registering at all. "Come on. What was the signature for Hitler's Gestapo?"

"You mean the Secret Service?" Phil asked.

"Yes."

"It was the SS, but what does that have to do with this dead bull in rural Arkansas?" replied Phil, exasperated that Father was playing "20 Questions".

"Hitler was into the occult big time. His entire Third Reich was empowered by demonic power. His prized possession was supposedly the Roman spear that pierced Christ's side while he hung on the Cross. His Secret Service was so possessed that they became pure evil and the atrocities that they committed against people were unheard of in the twentieth century. The SS that they wore on their uniforms was a tribute to a demonic principality. It is the cuneiform signature of the demon called Syrasohan."

"Syrasohan?" questioned Phil. "You mean some Babylonian demon killed Mr. Bowman's prize bull? Father, I respect your knowledge and position, but forgive me if I don't throw my arms around you and give you a big hug for solving this case."

"Phil," Father said laughingly, "a demon did not actually kill this animal. But someone, or a group of someones devoted to this principality did. He was invited into this area and he took the invitation. He has announced his arrival to all spiritual forces and established the boundaries of his territory with the blood of this bull. His signature is on the left side of the head of the animal. Our word sinister comes from the old English word for left. Left means away from God; right means toward God. The head represents the ability of the animal to think and control the rest of the body. The reason you found no blood is because part of it will be drunk by the person or persons who invited the demon to the area and the rest will be used to mark the actual territory of the principality."

"Pardon my French, Father," stammered Phil, "but why in the hell would anyone in his right mind drink bull's blood?"

"Anyone in their right mind wouldn't," replied Father Macon, "but someone who was in their left, or away from God mind, would to obtain the power."

"What power?" exclaimed Phil. "Somehow I'm missing something here."

"Phil, are you a Christian?" asked Father Macon.

"No, Father, too many hypocrites for me to get involved," he stated boldly with a slight sense of arrogance or anger.

"I guess you never read the Bible much either?"

"I could never get much out of it myself."

"Well, in the beginning of mankind, when man sinned he broke a spiritual Law called the Law of Sin and Death. It basically stated that if man disobeyed God, which was sin, then death would occur. Because God also stated that the LIFE of the animal was in the BLOOD, then the blood was poured out of the animal as a sign of its life being poured out. That's the reason God had Moses and Aaron kill and sacrifice animals and pour out THEIR life to cover the sins of the Israelites. The blood or life of the animal atoned for the sins of the people. Jesus, when he hung on that Cross and shed his Godly blood, was removing the sins of the people and giving them back their true Godly nature or life. Every time I celebrate Mass, the wine, through the power of the Holy Spirit, becomes His Blood. We then drink His Blood and, in doing so, drink into us His Life. This is a spiritual principle and Satan teaches his demons and his followers to use this same principle but sort of in reverse. As they drink the blood of an animal sacrificed to a demon the demon infuses his power or "life" into them through the blood. This has been known and done since the beginning of man."

"Whoa, boy," said Phil, rubbing his face with his hands and turning to Jamie with a look of questioning. "Jamie, what do you think?"

"I don't really know. We've seen a few of these cases around the state, but we've never gotten to first base with any of them. They've always just faded into oblivion and been filed away as unsolved cases. I think this is at least a lead worth looking into. I understand from Father that he thinks this is definitely occult in nature. What he is saying may not make sense in a logical setting, but maybe we need to look beyond the logical. Maybe that's where we've failed in the past."

As she finished speaking, Carl Bowman's truck came up to the yellow barrier tape and stopped. As he hurriedly stepped from the truck everyone's attention was drawn to him.

"Father Macon," he said quickly, "Mr. O'Leary just called from the hospital and his wife is pretty bad. He wants you to come as soon as possible."

"Thanks, Carl," said Father as he turned to the others. "Well, duty calls and I need to change before I head to the hospital, so if you all will excuse me."

"We appreciate your help, Father," said the sheriff. "Thanks for coming out."

"No problem, sheriff. I hope I haven't caused more confusion than assistance."

Phil extended his hand to Father Macon, "It was nice meeting you, Father. I would like to maybe talk to you again if this case warrants it."

"I'm available almost anytime," Father Macon replied as he turned to Miss McClain and extended his hand. "It was my pleasure, Jamie."

Jamie grinned and held on to his hand for a few seconds, then squeezed it as she let go. Father turned and headed for his jeep. He climbed inside and as he started to back it up he saw Jamie running toward his jeep with her hand waving in the air. He stopped the jeep and rolled down his window just as Jamie got there.

"Father, I've decided to stay at a motel in town and rent a car. Phil is going back to Little Rock. Would it be possible to meet with you again this afternoon?"

Father reached into the ashtray, pulled out a business card and handed it to Jamie. "I should be back at the rectory sometime this afternoon. Give me a call about 3:00."

"Thanks," she said with a grin, "and thanks again for your help."

"I'm glad I can help. See you this afternoon."

He hit the button that controlled the window and turned the jeep around. Jamie watched as his jeep became smaller in the distance, then returned to the three men who were still discussing the case. They had decided that Jamie would stay and do some further investigation, but Phil and the sheriff would devote no more time to the case unless there were further developments. Sheriff Martin would help Mr. Bowman file an insurance claim for the bull and state that foul play appeared to be the cause of death of the animal.

CHAPTER TWO

THE APPARITION

Driving back to the rectory, Father Macon tried to think of the beauty of Jamie McClain rather than the horror that those marks had brought to his memory. He had not let on and he didn't believe anybody noticed, but this was some heavy stuff and he was afraid he was the only one who knew how heavy. He quickly pulled his jeep into the rectory driveway, changed into his clerics and once again climbed into the jeep.

It was about seven miles into the town of Bettis Bluff and another two miles to the hospital. He spent time praying in the spirit as he drove and listened for guidance from the Holy Spirit. He could sense that something was up and he continued to pray until he pulled into the parking lot of the hospital.

The ministers' parking spaces were around the corner from the emergency room entrance. As he turned the key in his jeep, he noticed a lot of activity at the emergency room driveway. An ambulance still had its lights flashing as two EMT's hurriedly carried a patient into the emergency room. As he stepped from the jeep, he heard the small Voice say, "Plead the Blood."

As he walked into the hospital lobby, he could hear the commotion coming from the emergency room. Looking down the hallway, he could see the nurses and technicians scrambling as if every second were vital.

"Good afternoon, Father Macon," came a voice that pulled his attention away from the emergency room flutter.

"Busy day, huh, Barbara?" he answered as he turned and saw Barbara Johnson sitting behind the receptionist's desk.

"Well truthfully, it has been pretty quiet up until now, but this one seems to be serious."

"I'm headed for Mrs. O'Leary's room. If anyone needs me, feel free to page me."

"Thanks, Father. If you're needed I'll yell."

With a nod of the head, Father Macon passed on through the reception area and headed back to where he knew Mrs. O'Leary was staying. Bettis Bluff Municipal Hospital was small with only one floor, and he had been there enough times to know his way around well. He found Mrs. O'Leary's room and gently tapped on the door. He heard Mr. O'Leary's voice say, "Come in," so he pushed the door aside and entered the room.

"I sure am glad you could come, Father," said Mr. O'Leary. "Momma isn't doing so well."

As he spoke his voice broke and Father Macon gently put his arm around his shoulders. He could feel the fear and the concern as Mr. O'Leary's body trembled in his embrace.

"I thought the doctors said she would be out in a couple of days after her surgery," Father said, as he turned and faced the bed which contained Mrs. O'Leary.

"She was doing so well until last night, and then suddenly she took a turn for the worse. The doctors are still unsure as to why the turn, but I know they're doing everything they can."

"I'm sure they are, too," Father replied, trying to add confidence to the man's positive statement. "Still, let's pray and put the Lord to work on this problem. Okay?"

"Oh yes, Father, most certainly. That's why I called you."

Father prepared his stole and removed his anointing oil from his pocket. He opened his prayer book and as he made the sign of the Cross on the forehead of the listless woman, he began to read the prayer of the anointing of the sick. As he finished he very quietly began to pray in the spirit. He then prayed softly out loud, "Lord Jesus, Your Word says that if we will speak to the mountain and not doubt in our heart that what we have said will come to pass, we can have whatever we say. So Lord, in the Name of Jesus, I speak to this problem that Mrs. O'Leary is having and I command that it loosen its hold on her. She is your covenant daughter, and I break this sickness over her right now in the Name of Jesus. Father, I plead the Blood of Your Son and her Savior over her entire body to heal and make whole and by Jesus' stripes she is healed."

As he finished praying he turned to Mr. O'Leary. "Let's stand in faith together that the Lord has done a wonderful work, and we wait for it to manifest in the physical."

"I certainly hope so, Father," the man said as he dried his swollen eyes, "I couldn't do without her."

"God knows that, Ben," replied the priest warmly. "As you sit here and continue to pray for her, thank God that she's healed. Can you do that, Ben?"

"Yes Father, I can and I will," he snapped with a sudden burst of confidence.

Just as he finished speaking the intercom came on and Barbara announced for Father Macon to go to the emergency room.

"Ben, I'll check back later. You remain confident in God's healing power, and I'll expect to see Martha up and about next time I see her. Agreed?"

"Agreed," he said. "Thanks Father, I appreciate your confidence."

Father Macon grinned, turned and again made the sign of the Cross on Mrs. O'Leary's forehead, then left the room.

Walking down the hallway, he could feel his spirit starting to "churn" and he again quietly began to pray in the spirit. As he rounded the corner toward the emergency room he nearly ran into Barbara.

"Barbara, what's wrong?" he asked as he could see the concern in her face.

"It's Larry Geller. He was the one in the ambulance a while ago. They've been working with him for a long time. He's only twelve years old but something weird is going on with his heart. Come on, his mom wants to see you."

Trying to listen to Barbara while she almost ran down the hall, looking over her shoulder, was quite a feat, but Father was able to get the gist of the problem. The boy seemed to be doing fine until midday, when suddenly, he just collapsed in the den while sitting on the sofa. His mom had called 911, and the EMT's were able to get him stable until just a few minutes ago when his heart started going into fibrillation.

Barbara was still talking as she opened the door to the emergency room and held it back for Father to enter. The room was small and was very crowded with people and equipment. Larry was on the gurney in the center of the room with an IV in his arm, an inhalation tube in his nose. His chest was exposed and covered with leads that went to a cardiac monitor. The monitor was beeping rapidly and the small screen was a constant array of tall spikes. Two nurses surrounded the child along with Dr. Verney. Mrs. Geller was holding onto the arm of her child and sobbing lightly. She was the first one to speak as she saw the priest enter the room.

"Oh, Father!" she exclaimed, as her sobbing turned into

anguish, "My baby!"

Father held her and patted her back as he looked into the discouraged face of the doctor. His look caused the doctor to speak.

"Father, I have given this child every medication I know to help his condition and nothing works. It's almost like he's not even receiving it. I don't understand it."

"Is it his heart?" Father asked, remembering the information that Barbara had relayed.

"Yes, but it does not respond to any medication I give him. If it doesn't kick in shortly his heart will give out. It just can't stand this rhythm."

"May I pray for him?"

"Please do," answered the doctor. "I've run out of options."

Father let go of Mrs. Geller and walked up to the head of the boy. He took his anointing oil out of his pocket and with his thumb, he made a sign of the Cross on the boy's forehead. "You spirit of death and devour, I come against you in the Name of Jesus. I command you to let go of the heart of this child and release your control of his spirit."

Suddenly the sound of the heart monitor began to decrease. Both nurses looked up at the priest as the doctor encouraged his actions. "I don't understand it Father, but keep it up, it's working."

"Father God," the priest continued, "I plead the precious Blood of Your Son, Jesus over this child from the tips of his toes to the crown of his head, and Satan, I proclaim you defeated!"

Just as dramatically, the child began to awaken and cough. The sound of the monitor continued to decrease until it began to exhibit a normal sinus rhythm. As the young man became more cognizant of his surroundings, he began to move on the gurney. As everyone tried to assure him he was all right, he opened his hand and an object fell to the floor. One of the nurses reached down and picked up the object and handed it to the doctor. He examined it closely then shrugged and handed it to Father Macon. As his hand touched the object he could feel the hair stand up on his forearm.

"What do you think?" asked the doctor. "Looks like some kind of bone or ivory."

"I'm not sure. It looks like a ceremonial object of some kind."

"You mean like African or American Indian?"

"Yes, something like that, but I don't know for sure. Mrs. Geller, have you ever seen this object before?"

As the priest finished speaking he handed the object to the boy's mother. She examined it closely then shook her head and handed the object back to him. He placed the object in his shirt pocket just as the boy on the gurney began to vomit. The nurses quickly helped him to sit up and one placed a small basin under his mouth. He continued to throw up until the nurses realized that they would need another basin. They scrambled around until someone found a new one and placed it under the boy's mouth.

"My gosh, son," stated the doctor as the boy finally fell back on the gurney exhausted. The nurses replaced the electrodes he had dislodged in the process, and the monitor continued to give a reading that indicated all was well.

Father turned and walked out of the cubicle and into the emergency room hallway. The doctor was quick to follow.

"What went on in there just now, Father?" asked the doctor, overwhelmed by the whole occurrence.

"I'm not sure. How much do you know about demonic activity?"

"Not much," confessed the doctor. "I was raised Baptist and they talked about it a little, but I never really believed in the stuff."

"How long will you keep the boy?" Father asked, to change the subject.

"We'll keep him at least twenty-four hours for observation. But I believe he's going to be fine, thanks to you."

Father shook his head. "Not me, the Blood of Jesus."

"Well, whatever you call it, I'm sure the boy would have been dead without it. It was lucky for him that you were in the hospital, Father."

Father Macon nodded as he perceived the good doctor didn't have a clue about what he was talking about, and as he took the object out of his pocket he asked, "Mind if I keep this?"

"It's okay with me. I'll tell Mrs. Geller that you took it. If Larry wants it back, she can contact you at St. Mark's."

"Sounds good," Father Macon said as he extended his hand to the doctor.

"I'm really glad you were here," the doctor said solemnly as he grabbed the priest's hand with both of his.

"We're really in this together, you know," the priest replied, hoping to sow a seed in the mind of the good doctor.

"I think I'm beginning to understand that." He released the priest's hand. "Be careful."

Father Macon grinned, then turned and walked out of the emergency room into the main hallway. He found his way to the exit and was soon in his jeep heading back to Engleton. He took the object out of his pocket and placed it in the ashtray next to his business cards. He knew that in some way it was connected with the demon that had attacked the boy. He could almost feel the evil in it every time he held it. He wondered what it was and how Larry Geller had ended up with it in his hand in the emergency room of a hospital.

He had been in such deep concentration that the nine miles back to the rectory seemed to pass very quickly. Pulling into his driveway he gave the Lord praise for protecting him and for saving the young boy's life, and for healing Mrs. O'Leary. After parking the jeep, he unlocked the rectory door and went to his bedroom to again change clothes. He noticed that the clock on the night-stand said 2:30 and he knew that Jamie would be calling around 3:00 so he decided to go to the church and pray. He changed back into his jeans and tennis shoes but kept on his shirt and collar. He noticed that the light on his answering machine was flashing, but he didn't feel the urgency to check the calls. He left the rectory and headed for the church.

The rugged old church had been a witness in the small community for nearly a hundred years. It had been built by the parishioners and they had been excellent at their craft. Eight huge stained-glass windows graced the sides of the church, four on each side. The bell tower still had a bell that worked with a rope that hung down through the ceiling of the choir-loft. Father loved the old church the first time he saw it and was pleased to know that at one time the people of this community did want their God to be among them and a part of their lives.

He entered the church through the side door and knelt down on the steps facing the altar. As he prayed his eyes became attracted to the statue of Archangel Michael, spear drawn high and his foot resting on the head of Satan. It was a large statue which stood on a small pedestal about eight feet off the floor. The statue itself was about six feet tall and very beautifully painted. It brought to his mind the Old Testament story of the prophet Daniel and how he had prayed, in his distress, for twenty-one days until the Angel Gabriel appeared to him. Gabriel explained how the Prince of Persia had resisted the angel's attempts for the entire twenty-one days in the spiritual realm above the place where Daniel stayed. It finally took the help of Archangel Michael before the demonic power could be broken enough for Gabriel to get through.

Father's thoughts then went to the morning's activities. He knew that everything that had occurred was demonic in origin, but why all of a sudden, and where was it coming from? He wasn't sure about Mrs. O'Leary's condition, but the young Geller boy had definitely suffered a severe demonic attack. He was sure of that. The increased activity was certainly an indication that he was right about Carl Bowman's bull. But principalities and spirits had to have humans to work through. Who were those humans?

He put the whole thing out of his mind enough to spend the rest of the time in prayer. He thanked the Lord for reminding him to plead the Blood of Jesus this morning as he had gotten out of his jeep. Today, everyone in that emergency room witnessed the awesome power of God, and it made him feel very proud to be serving such a life changing Lord.

"Thank you, Father God, for saving Larry's life today. May his profound recovery open the eyes of others to Your love and power."

He made the sign of the Cross as he stood up and turned to leave by the side door. Suddenly, a gust of wind blew in his face almost taking his breath. Two of the votive candles by the door caught the impact of the wind and were blown out leaving a fine wisp of smoke rising above each of their smoldering wicks. He could feel the hair stand up on the back of his neck. He stopped and slowly began to pan around the entire church. His eyes suddenly stopped as he caught sight of a large dark figure in the corner at the far end of the church by the main entrance. He tried to focus his eyes for more detail, but the figure remained almost shapeless against the dark walnut stain of the interior walls. He could feel the power of fear trying to grip his mind but he began to pray in the spirit and fight the force of the attack.

Like the fire of a dart, he suddenly heard in his mind, "You cannot win, priest. You are a dead man."

The words caused the force of the fear to swell, but again he fought its unrelenting power. "That's a lie!" he shouted as he faced the dark figure in the corner. "God has not given me a spirit of fear, but a spirit of power, and nothing you have formed against me shall prevail. For greater is the Spirit within me than ANYTHING you can muster against me."

He began to walk toward the figure as he spoke. He could feel the coldness on his skin increasing. "I know who you are. I don't know why you're here, but I will not allow you to destroy these people. You are the reason I am a priest. I know now why you could not destroy me on that day in Iraq. You could not destroy me then, and you can't destroy me now."

Again in his mind he heard, "I am here because your people want me here. I am their god. I will kill them through their lusts and desires and you won't be able to stop me. They will for me to be here, and you know the Law! Nothing you can do will change the darkness in their hearts. That darkness is my power. I will prevail, priest, and destroy you in the process."

Father Macon had slowly been making his way toward the apparition as he heard its words in his mind, but as soon as the words stopped, the dark shape disappeared. The huge entrance door in the center of the vestibule suddenly flapped back and forth as if hit with some unseen force. Father Macon stood silently for a few minutes as he continued to pray in the spirit and listen for anything in his mind's "ears'. The silence was profound, and he was glad the apparition was gone. He again turned and walked toward the side door of the church. As he got to the entrance he stopped, turned toward the altar and made the sign of the Cross as he genuflected.

"Praised be our Lord and Savior Jesus Christ," he stated boldly as he stood up and walked out the side door.

Outside he could feel the warmth of the sun and for a moment he thought of the sheer coldness he had experienced during the time of the apparition. As he walked to the rectory, the words of the demon resounded through his brain, "They will for me to be here and you know the Law!" The Law of Sin and Death, he knew of its power and he knew of the ignorance of most Christians concerning this Law. Sin is darkness and where that darkness is, Satan, by design, has the right to be there. If people love the darkness more than the light and will not give up the sin, then that sin will empower the principality over the area, and death and destruction will result. Prayer is the only defense, and if the people of that area don't pray and seek the Lord, then the principality will run rough-shod over the entire community.

Father Macon entered the rectory and noticed that the big clock over the office desk read 3:45. He hadn't realized the time while in church and he wondered if Miss McClain had tried to call or whether she, too, had been delayed. He walked into his bedroom and noticed that the answering machine was blinking again so he punched play on the machine and sat on the edge of the bed to listen. The first two calls were from parishioners wanting to make an appointment with Father, but the third call was from Mr. O'Leary.

"Father, this is Ben O'Leary." His voice sounded very upbeat. "I just wanted to call and tell you that Martha is doing fine. Right after you left the hospital she woke up and has been doing fine ever since. She's already starting to get her appetite back which the doctors say is a good sign. I really want to thank you, Father, for your prayers and your compassion. We love you." As Mr. O'Leary spoke the last sentence, his voice broke indicating his relief and his appreciation. Father Macon grinned as he heard Mr. O'Leary's voice break and softly prayed, "Thank you, Father. Your mercy endures forever."

The third and forth calls were "hang-ups" but as call five started he recognized the voice. "Hello, Father Macon, this is Jamie McClain. I guess you're still busy. I'll call again later."

The next call was also Jamie, "Hello Father, this is Jamie again. It's 3:20 and I'm here at the Hilltop Motel, Room 14. Please give me a call when you come in. Bye."

That was the last message so Father Macon shut the machine down and picked up the receiver. He looked up the number of the motel and punched it into the phone. The hotel manager answered and Father asked to be connected to Room 14.

"Hello," was the familiar voice.

"Hello, Jamie."

"Father," she said, sounding relieved, "are you okay?"

"Yes, certainly, why do you ask?"

"Well, when you weren't there by 3:20, my imagination started going wild. I'm really relieved to talk to you. Can we still get together?"

"Yes, I would love to. Can you come out now?"

"Yes, I can be there in fifteen or twenty minutes."

"Good. I'll expect you."

After he hung up, Father went into the kitchen and started a pot of coffee. He was looking forward to meeting with Jamie but wondered how much he should share with her. He decided he would just go slow and make sure he didn't overwhelm her with the day's occurrences.

He heard her pull into the driveway and looked out of the kitchen window to see her small rental car pull up to the rectory. By the time he got to the door, she had managed to climb the rectory steps. He opened the door just as she was about to ring the doorbell.

"That's what you call timing," she laughed.

"Perfect," Father said, joining with her laughter. "Come in."

Father Macon stepped aside allowing Jamie to enter. She waited as he closed the door then walked ahead as Father extended his hand, motioning toward the rectory office. Father walked behind the desk and Jamie sat in one of the chairs facing the desk. She looked around the office and noticed all the degrees hanging on the wall.

"My gosh!" she exclaimed. "What is an educated man like you doing in an out-of-the-way town like this?"

"Obedience," replied Father Macon, grinning humbly.

"Obedience?" questioned Jamie. "To whom?"

"The bishop. I go where he sends me."

"I'm not sure this says a lot about the wisdom of your bishop," she said, mockingly.

"Sometimes things are not really what they seem. Our bishop is a very prayerful man. On this one I'm sure he had some divine inspiration."

The seriousness of Father's tone made Jamie realize that something was definitely going on.

"Were you assured of that today?"

"Without a doubt. In fact, this may be the reason I was ordained."

"Wow, this does sound serious," she said, leaning closer to the desk as if coercing an explanation.

"Jamie, are you a Christian?'

"Yes, Father, I am. I was born again when I was thirteen, in the Assembly of God Church in Crossville, Tennessee."

"That's wonderful," Father Macon exclaimed as her

proclamation seemed to give him a much needed boost.

"Then you know about demons?"

"Yes, I know they exist but I've never seen one. I've heard the people at church talk about them and I've read about them in the Bible but I really always thought that they were maybe a symbol for evil and didn't actually exist."

"I can assure you that they are very real. And as I shared with you and Phil this morning, it is the worship of these demons that killed Mr. Bowman's bull. I know also which principality we are dealing with because it appeared in the church this afternoon while I was praying."

Jamie looked shocked and Father Macon could already see the fear trying to grab her. He got up from his chair, walked around the desk and took her hand. "Jamie, I know this sounds frightening but the worst thing you can do is allow fear to come upon you. If you do, it will provide the atmosphere for demonic attack. I pray that you will understand the power of your baptism and resist the urge to become fearful."

It was strange but she could almost feel a surge of power go through her as he prayed for her. She could feel strength building in her mind.

"I'm okay, Father," she smiled. "You have to admit, however, that this is not your everyday conversation. What did the apparition look like?"

"It was only a large dark form in the back of the church."

"How do you know then which demonic power it is?"

Father Macon paused, then turned and walked back behind the desk. He pointed to one of the diplomas.

"Can you read this from where you are sitting?"

Jamie had to squint her eyes slightly but she was able to read most of the main lettering. "University of Stanford in California presents this degree in Archaeology to Rex Anthony Macon."

She tried squinting even more, then read, "in the year of 1996." Then shaking her head, she finally looked up and grinned. "That's about all I can read."

"This is how I know," he said, tapping his finger on the glass of the diploma over the word, Archaeology.

He could see that she didn't have a clue by the expression on her face. "Jamie, I've never told this to anyone else before but the seriousness of this situation dictates that the truth be brought to the light. This is a long story, however, so let me get us some coffee before I start. Is that okay?"

Jamie was anxious to hear the story, but she could detect his nervousness and thought maybe the coffee would be a good reason for him to stall long enough to gain the confidence he needed to share his story with her.

"I would love some. May I help?"

"No, thanks, I have everything ready. Just a minute and I'll bring it in."

As he left the room, she began to think about what he would say. What did Archaeology have to do with demonic power in Arkansas? How did he know what demonic power it was? Why would such an intelligent and nice looking man choose to be a priest? She fidgeted in her seat as she waited for his return and the answers to her questions.

CHAPTER THREE

THE EXPEDITION

Father Macon placed the coffee pot and two cups and saucers on a tray and started back to the rectory office. Looking at the tray he noticed that he had forgotten the napkins so he set the tray on the kitchen table and went back to the cabinet where he kept the napkins. Just then the door bell on the wall in the hallway began to sound. Father placed the napkins on the tray as he passed the table on the way to the rectory door. Opening the door, he was greeted with the figure of a man dressed in bib overalls and an old dirty ball cap. Father quickly recognized the man as Walter Foust.

"Come in, Walter. How can I help you?"

The man slowly walked up the steps and came into the rectory, keeping his head down the entire time. Father moved away from the door, leaving the man standing there with his head down.

"What can I do for you, Walter?" Father said again.

"I'm short of money this month and I need to pay my electric bill. They said they are gonna cut me off if I don't pay." His voice was muffled and Father had to strain to understand him.

"How much do you need, Walter, to pay the bill?"

"Eighty-five dollars," replied the man, shifting his weight from side to side nervously as he spoke.

"That's a lot of money, Walter. I may be able to help you a little but I don't have access to that much money. Why don't I call the electric company and see of I can get them to hold off turning your electricity off if you pay part of the bill?"

This was not what the man wanted to hear. As he looked up, Father could see the anger in his face. With gritted teeth the man spoke, "I don't want you to call the damn electric company. All I want is some money to pay the son of a bitches and get'em off my back."

His voice continued to rise as he talked and Father could tell that the anger in the man was building.

"Walter, I'm sorry," said Father calmly, trying to ease the tension, "but I don't have the money, but like..."

The man sharply spoke again, cutting Father off in mid-sentence. "You think you are some high and mighty dude because you wear that damn collar, but the people around here think you're a loser. You don't fit in here and you're worthless. You young priests come in here with your new ideas and shake things up when you're really full of crap."

Jamie had heard the man come in and she heard his voice continue to get louder as he talked. She could tell that the man was very upset, so she decided to see if she might offer some assistance. She left the rectory office and walked into the dining area where the two men were. The man was still lambasting Father when she entered the room. When he caught sight of her out of the corner of his eye, he suddenly stopped speaking as he turned his head to face her. Without saying another word, he cast down his head away from Jamie's view, quickly walked to the door and slammed it hard behind him.

"Who was that?" Jamie asked, apparently overwhelmed by the whole thing.

"That was Walter Foust. He lives with his brother about two miles from Mr. Bowman's farm. You know where we were this morning?"

She shook her head and tried to lighten up the situation. "Do all your parishioners think as highly of you as Mr. Foust?"

"Some probably don't have that high of an opinion," he laughed. "Change causes everyone to get upset and since I'm the instrument of change, I catch the brunt of the anger."

"That man was full of hate," she replied. "I hope they don't get any worse than that or you could be in danger."

Father laughed again, "Well, with Walter it's a little different. He was in the Marines when they fought the first Gulf War and ever since he came back from over there, he's been, well, uh, not right. He and his brother, Sam, live in a house down by the river and they help the farmers around here with bailing hay, harvesting crops, things like that. No one really has much to do with them because both of the brothers have a pretty short fuse. People say that Walter was really a wonderful guy until the Gulf War thing. Since then, it's almost like he's a completely different person."

"Did he have a nervous break down?"

"Nobody really knows. He just kind of lost it, they said. Some think maybe nerve gas poisoning, others just battle trauma. He doesn't ever come to Mass, and I don't see him but about once or twice a month and that's usually only passing on the road."

"Is he Catholic?"

"Oh, yes, his family was one of the first groups of people to settle Engleton. I know war is bad but for him it has really been devastating.

"We better drink this stuff before it gets cold," he continued, pointing to the tray of coffee, trying to change the subject. "Let me grab this tray and let's go back to the office."

He picked up the tray from the table and motioned for Jamie to lead the way. She took the gesture and together they walked back into the rectory office. She sat down in the same chair as before, as Father sat the tray on the desk and began to pour the coffee.

"Well, it looks like it's still hot." Steam rose from the two freshly poured cups. "I've got sugar, sweetener and cream so I'll let you help yourself, if that's okay?"

"That's great," she said as she leaned forward in her chair and prepared her cup.

Father Macon also prepared his coffee and when finished he sat down in the office chair behind the desk.

"Father Macon," Jamie asked, after taking a sip of the hot liquid, "how old are you, if you don't mind?"

"Oh no, I don't mind. I'll be thirty-two this October."

"How long have you been a priest?"

"I have been ordained for four years. I just celebrated my anniversary."

"How does archaeology come into the picture?"

"Like I told you it's a long story but now's the time, I feel, to tell it. Have you ever heard of a British archeologist by the name of Sir Austen Henry Layard?"

Jamie shook her head, no.

"He was a famous archeologist back in the 1800's. He was well known for his work around the old site of Babylon on the Tigris and Euphrates Rivers. He is the one credited with finding the old city of Nineveh. You know the story of Jonah and Nineveh?"

"Oh yes," Jamie responded. "He got mad because the people repented and God saved the city."

"That's right; very good," Father smiled as he continued. "In some of Layard's private notes he expressed that his greatest desire was to find and recover the skins that God had used to cover Adam and Eve after the Fall. He felt he was very close."

Father could tell by the questioning look on Jamie's face that she was already failing to understand. "You do remember that from the Book of Genesis, don't you?"

"Yes, I do. But I never thought that the story was real. I thought it was symbolic or just someone's theory of how the whole thing started. You mean the skins were real?"

"Layard thought so. He became almost obsessed with finding them because, for some reason, he thought they were buried with Semiramis, Nimrod's wife. He thought he was just on the verge of finding her burial site when he became sick and died."

"You're going to have to help me out here, Father," she interrupted. "I don't remember Nimrod or his wife, Semi…, Semro…"

"Semiramis," Father interjected. "Remember the flood and Noah?"

Jamie nodded and so Father continued, "There is a myth and Layard believed every bit of it, that the skins that Adam and Eve wore were passed on to their children until the time of Noah. Somehow the skins gave the wearer a strange spiritual power and control over all the animals and that's what Noah used to get all of the animals onto the Ark. Now according to scripture, Ham, Noah's son was cursed by God because somehow he shamed his father, Noah. Layard thought that even this verse had something to do with the skins because Ham gives birth to a son named Cush who in turn has a son named Nimrod. Now, it is interesting that Nimrod is called a mighty one in the earth and also a mighty hunter before the Lord. This man was somehow very gifted because he built many cities, and he is even given credit for the tower of Babel. Layard, however, believed the tower was instigated by Nimrod's wife, Semiramis. Somehow, she got into the worship of demons and became well versed in witchcraft and spiritualism. The tower, Layard thought, was her idea. He thought that it was through the wrong use of the skins that she became involved in the occult. Our modern New Age religions had their start there in the area of Nineveh or what is today called ancient Babylon. Semiramis was so enthralled in the occult that she would not let the skins out of her sight. She even made her husband swear that when she died, he would wrap her in the skins and bury them with her. Layard believed the skins would still be intact if he could find Semiramis' gravesite. Unfortunately he never saw his dream come to fruition."

"What did Layard want with the skins?"

"He believed they possessed a power that could be used to control all of nature. He had managed to accumulate other bits of information about the skins from other ancient writings, and he was convinced that the skins were unaffected by time and decay. He even speculated that Semiramis' body, if found, would be perfectly preserved."

"Did anyone take up Layard's work when he died?"

"Superstition is a powerful deterrent. So many people at the time thought that demons protected Semiramis' grave site so his work was completely abandoned. His entire scope of work was logged away for years until a professor from Stanford University happened to uncover it in the early eighties. His name was Bremlar Michaelson. Dr. Michaelson was a brilliant archeologist who became completely infatuated with Layard's work. After studying Layard's work, Dr. Michaelson himself came to believe that the skins did actually exist, and that somewhere in Iraq, buried in the sand, was the tomb of Semiramis and the sacred animal skins.

"During this time I was pursuing a degree in archeology at Stanford, and I became a primary student of Dr. Michaelson. I, too, studied Layard's work and wasn't quite as sold on it as

Michaelson, but I went with him to Iraq. We dug in the sands of Nineveh for two years and found nothing until one day a staff member found a small figurine carved from pure crystal. It was priceless, and Michaelson insisted it was part of the booty from Semiramis' grave treasure. From the day that figurine was found, strange things began to happen in our camp. One of the young Iraqi diggers had a heart attack. He was only sixteen. One of our vans ran off the road and down an embankment, killing three graduate students from Stanford. Many of the men claimed to have women appear to them at night and force them to have sex. The only women in camp, however, were the female students and none of them exhibited that kind of behavior. It became such a problem that even Michaelson was ready to abandon the project. Then, the day before we were scheduled to wind up the digging, we hit a burial chamber. Michaelson went in first and came out ecstatic. We had found it! We forgot about all the problems and proceeded full steam ahead.

"We set up the generator and the illumination system and three of us went into the tomb to survey the setup: Michaelson, another student by the name of Chad James, and myself. It was amazing! There were hundreds of statues all around the tomb, many of them strange looking creatures. The walls were covered with scenes depicting every form of sexual perversion anyone could imagine. Many of the scenes showed these same weird looking creatures having sex with women and men. Above each set of pictures was some cuneiform writing with each group of letters ending with the SS we saw on Mr. Bowman's bull. We spent three days mapping the room without touching a thing. Those were Dr. Michaelson's strict orders.

"Strange things continued to happen during those three days. Something happened to Chad one night that he refused to discuss.

It left him agitated and nervous and as jumpy as a cat. There was one wall of the tomb that had a large scene depicting a woman covered with something like skins having sex with this huge man-animal like creature. Michaelson was convinced that behind that wall we would find the burial place of Semiramis.

"On the fourth day we started carrying out the statues from the antechamber. The female students could not stand to go into the tomb without feeling terribly sick. Every one of them became so nauseated that Michaelson gave them the job of packing the crates. We were careful to catalog and crate each object separately because each statue was priceless. We're talking antiquity from almost the very beginning of the earth.

"About noon on that fourth day all hell broke loose. A sand storm came out of nowhere and blew relentlessly for two days. All of the Iraqis gave up and finally left on foot, along with a couple of the Americans. There were nine of us left in camp. On the third day of the storm we assumed we all would be killed because the storm was unrelenting in its intensity. Chad and I finally decided that the tomb was the safest place to shelter, so we left Michaelson and the others and went to the tomb. It was dark but at least we were out of the blowing sand. We lit a couple of torches and waited for the worst. The worst came.

Inside the chamber the torches began to sputter as if they were being blown by the wind. We couldn't figure it out. Suddenly, this huge creature about eight feet tall appeared out of nowhere and came toward Chad. I saw him reach into Chad's body and literally pull out his soul. Chad was screaming and fighting the thing furiously, but the thing overpowered him, holding up his soul like a prize. And then he started toward me with Chad's soul in one hand. I could see his soul in the hand of the thing, but his body was limp on the floor of the tomb. At first I thought I was hallucinating or that I was just imagining things but I can still hear Chad screaming as he fought that thing. I thought I was dead, but just before the thing got to me another being formed in front of me. He had a spear or sword that glowed like fire, and when he held it up to the thing, the thing backed off and disappeared, taking Chad's soul with it. I was so scared I guess I passed out or fainted. When I came to, it was as dark as pitch in that tomb, but I couldn't hear the storm blowing outside. I crawled past Chad's body and found the entrance to the tomb. When I got outside, the storm had stopped and the sun was shinning. I found one of the male students and three of the female students, all frightened and trying to figure out what to do next. No one knew what had happened to Dr. Michaelson or to the other students. John Davenport, the male student, said he heard Michaelson screaming like a wild man sometime the night before. However, the wind had been blowing so hard that he couldn't tell from which direction it was coming.

"The entire camp was a shambles. Nearly everything was covered with sand. The one lone vehicle was a goner, and we were at least forty miles from the nearest Iraqi settlement. It was John's reaction that first gave me a clue as to the reason for our survival. He suggested that we pray. As he prayed, I could tell it was a comfortable thing for the ladies also. In fact, they were much more comfortable with it than I was. I was a baptized Catholic who had been confirmed at age thirteen, but had never considered my religion very seriously. I went to Mass when it was convenient and prayed the 'Our Father' every once in a while but nothing of any magnitude.

"John suggested that we head north toward a settlement where they had stopped for supplies only two weeks before. We sifted through the debris and were able to find three canteens which we took with us as we headed out. It was terribly hot. We finished off two of the canteens very quickly. We walked for about five hours, and as the day came to a close we sat and rested as the heat quickly turned to cold. We huddled together and again prayed as we comforted and supported each other. It was John's strength and knowledge of God that impressed me the most. He would sit for hours and sing what he called praise songs to God. I didn't know any of them but the girls would join in sometimes on the ones they knew.

"'I'm doing what Paul and Silas did at midnight in jail,' he said. 'We've prayed and now we're thanking God that He is going to provide the answer. I promise you, we will be all right.'

"He said that with such confidence that I think I actually believed him. I fell asleep and the next thing I knew he was telling us all to get up.

"'Praised be Jesus,' he was shouting as he looked off into the distance.

"We got up and sure enough, two trucks were coming towards us in the distance. We began to jump up and down and wave our shirts and our arms as we watched the vehicles get closer and closer. When they finally got to us, we recognized two of them as the Iraqis from our group. They had managed to get through the storm and they had come back to rescue us. Riding back to the settlement, I thanked God and promised that I would get to know Him as well as John did."

"What happened to the tomb and all the relics?" Jamie asked, as Father finished the story.

"I don't know. Another sand storm hit the area after we left, and I don't know whether anyone went back. No one in our group wanted to go back. Dr. Michaelson was never heard from again. The University of Stanford closed the grant. As for myself, I took a year off from archaeology to sort things out. Every time I closed my eyes I could see that thing with Chad's soul in his left hand. I just couldn't get that scene out of my mind."

"You said that John's prayer was the first clue as to why you all were saved. Why were you?" Jamie asked, realizing that what she had just heard was probably one of the most incredible stories of her life. Had it not been coming from a priest, there was no way she would have considered believing it.

"On the plane back to the states I sat next to John. I told him about what had happened in the tomb. He listened, then with uncanny insight he said, 'Rex, we should never have been in that place. It had to be one of the most evil spots on this earth. God sealed that place, and we brought it back to life. There was so much demonic power in that tomb that it was almost physical. The perverted sexual demons were so strong that the women's spirits couldn't stand it and those poor Iraqis were constantly being attacked by those Succubus spirits. It was driving them crazy.'

"I had no idea what a Succubus spirit was," Father continued.

"I don't either," interrupted Jamie. "What is it?"

"This may sound strange, but a Succubus spirit is an evil spirit that actually has sexual intercourse with a male human. It seems so real to the man that even orgasm is achieved. An evil spirit that has sexual intercourse with a female human is an Incubus."

"This is for real?" Jamie asked, not wanting to believe his words even if they were coming from a priest.

"I promise you, it is very real and very devastating for the individual."

Jamie shook her head in either disgust or unbelief, she wasn't quite sure which. "What did John say about what happened to Chad?"

"He said that the ladies had been able to decipher one of the texts before the storm hit. It had been written in the earliest form of cuneiform and had taken them awhile. One of the texts had read, *The greater the abomination, the greater the honor to you, O Syrasohan. May our bodies be an instrument of your pleasure and a manifestation for your greatness. SS*

"While we were in the cave during the storm, it was Syrasohan that manifested. I don't know whether we unleashed something in the excavation or whether he was threatened by our discovery. I do know that what saved me was the Blood of Jesus."

"I don't understand," Jamie stopped him. "I know about salvation but how did that stop Syrasohan from taking you, too?"

"Syrasohan is one of Satan's chief demons. In fact, he is a principality, so he must have been an archangel in God's kingdom before the Fall. Chad was not saved and I understand now that because he wasn't, he was still in an unredeemed state with Satan as his lord and master. Syrasohan merely claimed what was his. It happens every time someone dies without being saved. Did you ever see the movie, *Ghost*?"

Jamie shook her head yes and said, "I know what you're talking about. When the bad guys got killed the demons came and grabbed them and took them away screaming. It was really a chilling part of the movie."

"Tell me about it!" Father agreed. "Now try to imagine that same thing happening seven or eight feet away from you."

"I would have died of fright right there on the spot," Jamie laughed. "How about the being that stood between you and the demon? Was that your guardian angel?"

"I really don't know, but I think it was Michael the Archangel, because Syrasohan definitely didn't want to mess with him. I'm not taking anything away from my guardian angel but I somehow feel it was someone with a lot of clout in the spiritual realm."

Jamie shook her head slowly. "That episode was most certainly a life changing event, wasn't it?"

"After I got back to the states, I finished my degree in archaeology at Stanford. I went through a lot of interviews and interrogations about the expedition, but I never said anything about what happened in the tomb. I just let everyone believe that Dr. Michaelson and the other students died from the effects of the sand storm. It caused the school some bad press but after about six months, the whole thing was forgotten. I left and moved to Jackson Hole, Wyoming to just get away and have time to think. I used to go to the little chapel in front of the Grand Tetons and just sit for hours and look at the mountains. It was while I was there that I knew I had to become a priest."

Jamie could tell from the spaced out look on his face that he was reliving those moments. But there was more she wanted to know so she deliberately broke his concentration. "What do you mean you knew you had to?"

He turned and looked at her with the most gentle look she had ever seen on a man's face. "Very few people have any idea that the spiritual realm is even out there. An even greater number fail to realize that there is a group of evil spiritual beings who are trying to kill them, both body and soul. I know that without a shadow of a doubt. No one, I don't care who they are, can convince me that they don't exist.

"When I went through seminary, I could not believe the unbelief among the professors. I wanted to cry when they would get up in front of us, men who would be millions of people's only spiritual connection, and teach that the devil and hell were not real. I've still got scars on my tongue from biting it so hard to keep from telling those guys that they didn't have a clue what they were talking about. Those were the hardest four years of my life. I realized very quickly, however, that if I wanted to get through the place I had better keep my mouth shut.

"The year before my ordination I went back to my home town, Rogers, Arkansas and while I was there a lady introduced me to the Charismatic movement in the Church. Man, I had come home! I read everything I could by anybody that taught about a life in the Spirit. I was on cloud nine and then my brother was killed and I realized that I needed to be ordained and get to work destroying the plans of the enemy. After ordination I was assigned to a large parish in the Little Rock area. Everyone was high on social justice and feeding the poor and helping the sick, but nobody seemed to realize who it was that was making these people poor, or sick, or crazy. No one knew anything about casting out demons or pleading the Blood of Jesus or binding the attacking demon. I soon realized that Catholics were more comfortable 'offering up' something than they were with fighting spiritual warfare. I thought the bishop sensed my frustration and sent me here to just cool off, but I know now that I am right where I'm supposed to be."

"Because you believe that Syrasohan is trying to move into this area?" Jamie asked, trying to discern his reasoning.

"I know he is. Remember, this morning after I left you to go to the hospital?"

Jamie nodded her head yes.

"I was called there to see a parishioner that had suddenly taken a turn for the worse last night. But while I was praying for her, Barbara paged me to the emergency room and Larry Geller, who is a twelve year-old parishioner, was suffering a heart attack. He would not respond to anything that the doctor administered. As I prayed for him and pleaded the Blood of Jesus over him, the heart monitor cleared up and he started waking up. As he did, he dropped something out of his hand onto the floor. The nurse picked it up and gave it to the doctor who then handed it to me. It looked like a piece of carved bone but nothing like anything I'd seen so I put it in my pocket."

"Do you have it with you?" Jamie asked, stretching out her hand, expecting Father to remove it from his pocket.

"No, it's out in the jeep. But wait a second and I'll get it."

He quickly jumped up and ran out the door. Jamie heard him open the jeep door. After a few minutes she heard him call her from outside, "Jamie, come here quickly."

Jamie obeyed and ran to the door which Father had left open. As she came outside he was looking at her. "It's not here."

"Look on the floorboard."

"I did!" he exclaimed. "I've looked everywhere in this front seat area and it's not here. I put it in the ashtray next to my business cards and now it's not there!"

"How could it just disappear?" Jamie asked as she climbed down the stairs to where Father was hanging half out of the jeep, still looking inside.

"It couldn't, but it's gone sure as the world."

"No one has been here except the man that got so angry and how would he even know it was in there?"

"You mean Walter Foust?"

"Yes, but how would he know that the piece of carved bone was lying in your ash tray?"

"I don't know. But no matter who it was, it seems to me we would have heard them open or close the jeep door."

"That's true unless….," Jamie stopped, not wanting to say what she was thinking.

"Unless what?" Father asked, looking out of the jeep at her. She didn't answer but just stared at him until somehow he knew what she was thinking. "Unless no human being took it?"

She shook her head up and down slowly.

“I don’t know. Poltergeist spirits are able to move objects around in the physical. But to actually steal something physical, I’ve never heard of it. They need humans to do their work in the physical realm. I just don’t think…”

Suddenly from within the church there was a huge crash. It sounded like the whole wall had fallen in.

“What was that?” Jamie exclaimed.

“I don’t know,” Father Macon answered as he crawled out of the jeep and cautiously started walking toward the church. As they slowly entered the side door, they smelled a strong odor of sulfur.

CHAPTER FOUR

THE INSTRUCTIONS

"What is that smell?" she asked, covering her nose, trying to see over Father's shoulder.

"That is the smell of hell. It's a sure sign of demonic activity."

"Oh, my gosh," Jamie cried softly as she grabbed onto Father's arm.

Entering the church they could see a small cloud of dust over at the front of the church by the side of the altar. Walking closer, they found the huge statue of the Archangel Michael laying in the floor, broken into a hundred pieces. It was obvious that the pedestal on which the statue had been sitting had somehow, mysteriously, broken loose allowing the whole thing to fall to the floor.

"Why is it so cold in here?" Jamie asked, breaking the silence.

"Look to the back of the church in the right hand corner and you'll find out," Father answered as he took her arm with his other hand.

"Ah," she screamed as she looked to the spot Father had indicated and saw the huge dark object that had been there previously. "What is that?" she asked, clutching closer to Father Macon.

"That is Syrasohan," Father said softly, standing as still as a statue.

As both of them stared at the demon, Father heard in his mind,

"You damn priest, you are a dead priest. Your people are mine. They have accepted me as their god and I will rule over them. You are alone and no one will help you. You are defenseless and I will kill you."

Jamie screamed and began to cry, "No, no, please no."

Father Macon turned her and held her in his arms, shielding her from the demon. "Syrasohan," he yelled, "in the Name of Jesus Christ, I command that you leave this sacred ground. You have no power here and I rebuke you and your evil henchmen in the Name of Jesus. I plead the Blood of Jesus over us and this church."

Both Father and Jamie heard an audible scream as they felt a sudden gust of wind blow by them. The demon was gone.

Jamie continued to sob as Father comforted her, "It's okay, he's gone."

"That was horrible," she sobbed. "I heard his awful voice speak to me."

"What did he say to you?" Father asked, trying to assure her that she was safe.

"He said he was going to enjoy using my body for his pleasure."

Father gritted his teeth, remembering the expedition and the scenes that he had seen on the walls of the tomb. He wished she had never gotten involved. He was not afraid, but he was afraid for her. She was a Christian, but it was apparent that she had no idea who she was in Christ and what her rights in Christ were. He knew that somehow he would have to quickly teach her and prepare her for the battle ahead.

"Come on," he said, still holding on to her as she continued to sob. "We have a lot of work to do."

"What about the statue?" she asked, as they stepped through the debris on the way to the door.

"I'll get someone to take care of it tomorrow. Right now we need to get you back to the motel."

As they exited the side door of the church, the sun was just setting over the trees. The light was getting dimmer and it would be dark in an hour or so.

"Jamie, let's go back to the rectory," he said, keeping a hold of her hand as they crossed the driveway. "I've got some things I need to give you before I take you back to the motel."

"Couldn't I stay with you tonight? I don't know if I can stay by myself."

"Under normal circumstances that might be all right," he said, almost laughing, "especially this day and time. But I don't think that would be a good idea with me being a priest and all. It would sure give my parishioners something to talk about."

She laughed. "I never thought about that. I guess that wouldn't be such a good idea."

He was glad to see her laughing, but he could still feel her trembling as they reached the rectory and went back into the office. He sat her down in her same chair and told her to wait there just a minute. He went to his bedroom and found a small bottle of holy water, a small container of blessed oil and a Bible. He brought them back to the office and handed them to her.

"Here, take these."

"What are they?" she asked, taking them and looking at each one.

"Ammunition. Come on. I'll explain on the way back to your motel. We'll leave your car here and I'll have someone bring it to you tomorrow." He escorted Jamie out of the rectory onto the first step. She waited for him as he turned and locked the rectory door, then both of them climbed into the jeep and pulled out of the parking lot onto the highway.

"Jamie," Father said, looking toward her seriously as he drove, "you are a Christian, aren't you? You have been baptized, right?"

"Yes, Father, I promise. But I really didn't believe this stuff was real. I just thought you lived your life out till you died then you went to heaven. I had no idea that we might encounter the spiritual realm here on earth. If I had, I would have taken my baptism more seriously. Right now I am scared to death and I know it really shouldn't be that way for believers. But I guess I didn't really believe until tonight. It's not too late, is it?"

Tears came to her eyes as she spoke, and she started to sob again.

"It's never too late, Jamie," Father Macon replied, gently trying to reassure her. "So many Christians are just like you, they don't understand that the Kingdom of God is now. You can see that it suffers violence. We experienced that this afternoon. But the violent take it by force. We have to fight for the Kingdom, Jamie. Most Christians don't have a clue what's really going on. This community is under a severe attack and many will suffer if they don't wake up. There is not enough prayer power going up from this community or Syrasohan could never have gotten such a foothold here. The people here have committed so much evil in the past hundred years and failed to repent of it that the way is paved for this demonic invasion. There is so much hatred and bitterness, unforgiveness, anger, pride, adultery, incest, and open sexual promiscuity in this area that darkness has overpowered the light and now somehow Syrasohan has been invited in."

"What do you mean invited in?" Jamie asked, clinging to Father's every word.

"Demons have specific territories. A principality is assigned by Satan over certain areas because he can't be everywhere at the same time. He is not omnipresent like God, so he has a chain of command, kind of like the military. Power is the only thing a demon respects. They are pure, unadulterated evil. They don't even respect each other. Someone, or something, specifically invited Syrasohan into this area and after surveying it, he decided it was worth his effort. I don't understand how anyone could have learned enough about him to invite him in."

"Is there any other way he could have been invited?"

"If someone had an object in their possession that was dedicated to Syrasohan and used it in their ceremonies, that could have given him an open door. That's highly unlikely around here, however, because these people are pretty much home bodies. No one does much traveling that I know of."

"Why did I feel violated back there in the church? I felt like I had been raped."

"Understand that demons have a certain propensity or inclination. They sort of specialize in a certain sin or evil. There are demons of anger, demons of unforgiveness, demons of death and devour, demons of fear, so forth and so on. Syrasohan is a principality of sexual deprivation and destruction of the human body. Your spirit felt his intrusion when he spoke to you and it picked up on his nature. Your spirit felt the sexual deprivation and death associated with him and transferred that to your mind. If we don't stop him, there will be a lot manifested in the physical, like you just felt in the spiritual."

"You mean rape will increase in this area?"

"Every kind of sexual sin will increase in this area along with the destruction of the people. Death will increase in every possible way, accidents, murders, sickness, disease. You name it and it will begin to manifest."

"What do we have to do?"

"We have to get these people to pray, fast, repent, and give up the sin that's empowering the principality over this area. Once the sin stops ascending to him and empowering him and his legions, he will be forced to leave. In other words, we have to increase the light and dispel the darkness."

"How do we do that?" Jamie asked with a look of despair.

"I really don't know, but I know God does and if just you and I stand together, we can build a big enough army to conquer this thing."

"Father, I don't know that I have the faith. Right now I'm still trembling. Couldn't I just go on back to Little Rock and let you find someone else more qualified?"

"Jamie," Father encouraged, "you are qualified. You've been baptized. That's all the qualification anyone needs. You've accepted Jesus as your Lord and Savior and this battle is really His. He will, however, fight it through us. Besides Jamie, you know too much now. Syrasohan would track you down and destroy you wherever you go if you don't come to know your rights in Christ."

"What do I have to do?" she asked, still not fully convinced that she was up for this sort of thing.

"I've given you a bottle of holy water. Demons hate holy water. It is a sacramental of our baptism and the death and resurrection of our Lord Jesus. It will deter demons. I've also given you a small vial of blessed oil. It, too, is a sacramental that symbolizes the power of the Holy Spirit. It is very powerful in the spiritual realm. Tonight when we get to the motel I want you to anoint the doorway and the window of your motel room with this holy oil in the name of the Father, and of the Son and of the Holy Spirit. Take the holy water and sling it around your room and cast out any unclean spirits in the name of Jesus. I've also given you a Bible. It is your sword of the Spirit. It is a powerful weapon. It is what Jesus used when he was tempted in the desert by Satan. I want you to read and re-read the Ninety-first Psalm. Can you remember all that?"

"Yes, without any problem," she said confidently. "Is there any thing else I need right now?"

"Yes, you need to be able to pray in tongues and to hear the Voice of the Holy Spirit, but we'll tackle that later."

"Tongues?" she questioned. "I thought that was only in the days of the Apostles."

"Ain't no way, I'm glad to say," Father laughed. "It's a powerful spiritual gift that Satan hates. That's why he fights it so much. It's available to every baptized Christian but most people are too prideful and fearful to ask for it."

She was pondering his words when he pulled the jeep into the motel parking lot.

"What number did you say, Jamie?" he asked, looking to see the numbers on each door of the motel rooms.

"Room 14, it's down at the end on the other side of that van."

Father Macon followed her direction and pulled the jeep into a parking spot in front of the room. They got out and Jamie found her key and opened the door. The light was on over the sink which kept the room from being dark.

"I'm sure glad I forgot to turn off that light," she said, putting her key on the dresser by the bed. "Are you sure I can't talk you into spending the night?" she asked, laughingly trying to cover the fear she was feeling.

"I'm afraid not." He walked to her and hugged her. "You'll be fine."

"I'm just so scared," she said, starting to sob again.

"I know." Father handed her a Kleenex off the dresser. "Just do what I told you and everything will be okay. I'll call you first thing in the morning."

"Can I call you if I need you?" she asked, still holding on to his arm like a child.

"Yes, any time. But don't talk to anyone else you don't know and don't let anyone or anything in this room. Hear me?"

She nodded and leaned up and kissed him on the cheek, "Thank you. I think you're wonderful."

The kiss caught him off guard and caused him to blush. "Good night, Jamie," he said, as he nervously pulled away, "and may God bless you and keep you in the name of the Father, Son and the Holy Spirit."

He made the sign of the Cross in the air over her as he blessed her, then turned and opened the motel door.

"Remember what I told you, Jamie?" he asked as he opened the door of his jeep and looked at her standing in the doorway of her motel room. She had tears running down her cheeks but she nodded and waved goodbye as he started up the jeep and backed it out of the parking spot. As he headed out of the parking area toward the highway, he noticed two men in a parked car near the motel pool. He didn't know if he was just paranoid but they seemed to be watching him as he passed their car and pulled his jeep out onto the highway.

CHAPTER FIVE

THE CONVERSATION

On the highway he kept looking back in his rear view mirror to make sure no one was following him. When no one came he breathed a sign of relief and began to think more of Jamie's kiss. She sure was a beautiful woman, and he felt a glint of shame as he admitted to himself that he had noticed her well proportioned body. She looked wonderful in her shirt and blue jeans. It was times like this that he really questioned the church's stance on celibacy. He reached up and felt his cheek where she had kissed him. That felt so good. He could easily see why so many priests had left the priesthood, but few had been given the grace that he had to understand the big picture. The eternal salvation of souls was much more important than his sexual needs. He praised God for his vocation and began to sing in the spirit as he drove back to the rectory.

He began to make a mental note of the things he needed to do tomorrow. He had to get someone to remove the pieces of statue from the church before Sunday. He didn't think that there was any way it could be repaired. He also needed to check on Mrs. O'Leary and see if he might talk with Larry Geller before his dismissal from the hospital. He had to remember first, however, to call and check on Jamie. In fact, he thought, he could see if she wanted to go with him to the hospital. He also wanted to spend some time in prayer to get God's answer on how to fight this battle and get Syrasohan expelled from the area.

When he got to the rectory, he parked his jeep and tried to unlock the rectory door. He had forgotten to leave the porch light on and it was as dark as pitch. He finally managed to find the key hole and unlock the door. He bypassed the rectory office and headed for his bedroom where he noticed the answering machine again notifying him that someone had left a message. He punched the play button as he sat down on the edge of the bed to remove his shoes.

"Anthony," the first caller said, "this is Bishop Landers. Please give me a call when you come in. God bless."

Father Macon began to wonder what he wanted as the machine continued to speak. "Father, this is Jamie. I'm sorry but would you please call me? Thanks."

He could tell from the sound of her voice that something was going on so he thought he had better call her first. He picked up the phone and dialed the motel. When the manager answered he told her room 14.

"Hello," Jamie answered cautiously.

"Jamie, this is Father Macon. Is everything all right?"

"Oh, Father," she replied almost apologizing for her fear. "When you left I watched and I believe there is a car across the drive way with two men in it watching my room. I just peaked out through the corner of the curtain a few minutes ago and they are still there."

"I saw them when I left too, but I'm not sure they're watching your room. I'll tell you what. I'll call Sheriff Martin and have him or his deputy check it out. Will that be okay?"

"I would sure appreciate that, Father," she replied in a way that made him know it brought a lot of relief to her mind.

"By the way, I'm going to go to the hospital tomorrow morning and talk with Larry Geller. Do you want to come along?"

"I'd love to," she answered with no hesitation whatsoever.

"Good, then I'll see you in the morning. Good night, Jamie."

"Good night, Father and thanks again."

Father pressed the dial tone button on the phone then re-dialed the sheriff's office. Sheriff Martin wasn't there but the dispatcher said she would send a car around to the area to check it out. Father thanked the lady dispatcher and again depressed the dial. Dread came over him as he paused before dialing the bishop's number. Besides his mom, the bishop was the only person who called him Anthony. The bishop said it sounded more holy than Rex. He finally gave into the inevitable and dialed the number. He wondered what the bishop could want.

"Hello," came the familiar voice on the other end of the line.

"Bishop, this is Anthony. You wanted me to call you?"

"Yes, Anthony, I did. Is everything all right there in Engleton?"

Father Macon paused momentarily, trying to think of what the bishop had possibly heard. He wondered if he had heard of the bull mutilation or the incident in the hospital. Quickly he decided to play ignorant. "Everything is about like it has been, bishop."

"I was just concerned, Anthony," the bishop responded. "I've had two calls from people who are supposedly your parishioners who are quite upset. They say you are running people off from the church and Anthony every person who leaves means less money to run this diocese. We are a poor diocese and we can't afford to lose people. Both of the people said they were disgusted with your blatant sexual antics with some woman you were seeing and even sleeping with in the rectory."

"What?" Father Macon exclaimed, forgetting who he was

talking to. "That is a lie."

"I was hoping you would say that," replied the bishop with a deep sigh of relief. "I don't know what you're doing but it seems that you've gotten a few of the people upset. Remember Anthony," the bishop continued, "try to be a peacemaker and not offend anyone. I know Engleton is a tough assignment but remember you are the shepherd of those people and they look to you for good leadership. I know the people are very set in their ways but basically they are good people."

Father Macon sat listening, wondering if he should tell the bishop about what was really going on, but he knew it would only cause a greater concern to the bishop so he decided to just play the game.

"Bishop, I assure you, there is not one ounce of truth in any of those accusations but I will attempt to find out what has the parishioners so upset."

"Good, Anthony," the bishop consoled. "I'll pray for you."

"Thank you, bishop, I appreciate your confidence."

"Good night, Anthony," the bishop said, indicating that the conversation was ended.

"Good night, bishop," Father Macon returned as he heard the bishop hang up the phone on his end.

"Satan, you louse," Father Macon retorted as he slammed down the receiver. Satan was using gossip to destroy the confidence of the people and divide his parish. He was a master at division and he knew that Father Macon was no push-over when it came to spiritual warfare. Satan was trying to get rid of him by having the people complain so much that the bishop would have him removed. Without him, Syrasohan would have a field day. The more he thought about it, the more excited he became. In this attack, Satan had revealed that he was concerned about Father

Macon.

"Hallelujah," he shouted as he began to dance a little jig. "Satan, I am going to kick your rear. I don't care what you tell the bishop. I know I've got you worried, and I'm going to prevail in this battle in Jesus' Name. I am an overcomer, and I overcome you by the Blood of the Lamb and the word of my testimony. I can do all things through Christ who strengthens me, and I'm serving notice on Syrasohan. You are defeated!"

Father Macon was so excited that he could hardly get to sleep. He was determined more than ever to do everything within his power to destroy this evil principality. As he prayed the prayers in his breviary, he praised God for having enough confidence in him to use him to fight such a strong demon. After his night prayers, he lay in bed, praying in the spirit and finally fell asleep.

As Father sat at the table drinking his morning coffee, he debated about when to call Jamie. He wanted to let her sleep as long as possible because of all she had been through the day before. He had already called someone to remove the statue and clean up the debris from church. They would arrive sometime this morning and Father had arranged with one of the parishioners to oversee the statue's removal and disposal.

Around nine-thirty he dialed the phone and again asked the motel manager for room 14. He was relieved to hear Jamie's voice on the other end and to learn that she had been up only a few minutes. She said she had slept fairly well but it had taken her a long time to fall asleep. She thanked Father for calling the sheriff's office but the men had left right after she had talked to Father last night.

"I'm really sorry for being such a big baby," she said, laughing lightly.

"You had every reason to be concerned, Jamie," he assured her. "You were put through quite an ordeal yesterday."

"You know, it all seems like a dream."

"Well," Father paused, "I can assure you that it was no dream but oh, how I wish it were. I'm afraid, however, that we've just touched the tip of the iceberg as far as this thing is concerned. I want to talk to Larry Geller this morning. I'm hoping he can tell us something."

"What kind of something?"

"If I'm right, Carl Bowman's bull was used in a boundary ceremony by a coven of Satanists. I was reflecting last night, and I have heard things but chose to ignore them because somehow I was hoping they were just rumors."

"What kind of things?"

"Rumors of possible Satanic activity in this area," he replied, being very blunt.

"Those seem to be all over," she responded, trying to encourage him for not taking the rumors more seriously.

"I know, but maybe we'll find out something when we talk to Larry. Can I pick you up in a little while?"

"Can you give me forty-five minutes?" she asked, fading into a young girl's voice. "We girls take a while to get ourselves beautiful."

"I understand," he said laughing. "I'll pick you up in an hour."

"You are most kind, sir," she replied in her most southern belle accent.

After hanging up the phone, Father took a shower and put on his clerics. He found his anointing oil and his small bottle of holy water and placed them in his pockets. He went to the office and found a pen and small writing pad and placed them in his inside coat pocket. He then went to the small chapel he had set up in the rectory and began to pray. He prayed until it was time for him to leave. He locked the rectory, climbed into his jeep and headed for Bettis Bluff.

Jamie was ready and waiting for him when he pulled up. She acknowledged his arrival and gave him a just a minute sign by holding up one finger. She disappeared back into her room for just a second and then came out with her sunglasses in her hand. She looked beautiful and as she placed the sunglasses on her face he decided that it made her look even more beautiful and mysterious.

"Was it worth the wait?" she asked, raising the sunglasses to look underneath them as she climbed into the passenger seat of his jeep.

"You look very beautiful this morning," he replied, trying to sound more complimentary and less sexual.

They continued to talk about the previous day as they headed toward the hospital. He mentally debated whether he should say anything about the bishop's call, but thought it might hurt her, so he decided against it. They parked in the ministers' parking spot at the hospital and found out from Barbara, the receptionist, that Larry was in a private room on the east wing, room 108.

They found room 108 and lightly tapped on the closed door. "Come in,' they heard a woman's voice say, so they pushed the door aside and found Larry sitting up in bed, watching TV. His mother was sitting in a chair at the side of the bed.

"Oh, Father," said Mrs. Geller, "please come in," as she quickly got up from her chair.

Larry grinned as he saw the priest and raised his hand to gesture a nervous hi. "Hi, Father."

"Larry, my man," Father encouraged, "you look great."

"Thanks to you, I hear," his grin growing in size.

"I wish I could take the credit, but my big Boss is the One really responsible."

Finally getting an opportunity, he turned and introduced Jamie.

"Larry, Mrs. Geller, this is Jamie McClain, a worker with the State of Arkansas. Jamie, this is Larry and Mrs. Geller."

He purposely didn't mention her role as an investigator because he was afraid it might scare Larry and maybe prevent him from sharing anything he might know about yesterday's events. They exchanged greetings, then found a chair for Father and Jamie to sit down.

"Larry," Father started, "how much do you remember about yesterday?"

"To be honest, Father," he replied, rubbing his head, "not a lot. I was sitting on the couch looking at this funny shaped bone and watching TV when I suddenly felt like someone had shot me in the chest with a hot spear. When I woke up I was here in the hospital."

"Where did you get the funny looking bone?" Father asked as he nodded his head, trying to convey that he believed what Larry was saying.

"I got it out of Patty's room. She had it taped to her dresser mirror. I wondered what it was so I took it, but I was going to put it back."

"I know you were, son," he again nodded as he turned to Mrs. Geller.

"Mrs. Geller, has Patty shown any strange behavior lately?"

Mrs. Geller turned her eyes down to keep from looking into Father's face, "Yes, for about four months now."

"Can you tell me what kind?"

"Well," she said, trying to hold back the tears, "she started being so rebellious. I couldn't get her to do anything. She would sass and talk back, and she started wearing only black clothing. She said it was what was in style. She even painted her fingernails and toenails black. The black lipstick was almost the last straw. I told her to not wear that stuff and she said if I stopped her she would run off. I asked her how she would get by and she said she had plenty of friends. She's not been to Mass, either, for at least three months and she refuses to go. She says it's boring and a bunch of crap. Father, you know since my divorce it's been hard without a man around."

Mrs. Geller started to cry and Father assured her that he understood.

"Her friends are so weird," Larry spoke up, trying to help take the pressure off his mom and show her some support.

"What do you mean, Larry?" Father asked, understanding his strategy and going along.

"All they talk about is death and how neat it's going to be to be dead and the power they'll have."

Father looked over at Jamie who was also on the verge of tears.

"Jamie, would you take Mrs. Geller down the hall and get her a soft drink from the machine in the lobby and get her some fresh air?" Father asked, trying to gesture with his tone of voice and his eyebrows.

"I could sure use that," she replied, quickly understanding Father's intentions.

Jamie got up and with her hand invited Mrs. Geller to go ahead of her.

"I'll join you in just a few minutes," Father said as he watched them enter the hallway and close the door behind them.

After he was sure they were gone Father turned to the young boy in bed and said as seriously as he could, "Larry, what else is going on that you know about but haven't told your mom?"

"I know Patty is sneaking out of her room at night a lot," he confided gladly, as if it was finally a relief to tell somebody.

"Where is she going, do you know?"

"I don't know but one night I was up to go to the bathroom, and I heard them outside her window. I got up and looked and there were, I think, about six other people outside with her. I think Billy was with her that night. He's been acting weird, too. He blasts us all out with that heavy metal music, and since mom works, he thinks he's the boss. His friends are always picking on me and they call me 'Testicle.'

"Lately these weirdo girls have been coming over when mom goes to work, and they all go into Billy's bedroom and lock the door. He told me that if I told mom he would see to it that I regretted it to the max."

"Do you know all of the girls, Larry?" Father asked.

"A couple, but there are two that I don't know. They are older."

"How old?"

"I would say at least twenty or twenty-one; and boy do they dress weird. They're worse than Patty. One told me she had an earring in her nipple and asked me if I wanted to see it."

Father had to bite his lip to keep from laughing from the way Larry rolled his eyes when he talked about the earring.

"Who else do you know in Engleton who is running around like your sister?"

Larry looked up to the ceiling as he tried to recall. "There's Elizabeth Krouse and P.J. Webster and P.J's older sister Rachel, but she's in college."

"How about with Billy?" Father pried even further.

"Some guy they call Brass. There's Mike Carson and Eddie Long. The rest I don't know."

"Larry, I'm going to kind of call this confession so I don't want you to tell anyone you told me this. It'll be our secret, all right?" Father was afraid that it might put Larry in danger if they knew Larry had told him so much.

Larry nodded his head yes.

"Can I pray for you before I go?" Father asked, as he sat down on the side of the bed.

Larry nodded again and then said, "For mom, too."

"For mom, too," Father repeated, almost breaking down as his heart broke for this family that was under such severe attack. "Father God," he started as he laid his hand on Larry's head. "Bless this young man and protect him, Father, because he is such a great young man. Father, in Jesus' Name, I plead Your precious Blood over him to protect him and to guide him. Give him strength in the storm to be strong and to help his mother. Bless him, Lord, for being so honest and may You use him for Your Kingdom as he helps draw souls to Your Son. Bless his mother and give her strength in this battle. Put Your angels around her and around Larry to guard and guide in Jesus' Name. Amen."

Larry shut his eyes as Father made the sign of the Cross on his forehead.

"Champ," Father said, getting up from the side of the bed, "you keep getting better and I'll see you at home. Okay?"

Larry nodded his head yes.

"See you later," Father grinned, as he gave the boy a thumbs up sign then opened the door and walked into the hallway.

Father walked down the hallway pondering over the information that Larry had just revealed. As he entered the lobby he found Jamie and Mrs. Geller talking over in the corner of the room. They both stood up as soon as they saw Father.

"You have one fine son there, Mrs. Geller," Father encouraged as he walked up to her and took her hand.

"It's just so hard raising kids this day and time," she replied, not able to receive the compliment.

"I know, but God always provides if we ask Him for help. In fact, could I ask you to do something that would bring God's blessing to your children?"

"Anything," she replied.

"Would you come by the church and pick up some holy water and a special prayer that I've written out that you can pray over your children?"

"Yes, Father, most definitely. Larry gets to go home this afternoon when Dr. Verney dismisses him. Could I come by then?"

"That would be great," he replied, squeezing her hand.

They exchanged salutations as Jamie and Father Macon left Mrs. Geller in the lobby and headed back into the hospital.

"Where are we going?" Jamie asked as she followed Father back down the main hallway.

"One more stop, then we'll be ready."

Father went back to where he remembered Mrs. O'Leary's room. The door was open as Father entered.

"Knock, knock," he said, as he paused at the entrance.

Mr. O'Leary was leaning over his wife helping her to get a drink of water. He grinned widely as he saw Father Macon.

"Father," he almost shouted, "come in here and see my beautiful wife."

"Ben," Mrs. O'Leary said as she let go of her drinking straw and slapped at him with her empty hand.

"Wow," Father exclaimed, going along with him. "Ben, you're the luckiest man in the world."

"I know," he said, continuing to grin from ear to ear.

"You boys," Mrs. O'Leary replied, enjoying every bit of the attention and flattery.

"Oh, I almost forgot," Father said, turning to Jamie and allowing her to come closer to Mrs. O'Leary. "This is Jamie McClain. She's a special investigator from Little Rock. She's trying to help me find out why all my parishioners can't be like you two."

Everyone laughed, then Ben spoke, "We're glad to meet you, Mrs. McClain."

"I'm glad to meet you, too," Jamie replied, "but I'm afraid it's Miss."

"Uh oh," Ben retorted, still grinning, "Father, we're going to have to pray a lot of strength for you."

"Ben!" Mrs. O'Leary chided as they all laughed.

"I haven't stopped since I met her yesterday," Father kidded as he remembered the bishop's phone call. "Have you been feeling better?" Father asked Mrs. O'Leary as their laughter died down and he thought he had better change the subject.

"I feel much better," her face returning to a serious look. "The doctors say that if all continues to go well, I can go home in a couple of days."

"Praise the Lord! That's wonderful," Father exclaimed enthusiastically.

"Yes, praise the Lord," Ben repeated. "And we owe it all to you, Father. I know she wouldn't be with us today if it hadn't been for your prayers. She was in bad shape." Tears began to well up in his eyes as he finished speaking.

"Ben," Father quickly cut in. "It wasn't me, it was the power of the Lord Jesus Christ. Your covenant rights include healing. By Jesus' stripes Martha was healed and we're seeing it manifested here today. To God be the glory."

"I know God did the work but your powerful prayers didn't hurt anything," Ben replied, regaining his composure.

"Prayer is powerful," Father agreed. "But it also proves that we need each other in the Body of Christ. In fact, right now I need your help with something."

"How can we help?" Mrs. O'Leary asked before Ben could say anything. He looked at his wife and grinned as he nodded his head in agreement, happy to see her back to her spunky self again.

"I believe Engleton is under a severe attack by Satan, but in order to fight him we must come together in prayer. I know you two believe in the power of prayer, and I need you to spend time in prayer for Engleton. I believe Martha's relapse last night was a direct result of the demonic activity being 'stepped up' against the people of Engleton. If we are going to beat this thing, we will have to come together in unity and defeat the principality over Engleton."

"Consider us part of the army, Father," Ben replied. "Martha is going to have to take it slow even when we get home. We can turn that time into a time of intercession."

"That's great!" Father exclaimed. "I knew I could count on you two."

"I've got my rosary right here," Mrs. O'Leary joined in, holding up her rosary beads.

"Wonderful," Father complimented. "Martha, I'm counting on you to wear those beads out."

"If I know her, she will," Ben laughed.

Father Macon prayed again over Mrs. O'Leary and Ben, then they exchanged good-byes. Ben told Jamie it was nice to meet her and Mrs. O'Leary squeezed her hand and whispered for her to look out after Father because he worked too hard. Jamie grinned and said she would try but she didn't know if it was possible for him to slow down. Mrs. O'Leary laughed and agreed.

Walking down the hallway of the hospital Jamie thought how truly amazed she was with this man. She was anxious to hear what Larry had told him while she and Mrs. Geller were out of the room. She had assessed that Mrs. Geller was a good woman but that she was just overwhelmed by the responsibility of being a single parent with three teenage children. She also realized that Mrs. Geller didn't have a clue about what was going on in the lives of her children. However, without a man's support and with all of the responsibilities dumped on her, Jamie didn't know how anyone else could do much better. She was beginning to understand something about how Satan seemed to work. He didn't come after those who were strong. She noticed that so far he had only attacked the weak.

CHAPTER SIX

THE TATTOO

It was getting close to lunch time as they drove back toward Bettis Bluff. Jamie had not said a thing, hoping Father Macon would initiate the conversation, but when he didn't, she couldn't stand the suspense much longer. She could tell he was deep in thought or prayer and she didn't want to interrupt but her curiosity got the best of her, and she finally ventured forth a slight cough to gain his attention.

"Jamie, I'm sorry," he apologized. "I didn't mean to completely ignore you. I was just thinking."

"About what Larry told you?" she asked, hoping he would share what they had discussed.

"Yes. I know now why Syrasohan decided to claim this area as his territory. Apparently we have a very active coven of Satanists in the area. They have been sending forth enough sin and evil to create darkness of a magnitude to make Syrasohan think it's worth his time to get involved in this area. Someone or something has given him the invitation and he has accepted. The thing that concerns me the most is that it sounds as if the young people are the ones most affected and mostly involved, but…."

He tapered off and she could tell he was back into a deep mode of concentration.

"But what?" she asked, trying to dislodge his concentration so that he would finish his train of thought.

"I don't think that a principality with the clout of Syrasohan would enter an area with just a bunch of kids involved in the occult. They're undependable. These things only work with the utmost secrecy. One loose tongue and the whole coven could be in jail. Satan doesn't want the PR. Anytime these things get in the news, it raises the awareness of the public that this stuff might be real. Satan doesn't want that. That's why very little is heard, even in a small community like Engleton. Usually a person can't stub their toe in this community without everyone knowing about it before nightfall. That gives you an idea how covert and secret this Satanist stuff is. In fact," he laughed to change the mood, "they've already got you and me sleeping together in the rectory."

"What?" Jamie laughed, looking at him and blushing brightly.

"The bishop called me from Little Rock LAST NIGHT just to check on rumors he had heard. That's after only one day."

"Whoa, that is heavy," she replied, trying to shield the thoughts that were coming into her mind. She wasn't sure but she was afraid she was falling in love with this man, a priest. Sleeping with him was not something she would turn down. She was glad he was a priest because if he had tried to make a pass at her, she would have probably accepted. Even though she was Christian, sex outside of marriage had never seemed that big of a deal to her. She had had sex with a couple of guys in high school and one guy since she had been on the investigation team, but no one had ever affected her like this man sitting next to her.

She had noticed that the last guy she had dated had the filthiest mouth. His vocabulary was terrible and as bad as she hated it, after a while she began to talk the same way. She realized after eight months that this guy was bad for her so she broke the relationship off. Her vocabulary had improved but some of those words still came out of her mouth every once in a while, sometimes so quickly that she didn't seem to have control, like a reflex action.

"That's part of Satan's strategy, too," Father continued, bringing her mind back to the moment. "If he can divide the people against me, the bishop will have me transferred and Satan will have a wide open field in which to work."

"Wouldn't he just assign a new priest to the area?" she asked, still trying to shake the sexual thoughts that kept whizzing through her mind.

"The church has a vast shortage of priests. There are not enough to go around. They might not get another priest or the one assigned might be old or not even know a thing about spiritual warfare. Satan could sit in the first pew and probably not be recognized."

"How is that possible? I thought all priests understood the power and the reality of Satan."

"That is not the case today, I'm sorry to say. People are being misled to think sin is a thing of the past. It's no longer our own fault when we sin. They think that either God made them that way, or that it was caused by a gene, or it was their parent's fault or their first grade teacher did something to them. It is generally thought that we are the way we are and that we have no power to change. Since sin is no longer real, God could not punish us for something that's His fault anyway. Hell becomes a thing of the past and Satan a personification of evil. When man finally gets his act together, evil will be destroyed and man will live in peace forever. They think man's salvation depends on man, and Jesus is not needed. To them He was a notable man in history but his true mission was to show us a better way just like Mohammed, Moses, Confucius, and every other mystic of our time."

"How in the world did it ever get to that point?" she asked in amazement.

"It was lost because the church lost its vision. Salvation of souls is no longer the primary ministry of the church, taking care of the poor is. Social justice has become the great 'windmill' of the church that we all charge forth to conquer. We're busy doing good things, trying to solve bad problems, but we fail to understand that those problems have a spiritual origin. People don't pray because they don't think a personal relationship with Jesus is pertinent. Self gratification is the source of happiness. If it feels good, then it's what I need, regardless of the spiritual consequences. When it doesn't work out, however, I begin to immediately look around and find someone else to blame."

"You paint a bleak picture, Father," she said, "but even I can see what you're saying in my own life. Just these last two days I've spent with you have been an eye opener."

"The prophet Hosea, three thousand years ago, said 'My people perish from lack of knowledge'. That's the exact problem today. Combine that with apathy and you can see why Satan is making such strong strides right now in this world. We talk to trees, and chant like a Montana wolf, eat tofu sandwiches and call the psychic hot-line for all our problems. God says 'Blessed is the nation whose God is the Lord'. God is no longer this nation's Lord and we are suffering the consequences."

"But it is so obvious," Jamie exclaimed, grabbing her arms and shivering. "That demon I saw in the church was as real as anything I have ever seen, and I could feel his terrible power."

"You now know the truth because you have experienced the reality of his presence. He's not going to show himself like that to everyone UNTIL it's too late."

"What do you mean, too late?" she asked, sensing the foreboding nature of his words.

"Jamie, have you not read the Book of Revelation? We know HOW this mess is all going to end. There will come a time when it will be too late for repentance. Many churches believe in what they call the Rapture. Many churches don't. Our Catholic Church is one of those who doesn't. All do agree, however, that a time of great trouble is coming. No one wants to ponder the extent of that trouble because Jesus himself said it was going to be not just bad, but super-bad! Again, we have some who have managed to convince themselves that there will always be another future generation when this terrible time hits. I get so tickled because at every Mass I say, the people respond, 'Christ has died, Christ is risen, Christ will come again'. Probably not half of the people who speak those words really believe them. Tradition has managed to destroy the power and the effectiveness of those words."

Just as he finished speaking, Father turned to Jamie and asked, "Are you hungry?"

"Yes," she answered, "I could eat something. I only had a small glass of orange juice for breakfast and that's wearing kind of thin."

"Good," he said, "me too. There's a Burger Royal right up ahead that makes great hamburgers. Does that sound okay?"

"Sounds wonderful," Jamie replied, as she started looking for the sign of the burger place.

She spotted the sign and Father slowed down to turn into the driveway. "We've got time to eat it here if that's all right, or we can go through the drive-through if you need to get back."

"I've got plenty of time," she quickly responded, wanting to make use of anything that might prolong her time with this man. He was undoubtedly the most intriguing man she had ever met, and she loved being with him.

Father Macon pulled the jeep into one of the parking spots and they both walked into the restaurant area of the burger joint. The place was not very crowded so they chose a booth over on the opposite side from the door.

"Hello, Father," the waitress said, setting down a glass of water in front of each of them. "You want your usual?"

"You know me well, Maggie," he said as he smiled, then took a sip of the water.

"How about you, ma'am?" she asked, turning to Jamie.

"I'll have a, ugh," she paused as she squinted, trying to read the menu above the counter. "How about the chicken special with a Coke?"

"Good choice," replied the waitress. "They'll be out in a few minutes."

As the waitress returned and brought their drinks, the door opened and a tall, rugged looking man with a cowboy hat came into the restaurant. He took off his hat and hung it on the coat and hat rack by the door. He glanced over at Jamie and when her eye caught his he quickly turned away and found a seat over in the corner. Jamie watched as the waitress waited on him and then turned her attention back to Father Macon.

"From what you said a while ago I somehow gather that you think Jesus' return is getting close?" she asked as she watched a stream of soda travel through his straw and disappear into his mouth.

"I really am not sure, and to be perfectly honest, I don't care. Now I don't want that to sound harsh but if Jesus comes tomorrow, there are a lot of people going to hell, and I don't want that and neither does God, my Father. I want as many people enjoying eternity as possible and His prolonged coming gives me a greater opportunity to bring more souls into the Kingdom."

She was simply amazed with the caring of this man. As she sat and listened to him, however, she noticed that the man in the corner booth kept looking at her. She could see him out of the corner of her eye and it gave her the chills. She started to say something just as the waitress brought their food.

"Boy, that smells good, Maggie," Father said as she sat his plate in front of him.

"Marry me and run away with me and I'll fix you one every day," she kidded, as she sat Jamie's plate in place.

"You know it would almost be worth it," he said, laughing as he took her hand and patted the back of it.

"Just as my mom told me," she said as he let go of her hand. "A way to a man's heart is through his stomach."

Jamie could feel a slight bit of jealousy quicken within her as she watched Maggie go back to the kitchen window. How many women would like to run away with him? She knew of two.

They continued to eat and talk and Jamie could feel the man in the corner continuing to stare at her. Finally, she just blatantly turned and fixed her gaze on him. He immediately finished his cup of coffee, put some money on the table, and walked over to the hat rack. He kept his face to the wall as he walked past them. As he fixed his hat on his head, his shirt sleeve fell away revealing a red and blue tattoo that read "Satan Rules". Before she could say anything the man opened the door and was gone.

"Father, do you know that man that just left?" she asked as soon as the door shut behind him.

"No, I never saw him before," he answered, trying to talk around a piece of food. "Why?"

"He stared at me the whole time and he had a tattoo on his left arm that read 'Satan Rules.'"

"Well, I can't blame him for staring, and that's not that uncommon for tattoos. Mothers, girlfriends, and the devil are the most common and, I think, probably in that order."

She was so surprised by his answer that she couldn't respond. In his own way, he had just told her that she was beautiful or at least something pleasant to look at. She giggled inside like a school girl and smiled to herself as she finished her dinner. It caused her to completely forget about the man and the tattoo.

After finishing their lunch Father paid the check and they once again climbed into the jeep. As he started the engine he turned to her and said, "Your car is still out at the rectory. I didn't find anybody to drive it to your motel room. Why don't I take you back out there and you can drive it back to the motel yourself."

"That's a good plan," she smiled, still beaming from his compliment.

Father pulled the jeep out on the highway and headed it toward Engleton. They drove quite a few miles before anyone said anything. Jamie could tell that he was deep in thought but she still wanted to capitalize on this time as much as she could.

"Why are there so many bridges in this area?" she asked, trying to find anything to bring his mind back to the now.

"This is farming land," he replied, "and a lot of drainage goes with level farming land, especially being this close to the river."

"What river?" she asked, not realizing that a river was close by.

"It's called Blue River," he answered. "It starts up in Missouri and runs into another river farther south toward you all in Little Rock."

"Where is it from here?"

"It's in that direction," Father pointed, as he extended his arm to the right over the dashboard, "about a mile, mile and a half, as the crow flies."

To her regret, they quickly arrived at the rectory. Her car was right where she left it, and Father pulled into his parking spot close to the steps of the rectory. As they both got out, Jamie fumbled in her pocket for her keys.

"I've certainly enjoyed it," she said, finally finding her keys.

"Me, too," Father replied as he came around the front of the jeep and took her hand.

"Are you following my instructions with the holy water and oil and especially Psalm 91?" The look he had on his face revealed that he was very serious.

"He that dwells in the secret place of the Most High shall abide under the shadow of the Almighty," she quoted as she grinned like a child trying for the approval of a parent.

Father smiled, too, as she finished the verse. "Jamie, I am so proud of you. If I could get a third of my parishioners to do in a month what you have done in a day, we could turn this thing around in no time."

His compliment only added to the wonderful feelings she experienced around him. It only made her departure more difficult, but she couldn't come up with any other reason to stay, so she finally said, "I guess I'd better get back to the hotel and check in with headquarters."

Father, still holding her hand, pulled her close to him and gave her a big hug. She quickly returned the hug which made leaving him even more difficult. He pulled away first and looked at her and grinned. He had been in love one time and he knew the feeling. He enjoyed being with her but he knew that more than fate had brought them together.

"Call me when you get to your room," he told her as she went around to unlock her car door. She nodded and got inside the car, buckled her seat belt and put the key in the ignition. When she turned the key, however, the car made a low grinding sound then stopped and made only a constant click.

Father immediately knew that the car was not going to start. "Jamie," he called, as she tried to start the car again.

She stopped, unbuckled her seat belt, got out, and stood looking over the top of the car.

"Sounds like your battery is dead."

"What should I do?"

"Come on into the rectory and we'll call a service station and see if we can get some help out here."

She tried to act disappointed but was actually excited that the car hadn't started. "Thank you, Lord," she said under her breath as she watched Father Macon unlock the door and stand aside so she could go in first.

"Where did you rent the car?" he asked as they walked into the rectory office. "They should be able to send someone out and take care of it."

She took out her billfold and pulled a card from the interior. "Murphy's Station and Car Rental, 763-4445," she read, then handed the card to Father.

Father Macon took the card and dialed the phone as he read the number softly to himself. He looked up at Jamie and grinned as he waited for someone to answer on the other end. Someone did finally answer but because of being short-handed, no one could come out and repair the car until later in the afternoon. Father told them thank you and that he would expect them sometime in the afternoon.

"Well, we have some time before they can fix your car. Let me change clothes and I'll fix us some coffee and then we can go check on the progress of the church clean-up."

Jamie shook her head okay and sat down to wait on Father. As Father entered his bedroom the answering machine caught his eye. "Father God, bless the man that invented this thing," he said as he punched the play button. There were three empty beeps before the first message. "Father, this is Mike Farron. The church clean-up went very well. Everything is fine and the church is ready to be used. Sure was sad to see that statue go. Kind of looks empty over in that area now. Talk to you later." Father praised God for the work being done and asked a blessing on Mike for his labor. Two more beeps went by until another message came forth. "Father Macon." He could hear desperation in the voice. "This is Eva Krouse. Something is terribly wrong and I need your help. Please, please call me as soon as possible."

CHAPTER SEVEN

THE ENCOUNTER

"Jamie," Father Macon yelled from the bedroom, "come here."

"Where are you?" she asked as she waited to hear his voice again.

"In here, in the bedroom."

She followed the sound of his voice and finally traced its origin to Father's bedroom.

"Come in and listen to this," he said as she stood in the doorway, waiting for an explanation.

She walked into the bedroom and sat down next to him on the bed as he leaned over and punched the button on the answering machine again. As the message replayed, the look on Jamie's face changed to one of concern.

"What do you think?"

"If I were a betting man I would say that this probably has something to do with our situation at hand."

"Oh really?" she replied, not making any connection.

Father turned off the answering machine then stood up and walked around the room thinking. "If I remember right, Larry Geller said that Elizabeth Krouse was one of the girls involved with Patty Geller. Somehow this has something to do with Elizabeth, I just know it."

Father walked over to the phone, picked up the directory and found the Krouse's number. He wrote it down beside the phone then dialed each number. Someone must have answered the phone on the first ring because the conversation became intense very quickly. Jamie could tell that whoever was on the other end of the line was very upset and frightened. As Father hung up the phone she could tell that he had been right in his assumption. His face looked very worried and she could tell by the way he had tried to comfort the other person that something big was coming down.

"Boy," he remarked as he hung up the phone,

"What is it?" Jamie asked, filled with anticipation.

"The Krouse home is having trouble with poltergeist spirits and it's got everybody in the family scared to death. They have furniture moving around, things flying through the air, and the small kids are seeing dark figures in their rooms."

"How about Elizabeth?"

"They haven't heard from her for two days, and her mom and dad are worried sick."

"It sounds like pandemonium," Jamie exclaimed. "What are you going to do?"

"I'm going to have to go over there and see what I can do. But I've got a problem."

"What's that?" Jamie asked, racking her brain, trying to figure out what kind of a problem he could have.

"I told Mrs. Geller that I would be here this afternoon when she came by to pick up the prayers I wanted her to pray, along with the holy water and the blessed oil. She needs to begin to use those things or we may have two haunted houses in Engleton."

"I'll be glad to stay here and give her those things while you go over to the Krouse's and tend to their needs. That way I'll be here when the mechanic comes to fix my car. Besides, I don't know if

I'm ready yet to have objects flying around me for no reason."

"That sounds great. I'll try to get back as soon as I can."

Jamie watched as Father gathered up his things. He found his stole and his anointing oil, and then he picked up a small suitcase that he had sitting next to his night stand and placed it on the bed.

"What's in there?" Jamie asked as she watched him open the lid.

"I may have to say Mass in order to cleanse the house fully and these are the things I will need for that."

He left the room for a couple of minutes and returned with a large manila envelope. "Here is what you need to give to Mrs. Geller when she comes by. In here is a bottle of holy water, some blessed oil and some prayers that she is to pray every day over herself, her children and her home. She can tell by reading them which prayer is to be used where. Tell her it is vital that she believe what she is praying and not let it be just something she reads off of a page. She must trust in God and in His might, not what the circumstances look like. Can you remember to tell her that?"

Jamie shook her head yes and took the manila envelope from his hand.

"Wait just a minute," he said as he started to pick up the things he had packed. He again left the room but returned this time with a book. "You will have some time on your hands while you are waiting. This would be something very valuable to read until I can get back." As he finished speaking he handed her the book. She looked at the cover and smiled.

"The Power of Speaking in Tongues," she read out loud, not sounding very excited about the subject.

Father picked up on her lack of enthusiasm and said encouragingly, "Jamie, this is one of the most powerful gifts we can use to grow in the knowledge of the spiritual realm. Anyone who is going to fight in spiritual warfare must have their prayer language. While I'm gone, spend some time reading that book and I think you will see what I mean. Then afterwards, if you want to, we'll pray for you to receive your prayer language."

"We'll see," she said, still not sounding convinced.

"I'd better go," he said as he gathered up his things and started toward the bedroom door. As he hit the doorway he turned and faced her again, "I'm glad God sent you here at this time. You don't know how much support you've been. Be careful while I'm gone and try not to talk to anyone except Mrs. Geller and the mechanic. Just let the answering machine handle any phone calls. Okay?"

She nodded her head, almost in tears from the words he had spoken. She was in love with him, she knew that now. Just those few words he had shared of her importance to him had caused her heart to flood with joy. She allowed the tears to roll down her cheeks as she heard the door to the rectory slam. She sat on the bed for a little while then took the book and went back to the rectory office. She opened the book and began to read.

The Krouse's house was only about two miles from the rectory so Father Macon began to pray in the spirit as he left the church parking lot. He listened for anything in his spirit, a word that might give him direction or discernment. None came.

"Lord," he finally said as he pulled his jeep into the Krouse's driveway, "this battle is not mine but Yours, in Jesus' Name."

Mrs. Krouse had seen Father's jeep pull into the driveway and she had run out to meet him even before he could shut the engine off and get out. Father could tell by looking at her face that she had been crying a lot.

"Oh, Father," she cried, almost dragging him out of the jeep before he could get his seat belt undone. "God is punishing us! We've not put enough effort into our faith and now He's punishing us."

"Calm down, Eva," Father said, grabbing her arm and trying to comfort her. "I assure you God is not the author of what's going on."

"But Father," she interrupted, "we've seen and heard things that can only come from God or His angels."

"How long has this been going on, Eva?" Father asked, removing his suit case and vestment bag that he kept in the back seat of his jeep.

"It started two nights ago and has steadily gotten worse. At first it was lights going off and on. We thought that was trouble with the electric company until we noticed that it didn't happen in all the rooms of the house at the same time. Then we started hearing voices that came out of thin air. The kids said they saw people standing in Elizabeth's room but there was no one in there. I called Ray. He's still on the boats and he said to call you. That's when things started flying through the air. Pens, dishes, one of my good vases and about an hour ago one of my dining room chairs just raised up into the air and came down, shattering into pieces."

"Where are the kids?"

"I sent them to their grandmother's in Bettis Bluff, except for Elizabeth and like I told you on the phone, I haven't seen her for a day and a half. The kids are scared to death. Jonathan thought it was the end of the world. Father, what is going on?"

"Eva, what I'm going to tell you may sound off the wall but it is the truth."

"Nothing sounds off the wall, Father," she interjected, "after what I've been through."

Father laughed lightly because he could see that she was beginning to calm down and lighten up some. "There is a group of Satanists in Engleton and they have invited a powerful demonic presence into this area. A lot of things have been happening as a result. I figure that what's going on in there," he pointed to the house, "is a direct result of your daughter's involvement with this group."

"Oh, Father!" Mrs. Krouse cried as she put her hands over her mouth and cheeks.

"Has your daughter been showing some strange behavior lately?"

"Oh, yes" she replied as she continued to cry, "so much weird stuff, clothing, make-up, those horrible posters in her room, that weird music. I even found drugs in one of her blue jeans pockets as I was going to wash them. It finally came to a head two days ago. I had talked to Ray on the phone and he told me to spank her butt. Father, she's as big as I am. How do you spank a sixteen year old? I told her I wanted those posters off the wall and she told me they honored her lover. I said who in God's name is your lover that needs honoring like that? She spouted off some weird name and I told her that was enough. I told her to go to her room and not come out until those posters were off the wall and she had cleaned up herself and took off all that black makeup. She apparently crawled out her window because a couple hours later when I went to check on her, she was gone."

"Eva, did her lover's name sound like Syrasohan?" Father asked carefully.

"Yah, something like that. I remember it sounded Iranian and I figured she had met some foreigner in Bettis Bluff that had influenced her to act this way."

Father cringed as he sat the suitcase on the hood of his jeep and removed the bottle of holy water and a container of blessed salt. "Eva, why don't you get in my jeep and wait there. I'll yell at you if I need you."

While Eva was following Father's instructions, he took the salt and water and began to walk around the outside of the house, sprinkling each sacramental as he went. "Father God, in Jesus' Name, I sanctify this property and this house. By the power of our baptism I call on our covenant rights and the power therein. As I sprinkle this water and salt let it be a testimony to our baptism and that we are indeed the salt of the earth."

He continued to pray and sanctify the ground around the entire house. As he came back around into Eva's view she could still see him sprinkling the salt and water and stopping every few feet in prayer. When he reached his original starting point he stopped and began to pray out loud in tongues. Then he raised his hands and said, "In the Name of Jesus Christ I declare this ground holy and sanctified and now, Father, I plead the Blood of Jesus over every inch of it."

The words were no sooner out of his mouth than from inside the house came a loud and spine chilling, "NO!"

Father looked over at Eva who was as wide-eyed as he had ever seen anyone. He could tell she was scared to death. "Eva, stay in the jeep. I'm going in the house and I'll be out in a little while. You pray while I'm in there. Okay?"

Eva nodded her head, and he could already see her lips moving in prayer. He came back over to the hood of the jeep, put the salt and holy water back in the case, then shut it and picked it up along with his vestments.

"Father, be careful," Eva said fearfully as he turned and headed toward the house.

Father opened the screen door then carefully opened the main door. A cold blast of air hit him in the face as he entered. It must have been below freezing. The cold was almost penetrating. He set his suitcase down on a nearby chair and opened the garment bag that contained his vestments. He methodically put each one on as he prayed in tongues. Suddenly a large vase that had been on the TV console flew past him and crashed into the wall behind him. The warmth of the vestments felt good. He leaned down and again took the salt and holy water out of the suitcase on the chair. Slowly he started making his way through the house. He could still feel the cold but it was now bearable. He found the hallway and started toward where he assumed the bedrooms would be. He stepped over broken glass from picture frames that had been hurled to the floor.

Approaching the first bedroom he carefully peeked in. Everything looked fine until the window blind on the far window began to go up and down in rapid succession. Father jumped from reflex, then loudly began to pray in tongues as he remembered what the lady who had taught him about spiritual warfare always told him. "No matter how frightened you are, never let a demon see you sweat." He grinned, trying to show confidence until from the next room down the hall he began to hear a low moan. It increased until he heard a low male voice say, "Priest, you are a dead man. I'm going to kill you and take over this entire area. There's nothing you can do, they want me here."

"Satan, you are a liar," he began to proclaim as he walked to the next room where he thought the voice was coming from. "I command you in Jesus' Name, whose I am and whom I serve, to leave these premises."

"You do not belong to Jesus, you are full of lust for that woman and I will use that lust to destroy you and possess her."

"That is a lie!" Father Macon exclaimed. "I have not lusted

after her and you will not lay one hand on her in the Name of Jesus."

Reaching the bedroom at the far end of the hall, Father quickly stepped into the bedroom doorway, expecting to confront the demon. There was nothing there, but he could feel the tremendous evil emanating from the room. The room was a mess with clothes every where, the bed unmade, and things strewn all around. Immediately he noticed the posters on the wall. The entire room was covered with posters showing vampires, weird looking robots, and grotesque monsters. In every scene the monster or robot was holding a half-naked woman in its arms. One poster showed a large breasted woman entwined with a fiendish looking robot and under the picture were the words: "Robot Sex Is Electrifying." It reminded Father of the scenes on the tomb wall in Iraq but they were not nearly as vile. As he thought of Elizabeth and how she had been deceived, his anger began to boil. He began to walk around the room and tear the vulgar posters off the wall. Shrieks and screams began to fill the room as he pulled each poster down, but he paid no attention.

He could feel the power of the Holy Spirit welling up in him as he began to exclaim, "Satan, in the Name of Jesus, I bind your strong man Syrasohan and his power over this house. I break his hold and his assignment over this family and command that he be cast to the foot of Father God for Him to do with as He pleases." As Father continued to pray, suddenly he began to hear a young woman's voice scream. "You're killing me, you're killing me."

Unfazed, he continued until every poster was down and in shreds. "I rebuke you in the Name of Jesus and command that you leave now!" he shouted. Father began again to pray loudly in the spirit, then he heard in his mind, "Bed." Continuing to pray out loud Father turned and looked in the direction of the bed. There on the headboard was the piece of ceremonial bone attached with a piece of scotch tape. He walked over to the headboard and removed the bone holding it by the piece of tape which stayed attached. He could feel the evil radiating from the fragment. The screams continued as he carried the bone fragment back into the dining area. The cold did not seem as severe, but it could have been because he was so angry at the demon for what he had done to this family. He went to the open suitcase and removed the bag of hosts and a small vial of wine. He lit two candles on each side of the table and laid a crucifix in the middle. He found a skillet and some bits of newspaper which he also placed on the makeshift altar. Then he placed the bone on the pile of paper in the skillet. He took one of the hosts and laid it on the paten and began to say Mass. All hell broke loose as he began the Eucharistic prayer for the Transubstantiation to take place. As the Holy Spirit came in, the activity reached a fever pitch. Things began to fly through the air. The lights began to go off and on until the bulb over the dining table which Father was using for an altar exploded. As it popped and went out, he flinched but continued saying the Mass. Things were hitting the wall all around him as he elevated the Body and Blood and began to pray in the spirit. Hundreds of voices began to scream and yell. It was almost nerve shattering but he continued with increased fervor. He knew he was winning. Tears streaked down his face as he suddenly saw the figure of Jesus on the Cross and above the roar of the voices around him he heard Jesus cry out, "It is finished."

After yelling the Lamb of God prayer for all creation to hear, he consumed the Body and drank the Blood except for a small amount. He then took the remaining amount and dripped it on the bone fragment. The most horrendous scream came from nowhere. Suddenly, the entire picture window in the living room exploded.

Glass fragments filled the front porch and the lawn in front of the house. The curtains and the attached rods were sucked by the explosion out into the yard almost to the bumper of Father's jeep.

Eva Krouse had hunkered down in the seat as the commotion in the house increased. She thought at one time about getting out and running away but she was afraid for the priest that was in her house all alone. When the window shattered and came flying her way, she screamed and covered her ears with her hands.

Inside the house Father took one of the altar candles and set the pieces of paper in the skillet on fire. He watched the bone fragment slowly blacken and shrink in size as the heat consumed it along with the paper underneath. The atmosphere in the house had changed completely. The window, now just a wide open space, allowed a fresh breeze to enter that caused Father Macon to grin. With everything he had he yelled, "Let us now go forth to love and serve the Lord."

From the open window he heard a faint, "Amen." Mrs. Krouse had gathered enough courage and concern that she had walked up to the window to peer in. A smile came to her face as she saw Father Macon finishing the Mass and she felt a strong burst of energy when he shouted the concluding prayer. "Father, are you all right?" she asked him as he began to take off his vestments.

"I'm wonderful!" he exclaimed. "And so is our Lord and Savior Jesus Christ. In His mighty Name and by the power of His Blood this house is free. Alleluia."

"What was it?" Mrs. Krouse asked, stepping into the living room through the open window.

"It was demonic activity of the strongest kind. I believe Elizabeth brought it in and it had made a claim to your home. Your daughter could be in a lot of danger. I'll call Sheriff Martin when I get back to the rectory. But Eva, you need to pray like you've never prayed before."

Tears began to well up in her eyes and trickle down her cheek. "Do you think she's in trouble?"

"I'm afraid so," he replied, reaching over and patting her on the arm, trying to comfort her. "But, our Lord is stronger than any foe so spend a lot of time in prayer tonight. When is Ray coming home?"

"He'll be in off the boats next week," she replied, still sobbing.

"Do you have someone who can help you fix this window temporarily until he gets in?" Father asked, using his head to point at the open window.

"Yes," she said, wiping her eyes, "I'll go to mothers and get Jonathan and he can help me. Should I tell him what went on here?"

"He'll have to know sometime, Eva. He's big enough to handle it and he really needs to know what's going on."

Father gathered up his things as Eva surveyed the damage.

"I don't know that I can stay here after this," she said, beginning to cry again.

"I know it's tough, Eva, but with enough love and prayer this can be a loving home again. You and Ray may have to make some adjustments, but it can happen. I promise you."

CHAPTER EIGHT

THE SUCCUBUS

Jamie sat and read the book with fascination. Why hadn't she been shown these things in her church? The stories in the book made her hungry to know Jesus the way the people in the book did. Story after story told how ordinary people overcame tremendous odds. People rescued, people healed of incurable diseases, people set free from addictions and demonic attack, and the one common denominator was the gift of tongues. Each person related how they had prayed in tongues for extended periods of time and how they had become sensitive to the Spirit of God through the gift.

She had not read all the book but a major part of it when she heard someone drive up in the parking lot. She got up from the chair and as she did, a small slip of paper fell to the floor out of the back of the book. It read: "Jamie, if you want your prayer language just ask God for it. He wants to give the gift to you even more than you want to receive it. He's waiting for you to ask." The note was signed by Father Macon. She folded it up and put it in her blouse pocket. She then went to the door to see who had entered the driveway. Immediately, though the window, she recognized Mrs. Geller and Larry. She opened the rectory door to greet them as they started up the steps. Mrs. Geller was surprised to see her but quickly responded to Jamie's invitation to come inside.

"You look great, young man," she said, as Larry came through the doorway.

He smiled and Jamie closed the door. "Father has a package for you in the office. Come on in," she said as she stepped around the two and led them to the rectory office.

They followed and Jamie handed her the manila envelope from the desk. She related everything that Father had said and stressed the importance of fervent prayer for her children and for her home. She explained that Father had been called out and that her car had a dead battery and that she was waiting on a mechanic.

"In fact," she said finally, "he should be here anytime. It's almost four and I know they probably close at five."

Mrs. Geller and Larry thanked Jamie and asked her to tell Father thanks. Jamie walked out with the two and stood talking to Mrs. Geller as she got into her car. Just as Mrs. Geller started her engine Jamie saw a truck pull into the driveway with Murphy's Auto written on the side.

"There he is now," she said, relieved to know that she hadn't been forgotten.

"Good," said Mrs. Geller, "we'll go and get out of his way."

Jamie waved good-by to the Gellers as she watched the two vehicles pass in the driveway. She waited until the truck pulled up and stopped and the driver got out.

"Ms. McClain?" he asked, looking through the door he had just opened.

"Yes," she answered, "here's the car." She turned and pointed to the dead automobile. The man shut the door and leaned over into the bed of his truck. He pulled out a car battery and as he passed her he said, “We ought to have you up and going in just a few minutes.”

She watched him raise the hood of the car and start to work, unhooking the old battery. She turned and went back into the rectory, returning to the office to read her book. As she did she remembered the note. She removed it from her blouse pocket and re-read it. Refolding it, she put it back into her pocket again and sat there quietly, gathering enough courage to ask for her prayer language.

“Jesus, I don’t know You like I should,” she said, as tears filled her eyes, “but I want to. I don’t know whether You remember or not but I was saved in Your Name many years ago. I’d like to renew my relationship with You now and get to be as good a person as Father Macon. He says I need my prayer language, and I trust him with all my heart. In fact, You know I’m in love with him. In Your precious Name, fill me with Your Holy Spirit and give me my prayer language.”

She sat there still, waiting to be hit by a bolt of lightening. She felt nothing and nothing came out of her mouth. She sat silently a little longer, waiting, but nothing seemed to happen. Disappointment was starting to take hold of her when the door bell rang. She got up, went to the door and found the mechanic standing on the top step.

“Ma’am, I’m sorry,” he said,” but it’s not the battery, it’s the starter. I put the new battery in and it still does not start. I won’t be able to fix it until tomorrow.”

“Oh my,” she said, grabbing a strand of hair and twirling it in her fingers. "I need to get back to the Hilltop Motel. Can I ride with you?"

"Sure, it's right on my way. I apologize for the inconvenience this is causing you."

"Oh, that's okay. Wait just a minute and I'll leave Father a note so he'll know what has happened and where I've gone."

"I'll wait for you in the truck," the man said as Jamie turned to go back into the rectory.

"I'll be right out."

Inside she found her book and put it under her arm. Then she found a pen and a piece of paper. She wrote: "Father, the car is still broken. The mechanic said it was the starter and not the battery. I rode back to the motel with the mechanic. I'll see you tomorrow. Call me tonight and let me know how things went at the Krouse's. Love, Jamie. P.S. I prayed for my prayer language. Nothing yet."

She looked around for a place to put the note so he would be sure and see it when he came in. She decided on the corner of the dining room table just inside the door. She thought that there, he couldn't miss it. She then turned on the outside porch light, locked the door and pulled it shut.

She walked over to the truck and climbed in the passenger seat. As they drove out of the driveway, she wondered how Father was getting along.

Eva had decided to spend the night at her mother's house in Bettis Bluff. Father helped her tack a large quilt over the window opening, hoping it would keep out any animals that might wander by. She thanked him over and over for what he had done, and she had made a vow to become a much more faithful prayer warrior. Father gave her a hug and watched as she pulled her car out on the highway, then he climbed into his jeep and started back toward the rectory. He was anxious to tell Jamie about what had happened and to share this first victory in the encounter.

He sang in tongues as he drove and he laughed when he thought about the demon accusing him of lusting after Jamie. She was beautiful and he enjoyed being with her but that did not constitute lust.

The sun was just setting as he neared the rectory. As he pulled in the driveway he was glad to see that her car was still where it was. He assumed that the mechanic had fixed her car and she had decided to stay and wait for him to return. He thought it was strange that there were no lights on anywhere. He parked his jeep and unlocked the rectory door. There was just enough light that he didn't have any problem finding the key hole. Opening the door, he turned and flipped on the light. Nothing happened.

"Jamie," he called out.

"In here," she replied, "I've been waiting for you."

Father followed the sound of the voice but could find no one in the office.

"I'm in the bedroom," she said softly. "I thought you'd never get back."

Standing in the doorway he could see her in his bed under the covers. "Why don't you come on in and lay down with me. I know you've got to be very tired," she said seductively.

Father didn't know what to do or what to say. He stood mute, just staring at her.

"If you won't come to me," she said, acting hurt, "then I'll come to you."

With her hand she threw back the covers revealing to him her nude body. She put her legs over the side of the bed then stood up facing him, revealing her entire body to him.

He was spell bound. She was beautiful. Her figure was perfect and he watched as her breasts rose and sank with each breath.

"I know you like what you see," she said, taking her hands and pushing her breasts toward him. "I'm all yours to do with as you wish."

Father could feel the power of the temptation pulling him to shreds. How could any man turn this down? He thought he was strong but this was just too much. Maybe the demon had been right. Maybe he was lusting after her and didn't even realize it. Right now the only thing he wanted to do was take her in his arms and make passionate love to this beautiful woman who was only fifteen feet away.

"I'm waiting, Rex," she enticed. "You're not going to disappoint me are you? I need you. I want you to make love to me. Tonight, right now. Take me in your arms and have your way with me. Hurry, Rex, I need you." She dropped her hands from her breasts and extended them to him.

With all the power and control he could muster within him he began to lightly pray in tongues. As soon as he started praying, he heard in his mind, "Succubus."

The word gave him strength and he asked her, "What happened to the lights, Jamie?"

"I don't know, honey," she replied. "They went off about 4:00. But don't worry about that, we've got plenty of light to do what we want to do."

He noticed that she would not leave the position by the bed. "Come on out into the light a little more, Jamie," he motioned with his hand, "I want a better look at that beautiful body."

"You can see me well enough where I am," she responded, losing some of her seductiveness. "You don't need to see me. I want you to feel me."

As she said that she bent forward slightly, trying to entice him with her cleavage. He caught a glimpse of her eyes. There were none there.

"Praise God," he said under his breath. "Jamie, I will make love to you if you will answer one question."

"Ask me, Rex, and hurry," she cooed. "I'm getting so hot waiting for you."

"Did Jesus Christ come in the flesh?" he exclaimed.

"Jesus is the son of God," she replied, "but let's not talk religion at a time like this. I need to make love to you."

"But did He come in the flesh?" he persisted.

She just stood there.

"Did Jesus Christ come in the flesh? Yes or No! Answer me!"

"You goddamn priest," she said, but with a much deeper voice. "You think you're so goddamn smart, but I will prevail." A long slender tongue came out of her mouth as she finished speaking. Her form began to change and as he watched, the beautiful form that had been before him slowly turned into a horrid, grotesque shape. "I will kill you, priest, and this territory will be mine."

"Satan, hell is the only thing that will be yours," he said boldly. "Jesus Christ did indeed come in the flesh and because He lives I have the power to tread you under my feet. You are defeated and my people will rise up against you."

"Your people are mine," the demon said in a mocking, raspy voice. "They love me much more than they do your Jesus. They love me because they love what I've got to offer. Sex, drugs, alcohol, abuse, mammon, I'm their god. How many ministers of your puny gospel would turn down what you did tonight? They all talk a good talk but underneath I know their hunger for what I have to offer. I have ruined many, and I will destroy them all, including you, priest." He pointed his scaly finger at Father Macon. "No one can stay strong by himself forever," he continued, "and when you get weak I promise I'll be there and you'll be mine." As he finished speaking he began to laugh in a horrible mocking manner, then suddenly the demon was gone. Father could hear the laughter still ringing through the rectory even after the demon had gone.

Father was still standing in the hallway when the lights flickered and then came back on. He immediately went to the office, grabbed a bottle of holy water and began to go through the rectory, slinging the water and casting out any remaining demons. When he got to his bed he poured the entire amount remaining on the bed clothes. He then changed his sheets. "How close I almost came to giving in to that demon," he thought. He fell to his knees on the side of the bed and began to give thanks to God for giving him the strength to resist such a powerful temptation. As he prayed his thoughts turned to Elizabeth Krouse. He quickly got up and dialed the number of the sheriff's office. On the third ring someone answered and he recognized Sheriff Martin's voice.

"Hello, sheriff's office."

"Sheriff Martin, this is Father Macon."

"Hello, Father. Boy, you just barely caught me. I was on my way out when I heard the phone. What can I do for you?"

Father told him that Mrs. Krouse and Elizabeth had had a quarrel and Elizabeth had run away. That had been two days ago and no one had heard anything from her since.

"You know these teenagers," the sheriff said assuredly. "When the hormones start flowing they all go kind of wacky. I raised two myself, and it was the worst time of my life. I wouldn't do it again for all the money in Fort Knox. She'll be back when she gets hungry. Tell Mrs. Krouse that I'll come out and take a look around tomorrow, but Father I see this all the time and it always works out. This will too."

"I hope you're right, sheriff," Father replied, thinking about the posters on Elizabeth's bedroom walls.

After hanging up the phone, Father decided to take a hot shower and get to bed. He had experienced a full day and it had drained him both physically and spiritually. He went through the rectory turning off any lights left on and as he passed the dinner table on the way to turn off the porch light, he found Jamie's note. He grinned as he read it and asked the Lord to give her a bold prayer language.

The shower felt great and after saying his night prayers, he climbed into bed and was soon sound asleep.

Suddenly he was in a barn loft fighting with Walter Foust.

Walter was cussing him as they fought, and he was getting too tired to go on. Walter seemed to be getting the best of him. Walter finally pinned his head to the floor with his boot. The straw on the floor was so thick that he could hardly breathe. He tucked Father's hands behind his back and held him up immobile. Father's head was so heavy but when he managed to raise it up there was the demon laughing and mocking him. "I told you I would win, you worthless piece of humanity," the demon snarled. As the demon started to kill him, the woman in Rogers who had taught him spiritual warfare flew in the hay hole of the barn loft and along with her were hundreds of people. They began to slap and hit at both the demon and Walter Foust. After a while both fell to the floor in a heap. The woman turned to Rex and said, "Father, that's how it's done." Then they started shouting and yelling and someone started ringing a bell as they celebrated. The bell seemed to get louder and louder, and....

Father Macon sat up in bed as he realized he had been dreaming. The phone was ringing and he laughed as he picked up the receiver.

"Hello," he said, too sleepy to remember the proper greeting.

"Father, this is Sheriff Martin," he heard in the phone.

Father had been in such a deep sleep that he had trouble waking up.

"Father, are you there?" he heard the sheriff ask on the other end.

"Yes, I'm here," Father said with a yawn as he put his legs over the side of the bed, trying to wake up. "What's the matter?"

CHAPTER NINE

THE VICTIM

"Father, I'm afraid you were right about the little Krouse girl. This one didn't turn out so well."

"Why? What's happened?" he asked, fully awake and aware that something terrible had happened.

"Some fishermen found her hanging from a tree down by the river right before daybreak. It looks like suicide. I'm headed back now to the scene and I thought you might want to ride with me."

"Yes, sheriff, I would," Father replied quickly. "Would you mind calling Miss McClain at the motel and picking her up also?"

"Do you think that's necessary?" the sheriff asked.

"Sheriff, if I'm right, this may appear to be a suicide but it's really a lot deeper than that. At the very least it was premeditated, assisted suicide."

"Okay Father, you've been right so far," the sheriff responded. "I'll call Miss McClain right now and pick her up on the way out to your place."

"I'll be ready," Father replied as he hung up the phone. He realized the victory was short lived. Satan is like a disease, he never gives up. He sat on the edge of the bed, realizing the magnitude of the battle and how small he was. He realized that he could not fight this battle by himself even with Jamie's support. He had to somehow make the people of Engleton understand. Unless they changed and repented and sought the light of the Lord, Satan would rule this area and their lives. More death would result. How many would have to die before they were willing to change?

"How do I do it, Lord?" he said, looking up to the ceiling. "How do I make the people see?"

By the time he got up, dressed, and downed a glass of orange juice, the sheriff's car was pulling into the driveway. The sun was still below the tree-line as he turned and locked the door to the rectory then walked down the steps to the sheriff's car. He could see Jamie sitting in the front seat with the sheriff so he opened the door behind the sheriff and sat down in the back seat.

"Morning," he said softy as he shut the door, leaving off the "good" on purpose because it was, as yet, anything but a good morning.

Jamie turned around and smiled as they exchanged greetings. The sheriff pulled the car back on the highway before anyone spoke again.

"Father, this is not a pretty sight," the sheriff said, breaking the silence. "The death of a child is never an easy thing to see."

"What makes you think it was a suicide?" asked Father, trying to reassure the sheriff that he could handle the situation.

"There was a note found on the ground below her body," he replied. "We think it fell out of her hand when she jumped from the tree."

"What did the note say?"

"Really strange stuff about her lover making her a queen and ruling with him in a kingdom much grander than this ugly world, but first she had to shuck off this flesh body to join him. I figure it was drugs."

"I'm afraid it's much more powerful than drugs," Father added, remembering the posters on the young girl's walls and associating them with the words of the note.

"What do you mean, Father?" the sheriff asked, trying to turn around to look at Father and drive the car at the same time.

"Sheriff, I don't know how much you've been exposed to Satanic worship but it is trying to get a stronghold here in Engleton. I know Elizabeth's death is a result."

As the sheriff and Jamie listened, he told them about the encounter the day before at the Krouse's home. He also shared with them what had happened with the Gellers and his "run in" with the demon in the church. He explained about Syrasohan and that somehow the principality had been invited into the area. He did not feel led to share about his experience with the Succubus spirit in the rectory the night before. He knew it would seem too far out and it might really embarrass Jamie. He continued to reveal to the sheriff the nature of the principality, Syrasohan, and what to look for and expect. Sexual perversion and death were his specialties, and if the Satanists weren't stopped, Elizabeth would not be the only victim.

"Father, that's pretty heavy," the sheriff replied, as Father finished speaking.

"I have seen the demon, too, sheriff," Jamie joined in, trying to lend support to Father's story.

"Both of you are convinced that this is what we are dealing

with, aren't you?" the sheriff asked, sensing the sincerity in Jamie's voice.

"Without any doubt," Jamie exclaimed, looking back at Father.

"Sheriff," Father said somberly, "this is more of a spiritual problem than a physical problem but convincing others of that will be difficult."

"You're telling me," the sheriff replied. "I will do what I can to help but the state boys may have a different opinion."

"I called Phil Bellows before I left," Jamie interjected. "I think he can help us out there. He should be here in an hour or two."

The sheriff had long since pulled off the main highway and had been turning here and there on gravel roads as they talked. They finally came to a straight stretch of ground, and Father could see some vehicles up ahead. As they drew closer, he noticed a deputy's car, two state trooper's cars, and the coroner's ambulance. The sheriff pulled along side his deputy's car and stopped. It was then that Father noticed the young girl's body still hanging in the tree.

"Oh my," Jamie cried as she, too, caught sight of the body hanging limp.

All three stepped out of the car as they were greeted by the other officers. Sheriff Martin introduced Father to the state troopers. He knew the deputy and Jamie had met the troopers previously in her work. The sheriff then introduced her to the coroner.

"This is a first for me," the coroner said as he shook Jamie's hand. "Kids are tough any time but this kind makes it worse."

Jamie nodded her head in agreement, then everyone walked

over to the tree where the young girl's nude body was hanging. Father felt pressure in the pit of his stomach, but began to pray in the spirit under his breath. A red flag was stuck in the ground below her body.

"What's this for?" Father asked, pointing to the flag.

"It marks the spot where we found the suicide note," Sheriff Martin replied.

"May I see the note?"

"Get the note, Paul," the sheriff commanded, looking up at the deputy.

The deputy left the group and everyone watched as he went to his car and pulled out a briefcase. He set the briefcase on the hood of his car and after opening it, he pulled out a baggie with a piece of paper inside. He then brought the baggie over to the group. The deputy handed the bag to the sheriff then turned and handed a rubber glove to Father Macon.

"Here, Father," he said, "put this on before you touch the note."

Father put on the glove as the sheriff opened the plastic bag. Father reached in and took the note. Then with one hand he straightened it enough to read. Father read it out loud.

"I have been asked by my lover to join him. He has chosen me to be his queen and to join him in ruling his kingdom. He has promised me immortality if I will but shed this body of flesh and cast off the limitations it holds for me. I honor my Lord Syrasohan with the death of my body."

"Man," said one of the troopers. "How screwed up can you get?"

Father ignored the trooper's comment as he placed the note

back into the baggie. He peeled the glove off of his hand as he turned and walked back over to the sheriff's car. Tears came to his eyes as he thought of how the young girl had been deceived. She was a young girl so hungry for love that even death was not out of the question if that is what it took to find that love. How could families get so caught up with the things of this world that they became more important than the love and life of each family member. He was pondering the question when he felt a hand grab his arm.

"This thing is really serious, isn't, it?" Jamie said as she slipped her hand down his arm to his hand, then squeezed to comfort.

"Much more than even I realized."

"Sheriff just asked me if you would notify her family since they are members of your parish?"

Father nodded, but with tears in his eyes he turned and looked into her face. "It's times like this that I hate this vocation."

"I know," she said, "but maybe God can use this girl's death to open the eyes of the people. I would hate to think it was a total waste."

"I pray that you're right, Jamie, because if it doesn't, there will be more."

They watched as the sheriff and the other men finished investigating the scene. Then Paul, the young deputy, crawled up the tree and cut the rope which held the girl's body. The other men caught the body as it fell and helped the coroner put it in a bag then they placed the bag on the coroner's gurney. Father put on his stole and with his anointing oil he approached the gurney. The coroner opened the zipper far enough to expose the head of the child and

Father administered Last Rites as Jamie and the coroner looked on. As Father finished and the coroner started to close the bag, Jamie shouted, "Father, look!"

Father leaned over along with the coroner and looked at the place Jamie was pointing to. There on the left side of the head of the young girl, cut in her hair was the SS.

"What's that?" asked the coroner, looking up at Jamie for an explanation.

"That's a sacrificial mark," Father replied. "It means the sacrifice was dedicated to a certain demon."

"Holy smokes!" the coroner exclaimed. "We had better ask for an autopsy. This may not be as cut and dried as it looks."

"I think that is an excellent suggestion," Father agreed, "and when I talk to the family I'll explain the importance of giving the state permission."

The coroner slid the gurney into the vehicle and Father watched as it collapsed and came to rest in the bed of the ambulance. As he and Jamie walked away, he suddenly turned back to the coroner. "Do you think I could get a copy of the autopsy report when it is finished?" The coroner looked around and feeling safe that no one could hear, he said, "I can't give you a written copy but I could call and read it to you."

"Would you do that, please?" Father encouraged, even though he knew he may be overstepping the law.

"As soon as I see it, Father, I'll give you a call."

"Thanks a lot," Father said as he turned and walked back to the sheriff's car. The sheriff had been talking to the deputy and the troopers, but as Father and Jamie approached, they broke up and went back to their own vehicles.

"Our job is done here for now, Father," the sheriff stated as Father and Jamie approached the car. "Miss McClain, Mr. Bellows just called in on the radio and said for you to wait here with the deputy until he gets here. He said he was about fifteen minutes away. I'll take Father back to the church so he can make preparations to notify the family and have them come down and make a positive I.D."

Jamie nodded to the sheriff, then looked at Father and grinned. He returned the grin as he walked around in front of the sheriff's car to get in. The sheriff backed the car away from the deputy's car then drove back down the path until he hit the gravel road.

Jamie watched as the car drove away, then said a prayer for Father. She didn't envy him one bit right now. Losing a child was a hard strain on any family. To lose one under these circumstances was going to be very difficult.

The sheriff asked a lot of questions as he drove Father back to the rectory. He was not a Christian but had been to church with his wife a few times. He had heard about "stuff like this" as he called it, but had never taken it seriously. In his job he had heard of these things but he had written the whole thing off as just crazy people getting their kicks.

Father shared as much as he felt the sheriff could receive and told him there would be more of the same, if things didn't change. He also told the sheriff that Jamie had thought she was being stalked and he might have the deputy on duty drive by her motel room each night while on his rounds. The sheriff agreed but wondered who would be stalking Jamie and what would be the purpose. Father stated that he didn't know, but just to reassure Jamie he would appreciate them checking on her.

Sheriff Martin dropped Father off at the rectory and told him he would be in touch if there were any further developments. Father spent about thirty minutes in prayer then called the Krouse's home. No one answered, so he called Eva's mother's house and found Eva there. The news was very painful for her. He told her to remain there, and he would pick her up and go with her to make certain of the identity.

He took a quick shower, put on his clerics and began the drive toward Bettis Bluff. He prayed in the spirit as he drove, thinking of the terrible evil and pain that Satan was causing so many people. He still didn't know how to fight this attack, but as he continued to pray, last night's dream popped into his mind. He wished he had written it down but the circumstances had prevented that. He remembered the bell and laughed to himself when he thought how the bell the people were ringing had turned into the telephone ringing. What were they rejoicing about? "Father God, help me remember the dream if it is important," he prayed, trying to remember the details. He prayed and listened until he drove into Bettis Bluff but nothing came. He redirected his attention to dealing with Mrs. Krouse and Elizabeth's funeral arrangements.

He found the home of Eva's mom and after a time of dealing with the grief, Father and Mrs. Krouse drove down to the funeral home. Father cried as Mrs. Krouse grieved aloud when she saw her daughter's body and identified it as Elizabeth. He made a vow to do everything in his power to destroy every tiny bit of Satan's kingdom.

Driving back to Eva's mother's house, they discussed the funeral. She had already called Ray, and he would be in that afternoon. She hoped Father would be around when he came in, and Father said he would because he wanted to talk to them both together about the funeral Mass.

Jamie waited with the deputy for about ten minutes before they saw Phil Bellows' car pull onto the dirt path from the gravel road. Phil was by himself and he shook hands with the deputy as Jamie introduced him. Jamie showed him the tree and the red flag and tried to share as much of the note as she could remember. Phil asked a lot of questions. She and the deputy were able to answer most of them to his satisfaction. She noticed he became irritated when she shared that Father said this or Father believes that. When she mentioned the two SS marks on the girl's head and said they were the same marks as on the dead bull, he snapped angrily at her.

"So you think this whole thing is the result of a demon from Babylon who now wants to live in a Podunk town and be chased around by a Podunk priest? Come on, Jamie, give me a break! This is not the third century, this is the twentieth century and this kind of thing just doesn't happen. You know we have seen cases similar to this one before."

"And how many of them have we solved in a so called logical manner?" she broke in. "I'll tell you how many, none. We come in and say, 'Wow, this is weird,' then move on to another case and never solve any of them. Doesn't that bother you, Phil, that we never solve one of these cases?"

"I don't give a damn, Jamie," he shouted. "I get paid whether I solve none or solve them all. If you think I'm going to march into the boss's office tomorrow and say 'Boss, a demon killed this bull then killed this girl,' you're crazy. I plan to be on this team until I retire and I'm not going to let your screwed-up idea about a Babylonian demon wreck my pension. And as for your friend Padre Exorcist, he can chase these spirits of Podunk all he wants, but I advise you to keep away from him or you may find yourself working for the parking meter patrol."

"Then what you're saying is you're ready to file a report right now, without doing any more investigation?" she asked, allowing her temper to flare.

"Yes ma'am, I am," he replied. "Some sweet, young Catholic girl gets involved with the wrong crowd, gets hooked on drugs, and then kills herself because she talks to hallucinations. That's simple and it's non-threatening to everyone."

"Everyone except God," she exclaimed, not really knowing where that came from.

Phil looked straight at her and pointed his finger into her face, "Jamie, don't give me that pious bull crap. You know what I think of God. Any God that would allow the pain and suffering to go on like it does in this world, can't be a God that someone would want to spend an hour with, let alone eternity. He doesn't look out after my ass, I do, and if He doesn't like the way I write up cases, let Him find someone else to do it."

She could see she was making no headway with him so she just dropped the conversation. The deputy had apparently been turned off by the argument and had gone to his car. She walked over to his car and thanked him for his help and for waiting with her until Phil had shown up. He tipped his hat, smiled, and told her "any time." She walked over to Phil's car and got in on the passenger side.

"Did the coroner take the body?" Phil asked, as he started the engine.

"Yes, but I'm not really sure where. You might radio the sheriff and let him tell you."

Phil picked up the radio and called the sheriff's office. The sheriff wasn't there but the dispatcher said that the body was being kept at Montgomery Funeral Home in Bettis Bluff. She then gave him instructions on how to get there.

CHAPTER TEN

THE AUTOPSY

Father and Eva had stayed at her mother's house waiting for Ray to get home from the boats. He usually worked thirty days on the river then was off for thirty days. He had gone by his house first to change into some nicer clothes and was shocked by its condition.

After kissing his wife and greeting Father he asked, "Babe, what's going on around here? I just came from our house and it is in shambles."

Eva looked at Father. He knew she was expecting him to explain, so he encouraged all of them to sit down.

"Ray, what I'm going to tell you may sound strange, but it will be the truth."

Father told Ray everything that was going on in Engleton and about the principality, Syrasohan. He related that somehow Elizabeth had been deceived into joining the coven and that her involvement with the group had caused her rebellious behavior and had eventually caused her death.

When Father finished Ray got up and walked around the room rubbing his head with his hands. Father could tell that he was trying to deal with all of it and understand how something so strange could cause his daughter's death.

"How could something like this happen?" he finally turned and asked Father.

"Do you want the truth, Ray?" Father asked, looking up at him.

"Is it that painful?" he asked, as tears began to crawl down his cheeks.

"I'm afraid so. Sometimes we want to give our kids so much that we fail to realize that all they really need is our love and our presence in their lives. When it's not there, they always find that love somewhere. That somewhere becomes the problem.

"It's the same way with God. We need His love in our lives to sustain us and to nourish us, but when we don't receive it from Him, we look for it in different places, in different things. The more power and time we give those things the farther we get from God, and that gives Satan an opportunity to move in big time. That's what has happened to Engleton and your daughter is the first victim. There will be more."

"But we go to church!" Ray exclaimed. "We've gone to church all our lives."

"That's the problem, Ray," Father explained. "We all went to church, thinking that was all God required. We fulfilled our obligation, but we had no time or use for our neighbor or anything else God had to offer. In the process we cut ourselves off from really knowing God."

"I don't understand how that could lead to my daughter's death," Ray said angrily.

"Anywhere there's darkness, Satan has a right to be there and sin, no matter what the cause, is darkness. Let me give you an example. Do you remember last year when Mr. Kranz killed your dog for getting in his garden?"

Ray nodded.

"You haven't talked to him since, have you?" Father asked.

"No, Father, but I loved that dog." Ray explained. "It was the best cattle dog I had ever trained. He had no right to just up and shoot him."

"It doesn't matter, Ray. God calls that unforgiveness and that is sin. Your unforgiveness for Mr. Kranz has added to the darkness that is empowering this principality over Engleton. Now multiply that by the number of others who feel the same way about somebody, and multiply that times the number of families that have ever lived in Engleton and you have the darkness this principality needs to thrive and rule."

"Our hate, unforgiveness, dishonesty becomes the gasoline that runs this thing's engine, doesn't it?" asked Ray, now understanding the situation.

"Exactly," Father replied.

"How do we stop it then?" Ray asked, gritting his teeth as he realized his contribution to empowering the demon.

"We make sure that Elizabeth hasn't died in vain. First we give the coroner the permission to do an autopsy to prove what really killed Elizabeth. Then we use her funeral Mass as a platform to reveal the truth to every person who comes and who will listen. I need your permission to do that. We must not let fear or embarrassment keep us from telling the truth of what she was into and why."

Ray looked at Eva. "Momma, what do you think?"

Eva, with tears in her eyes, responded, "Ray, I think we owe it to our other children, to the people of Engleton and to God. I think it's time we made God's will a priority in our lives."

"Father," Ray replied, clinching his fist, "let's bring this principality down. I'll try my best to do my part and you give us everything you've got at my little girl's funeral. Tomorrow I'll have a talk with Mr. Kranz."

Tears welled up in Father's eyes as he stood up and embraced Ray. They both cried as they continued to hug each other.

Jamie and Phil drove to the funeral home in Bettis Bluff without saying much to each other. She knew he would not listen so she just kept her mouth shut. The coroner showed Phil the girl's body and Jamie pointed out the SS marks on her head. The coroner told them that the state would be there in the morning to do a complete autopsy. The family had given full consent and the sheriff especially wanted to know if there were any drugs involved.

Phil had seemed unimpressed with the circumstances of the girl's death. He had already formulated in his mind that the girl was on drugs and that she had killed herself while under the influence. The fact that she was miles from anywhere without any clothes, and the content of the suicide note, was more than enough evidence to prove that she had gone off the deep end. There were no bruises on the body to indicate fowl play, so drug induced suicide looked to be the obvious answer.

"What if the autopsy shows your 'obvious answer' to be wrong?" Jamie asked.

"It won't," Phil replied arrogantly. "I don't see any sense in even doing an autopsy. Drug induced suicide is the only possible explanation."

"We'll just have to wait and see," she said, still holding on to the thought that he might consider that the young girl was victimized.

"I'm not waiting for anything," he replied harshly. "Tomorrow morning we're going to write our report just as it stands. I promise you right now there will be none of this demon crap in it. We will both sign that report, and by tomorrow night we will both be back in Little Rock."

Father had left Eva and Ray and had driven back to the rectory. His mind was on his homily for the funeral Mass. He had to tell the truth but he knew that very few would believe him. How many deaths would it take before they realized what was going on? He had to give it a try, however, because it was their only hope. Unless they came together and fought this thing, the principality would eventually destroy the entire community of Engleton. He prayed that the people would come to know the truth for he knew it would set them free.

His prayer time was interrupted by the young mechanic from Murphy's Auto. He told Father he should have Miss McClain's car ready in about an hour. Father explained that she was staying in town, but offered to call her and let her know that it was fixed.

Father went back to his prayer time. He could hear the young man working on Jamie's car outside. He missed her company, and he would miss her when she had to go back to Little Rock. He had hoped that she could stay until this thing was over. She knew too much for Syrasohan to leave her alone, but she still did not know enough to fight the demon by herself. He didn't know how to pray for her so he began to pray in tongues. "Father God," he said humbly, "You know what Jamie needs. As I pray in the spirit, let my prayers be for her in Your will." He then continued to pray in the spirit until the doorbell rang. It was the young mechanic notifying Father that the car was fixed. Father thanked him and told him he would call Miss McClain and let her know. The young man thanked Father, then left.

Father called the motel and asked for room 14. But after it rang six or seven times, he hung the phone up and made a mental note to try again later. He spent the afternoon working on parish business that had fallen behind since this thing had started consuming most of his time. When it got late enough for him to turn the desk lamp on in order for him to see, his eyes began to get tired so he laid down on the bed to rest for a little while.

Suddenly he is fighting a group of renegade Indians. He is a Union soldier and he is completely surrounded by the band of attacking Indians on horses. Jamie is there, reloading his guns as he empties each one in the heat of battle. The chief of the Indians charges his position, jumps off of his horse and begins to fight Father hand to hand. He recognizes the Indian as Walter Foust. In spite of Father's strength, the chief begins to wear Father down and push him to the ground. Jamie slaps at the Indian, but he uses his foot and kicks her to the ground. She hits her head on a rock and is knocked out. The Indian begins to yell and chant as he realizes he is going to win and kill Father. Father begins to pray in tongues as he knows he is about to be killed. Out of the blue, he hears a bugle sound which startles the Indian. As they turn to look in the direction of the bugle, a group of cavalry soldiers on flying horses come to the rescue. Leading the charge is the woman from Rogers who had taught Father about spiritual warfare. They attack the Indians and drive them off. The chief is knocked to the ground and disappears.

Father awoke and realized he had been dreaming. He reached and picked up the pen and notebook on the night table that he used to write down his dreams. He wrote down everything he could remember about the dream, and as he finished, he noticed that it was 2:00 in the morning. He had slept a lot longer than he had intended. He removed his clothing and crawled back in bed. He thought about the dream until he dozed off to sleep again.

The forensic team from the state who were scheduled to do the autopsy had a flat on their van and didn't arrive until late in the morning. Jamie and Phil had worked on their report most of the morning and had finished it by lunch time. Phil was upset because now he wouldn't get back into Little Rock until late in the night. He didn't want their report to get there ahead of the autopsy results just in case something might show up in the autopsy that he had not covered in their report. They called in a pizza for lunch, afraid they would miss the call from the team if they left. They watched TV most of the afternoon and Phil seemed to get more antsy as the day passed.

"Damn," he finally said, throwing the TV remote on the bed, "what's taking those boys so long?"

Jamie kept her mouth shut. From experience, she knew what he was thinking. The fact that it was taking so long meant that maybe it wasn't as cut and dried as Phil wanted it to be. About five o'clock the call came. She could tell by the way he was talking that he didn't like their results.

"Not enough, huh? Gosh, damn, busy little whore, wasn't she? Yea, boy, I'd like to have gotten in to some of that myself." She heard him say, then laugh. "I believe I'd leave that off. It would only cause a lot of trouble," he continued. "Sounds good. Country girl overdoses and hangs herself while under the influence. Good job. Yea, we'll wrap things up here, then try to beat you guys to Rock City. Okay. Good-bye."

"Leave what off?" she asked as soon as he had set the receiver down.

"Oh," he paused, "they ugh, they wanted to describe how much the rope dug into the girl's neck and I told them it wasn't necessary. I said just to leave it off."

"What did they find out?" she asked, not really going along with his answer.

"Just as I told you they would," he replied confidently, "enough dope in her blood to kill a bull."

Jamie hung her head in disbelief. Why hadn't something shown up that would have given credence to her being used as a sacrifice? Then everyone would have understood what was going on in Engleton. Now Father would still be alone. She thought she had better go to her room and let him know the results of the autopsy. She started toward the door then turned and looked at Phil. "What did you mean by 'busy little whore'?"

"Come on, Jamie, a young sexy girl running around naked down by the river at night?" He threw up both hands and shrugged his shoulders as if to say, "What would you call her?"

Jamie had started out the door, disgusted with his remarks, when he yelled back at her, "Jamie."

She turned back to face him.

"We need to get on the road. Think you can get your things together fairly quickly?"

She nodded, then slammed the door hard to show her reaction. Of all the men to work with she had gotten stuck with Mr. Pension Plan.

She went to her room and immediately phoned the rectory. Father was very glad to hear her voice and he told her so. She returned the compliment then shared with him the results of the autopsy. She heard a long pause and she knew he was deep in thought.

"Father," she said, trying to bring him back.

"Jamie, I'm sorry," he apologized, "but that can't be possible. I can't believe a professional forensic team couldn't find something to document foul play. How about the two SS marks on her head?"

"They didn't say a thing about them as far as I know." She replied, sharing his contempt.

"Jamie, it just doesn't make any sense. This makes Elizabeth look like a junky who just went berserk, and I know that is not the truth. This makes our case very weak, and I was sure counting on the results of that autopsy to give me more material to share with my parish."

"Father, I'm really sorry," she said, feeling his disappointment. "I guess, too, this is my good-bye call. Phil and I are going back to Little Rock tonight."

"I will miss you, Jamie. Keep growing in the Lord and remember to pray your 91st Psalm."

Tears rolled down her cheeks as she realized she was leaving the man she loved but could never have.

"Your rental car is still here. How do you want to handle that?" he asked, realizing that she was struggling with the good-bye.

"Oh, shoot!" she exclaimed, wiping the tears from her face, "I forgot about that dumb car. I'll have to come out and get it and return it to Murphy's."

"I would bring it to you, but I've got Elizabeth's rosary service in about thirty minutes, so you'll have to come out and get it yourself."

"That's okay, Father," she replied, not wanting to burden him. "I'll have Phil bring me out in a few minutes."

"Better wait about an hour, Jamie. People are already arriving for the rosary and by the time you get here you won't be able to get the car out."

"I'll see you in about an hour," she said as she hung up the phone. She knew Phil was not going to appreciate the news.

She waited about ten minutes then went to Phil's room and told him about the delay. She was right, he was upset. He told her to have everything ready to go so that when they dropped off the car they could head out of town. She went back to her room and began to pack her things.

Father couldn't get the autopsy report off of his mind. They had not listened to a thing he had said and neither would his parish. Without that support, he would only bring more speculation and ridicule to the Krouse family.

As he locked the door and started for the church, it began to rain. Turning around, he ran back up the steps, unlocked the door and went to his bedroom where he kept his umbrella. As he picked it up the phone rang. He looked at his watch and decided he had the time to answer it instead of catching it on the answering machine, but he didn't have time for a long conversation.

"Father Macon," he answered as he picked up the phone and placed it to his mouth.

"Father?" a voice asked quietly on the other end.

"Yes, this is Father Macon."

"Father, this is Mike Broadway, the coroner."

"Oh, Mike. Yes, Miss McClain has already called me with the autopsy report," he said, trying to hurry and anticipate the man's business.

"It's not the truth," he stated, again very softly.

"What do you mean?" Father asked, not caring how long it took for an explanation.

"The forensic team wrote the report up the way Mr. Bellows wanted it written, but it is not the truth. He's scared to death that if too much is made out of this case and it gets a lot of bad press, then he'll make the special investigation department look like a bunch of goofy Ghostbusters and he'll lose his job."

"Mike," asked Father, "what did they find out?"

"They found that she had only a small amount of drug in her blood. Not nearly enough to cause her to go crazy and kill herself. They also found signs of other's fingerprints on the note, but not enough to really identify. The strangest thing they found....," he paused.

"What was that, Mike?" Father asked, trying to break the silence.

"They found that she had been gang raped."

"What do you mean, gang raped?"

"They found five different DNA's in the sperm sample that they found in her vagina."

He had been right. She had been victimized by the coven and used as a sacrifice to the principality, Syrasohan. She wasn't high on drugs she was high on demonic power!

Father thanked Mike and promised he would not tell where the information had come from. Mike said that Sheriff Martin didn't know anything about the falsified report and that he would only get a copy of what Mr. Bellows submitted to Little Rock. He had overheard the forensic team talking to Phil on the phone, but they had not known he was there.

The rain was coming down pretty hard as Father locked the rectory again and headed for the church. He was late but what he had just heard made it well worth it. God is so good, he thought. He remembered the words of Jesus, "What is done in the darkness will be brought into the light." As he stepped inside the side door of the church, he broke down his umbrella and made his way to the sacristy.

CHAPTER ELEVEN

THE FUNERAL

Phil looked out of his motel room and complained as it started to rain. "Crap! I was hoping to get out of here before this mess started."

"I know and I'm sorry," Jamie replied. "Things have happened so fast that I completely forgot about that stupid rental car."

"Well, let's go," he said, closing the window curtain and avoiding her apology. "The church service should be over by now."

It was raining very hard as they loaded their suit cases into the trunk of the car. By the time they got their things loaded, both of them were fairly wet from the rain. Before pulling out onto the highway, Phil pulled into a nearby gas station and filled the tank of the car then headed toward Engleton.

Jamie complained about being cold so Phil turned the heater up more and joked that she could take off her wet clothes if she wanted to. She gave him a dirty look as he laughed and made a comment about that being the normal dress code in the hick town of Engleton. He said he could even let her off down by the river if she wanted to run around.

"That's getting pretty bad, Phil," she scolded.

"I don't know what's come over me," he kidded. "Think I'm

possessed?"

Jamie looked at him and shook her head. "More like crazy."

He laughed and continued to kid her as they drove, and the rain increased.

"Man!" he exclaimed. "It's coming down in sheets."

"Maybe you shouldn't drive so fast with it raining as hard as it is," she warned.

"I can see fine. I want to get away from this place as fast as I can."

"Why's that?"

"I don't know. Something about this place gives me the creeps."

The rain continued to pour and a couple of times she warned him to slow down as she felt the car catch water and hydroplane.

Suddenly, as they crossed one of the bridges, a huge creature, standing about eight feet tall, stood directly in the path of the car.

"What in hell's name is that?" he screamed as he turned the steering wheel sharply, trying to avoid hitting the creature.

Jamie looked up just as the "thing" went by on her side. "Oh, Jesus," she screamed.

Phil had been traveling so fast that when he turned the wheel, the car started hydroplaning and he lost control. The car caught the corner of the bridge, glanced off a road sign which caused the car to flip in the air and turn over. It hit on the driver's side, slid down the sharp incline and landed in the ditch at the bottom of the embankment upside down.

Jamie never lost consciousness and was held in place by her seat belt. She could smell gasoline, and she was afraid that the car might catch fire. She tried to see if Phil was okay but didn't see any movement or hear anything but the rain hitting the bottom of the car. She unbuckled her seat belt and crawled out her side window. The glass had been knocked out in the impact. She did not feel any pain in her body as she stood up and began to look around. The car was starting to smoke as she called out Phil's name. She walked around the end of the car as she heard the full gas tank emptying its contents on the ground. The rain had let up slightly and when she rounded the end of the car she saw Phil's body hanging half in and half out of the driver's side window. She heard a pop and jumped as she saw flames begin to burn on the side of the car where she had been riding. She knew the whole thing would soon be going up so she grabbed Phil's limp body, and with everything she had, pulled it free from the burning vehicle.

She could smell electrical wire burning as she pulled Phil's body further up the embankment. She stopped and felt his pulse and found a faint but steady heart beat. She could see blood on his clothing but she couldn't see where it was coming from.

With a loud bang, the fire ignited the spilled gasoline and the entire car was engulfed in flames. She tried to drag Phil further from the burning car but it felt like he weighed a ton. She was beginning to feel light-headed, and she could feel her strength going out of her. She knew she was about to pass out but she knew she had to get Phil pulled further to safety. To the side of her, from under the bridge, she heard a loud wild cry, and when she looked, she saw the huge creature which had run them off the road. She was down on her knees next to Phil, and when she saw the creature coming toward them, she tried harder to climb up the embankment, leaving Phil's lifeless body alone. She had managed to get half way up the bank by the time the creature reached Phil's body. With one hand, the creature reached into Phil's body and pulled out a clear, carbon copy of Phil Bellows. At first the form was lifeless, but then it stirred and woke up. It seemed dazed until it realized what held it captive, then it began to scream and fight, trying to break free from the clutches of the creature. The creature laughed and shook Phil like a dog would a bone as he continued to cry and scream for help. Jamie began to cry and scream also as the creature started up the embankment toward her.

"You're mine, too," the creature laughed as it drew closer up the bank.

"No," she shouted as Phil's soul continued to fight and kick futilely against the strong arm of the demon. "I belong to Jesus Christ."

The demon stopped momentarily then continued its stalking up the bank. The car was now blazing and she could see everything as clear as day by the light of the fire. The huge demon continued his pursuit until he was within five feet of her. As he started to reach for her, he suddenly stopped and drew back. The fear in Jamie was almost more than her mind could stand, and she could feel herself starting to lose consciousness. She fell over on her side and between her and the demon she could see another creature standing with a sword drawn. It was transparent just like Phil but gave off a golden glow all around its body. It looked at the huge demon and shook its head from side to side as it pointed to Jamie. The demon cussed and stomped it's feet and shook Phil's soul violently, then turned and walked into the flames of the burning car. The other creature looked at her and smiled, then pointed its sword toward the highway above the embankment. As she turned to look, she saw a truck come to a stop and two people get out and run down the embankment toward her. Then she passed out.

A lot of the people from Engleton were at the visitation and rosary service. Everyone had heard where and how Elizabeth Krouse was found, but it was too early for anyone to know the results of the autopsy. After the rosary Father announced for everyone to be seated. He then waited for the church to become quiet. He could hear many crying and sniffling as he looked down at the casket which held the young girl's body.

"You will probably hear tomorrow," he said softly as the tears welled up in his eyes, "that this young girl was high on drugs and that because of the drugs she decided to take her own life. As your pastor I tell you that is a lie." He could hear some of the people mumbling. "This girl was killed on the battlefield, a battlefield that touches each and every one of our lives. The body lying here could just as easily be your son, or your daughter or even your wife or husband. In fact, what killed her is, even now, stalking each one of you. If we don't fight it together, it will pull us down one by one." Father could tell from the reaction of the people that they were becoming nervous, so he decided to save the rest of his talk for tomorrow's funeral. "Tomorrow as we lay the soul of this beautiful creature to rest, I will tell you all how she died and what we, as people of God, must do about it."

He then went back into the sacristy to change out of his vestments. Ray and Eva got up and went over to the casket as the people began to file out of their pews and come forward to share their condolences.

Father came back into the main sanctuary and sat down behind the altar. He prayed in the spirit until most of the people had left then he went down and hugged Eva and Ray.

"This is not going to be an easy thing, Father," Ray said as he wiped the tears with a handkerchief which he had been holding. "A lot of people walked out of here tonight threatened. I could see it in their faces. A lot of pride and a lot of old tradition is being challenged, but I want you to know that we're with you all the way. We hate like everything to lose our daughter, but we don't want her death to be in vain."

"Ray, I feel the same way," Father replied, proud of Ray's stand, "and I know it is an uphill battle, but we have to trust that God has a plan if we can just be open enough to receive it and humble enough to implement it."

He hugged each of them again and told them he loved them. He told them to try to get some rest because it would be a long day tomorrow. He turned, genuflected toward the altar, then left the church out the side door. The rain had stopped so he carried his folded umbrella and walked back to the rectory.

Walking up the steps he became aware that Jamie's rental car was still parked in the same place. He thought it odd, and wondered why they had decided not to return the car to Murphy's.

He unlocked the rectory and went immediately to his bedroom to check the answering machine. The light was not blinking which made the mystery even greater. He suddenly got the idea that because of the rain and because they were running so late, they had decided to let Murphy send someone out tomorrow to pick up the car. That seemed like the most logical explanation, so he accepted it and put the whole thing out of his mind. After all, if something had gone wrong, he would surely have heard.

He went through the rectory and turned off the lights then knelt down beside the bed and said his night prayers. He prayed especially for Eva and Ray and their children; that God would give them the joy of seeing their daughter's death turned into something glorious for the Kingdom of God.

He prayed in tongues as he got ready for bed, and listened for the Voice of the Spirit until he fell asleep. The Voice was silent.

Father was up early the next morning. He had not slept well, but had awakened several times and had trouble going back to sleep. He sensed in his spirit that something was happening but he thought it was just the warfare centered around his homily for the funeral Mass. He knew it would be tough on the people, the truth usually was, but it would be ONLY the truth that would set Engleton free. It was up to him, the pastor, to give them the knowledge of that truth. As the time for the funeral drew nearer, he could feel God's grace in him growing stronger. "I can do all things through Christ who strengthens me," he said, as he locked the rectory door and headed for the Church.

The church was packed as he expected it would be. Some had come to pay their respects, others had come out of curiosity. Some had even come from Bettis Bluff after hearing the strange circumstances surrounding the girl's death.

The family had chosen young people as pallbearers, and as the Mass started, Father wondered how many of them were involved in this terrible thing. The Mass proceeded and after the readings of the scripture, it came time for Father's eulogy. Walking up to the podium Father Macon asked the Holy Spirit to fill his mouth with the words of God.

"A very long time ago, there was a town called Nineveh. It was in Babylon. The people of that city had chosen to embrace a way of living that caused Nineveh to become very dark in sin. God sent a man named Jonah to warn the people. He was reluctant to go because he didn't like the people. Finally, he did go. He warned the people that unless they changed and turned from their way of darkness, God would destroy them and their city. They had forty days to decide.

"The people believed Jonah and repented of their wicked ways. God forgave them and the people were saved.

"Elizabeth, in her own way, is a Jonah to the community of Engleton. Her death is a warning to us that something is happening that is so powerful, that we, too, might compare ourselves to Nineveh."

Some of the people began to look around, obviously already convicted by his comments.

"Because of the darkness over Engleton, we have invited a very powerful spiritual principality to move into the spiritual realm above our community. I know some of you do not believe in this sort of thing. But I assure you it is very real. The apostle Paul makes this a certainty in his letter to the Church at Ephesus. He says that we war not against flesh and blood, but against principalities, against powers, against the rulers of the darkness of this world, against spiritual wickedness in high places. That battle he is talking about is now taking place in the spiritual realm over Engleton. Elizabeth is our first casualty of that battle.

"You see, people," Father moved away from the podium, checking his lapel mike as he moved closer to the people, "sin, regardless of its nature, goes up as power to empower the evil spirits above any area. As those evil spirits receive that darkness, they gain more control over an area which causes them to gain more influence over the MINDS of the people. When that happens the people begin to think, and then do, things that they wouldn't have thought they would ever do. They begin to take on the spiritual nature of the chief, or lead demon, of their area. That demon is called a principality and is like an Archangel, only working against God instead of for Him.

"What type of principality rules over San Francisco?" Father waited, looking around the room. "It's a principality of homosexuality. The sad part about this whole thing is that the more sin the people commit, the more power they give to the principality ruling over them. In return, that gives the principality more influence over the people to lead them even deeper into sin.

It is a vicious, vicious circle that can only be stopped when the people decide to repent, come together in battle, and through prayer power and fasting, pull the principality down. When the sin stops going up in an area, the principality loses its power and becomes weak. Rather than hang around, the principality then pulls up stakes and leaves. The people in that area will immediately notice a difference.

"I know who the principality is that is trying to move in over Engleton. It is the principality Syrasohan. He is a Babylonian demon that is full of sexual depravity and death. I've had a couple of encounters with him already this week. One was in this very church."

Father could tell that the people were getting very uncomfortable but he was determined to tell them the truth. He was under obligation to do that. They could then decide which way they wanted to go.

"In fact," Father continued, "the destruction of our beautiful statue of Archangel Michael here in the front of the church," Father took his hand and pointed to the empty wall where the statue used to reside, "is a result of his handiwork.

"What I am sharing with you may sound frightening, and it can be, if we forget who we are in our Savior Jesus Christ. If He is Lord of our lives, then there is nothing to fear. It is only when we get out away from Him that we become vulnerable to the enemy's attack.

"Someone, or something, has caused this principality to take notice of our community. Most of you know about Carl Bowman losing one of his prize bulls the other day. That bull was used in a ritual ceremony to announce the principality's arrival and to mark his territory. This principality has only one thing on its mind." Father paused as he held up one finger. The entire church was so still that the silence was deafening. Every eye in the church was on Father Macon. “He wants to kill and destroy every one of us. We cannot fight this thing separately. We must come together as a group of Christians and fight this thing together, using spiritual weapons.”

Father walked over to the casket and looked down at the beautiful girl that lay inside. He fought back the tears as he once again knew he must reveal the whole truth. “This beautiful girl lying here today became deceived by the false promises and lies offered by the principality. Today or tomorrow when you hear of the autopsy report, it will say that she died of suicide and overdose. That is not the truth. If the truth were revealed, it would show that she was coerced into, and became a victim of satanic worship.”

The mumbling and talking among the people increased to such an extent that Father held his hands up to silence the people.

“I know this sounds far-fetched and from the Middle Ages. But unless we believe and come together and fight this presence among us, it will continue to kill and destroy the people of Engleton. Elizabeth is the first. We can heed her words today as she, like Jonah, calls us to repent and pray, OR,” Father increased the volume, “OR we can sit back, fail to believe, and come together like THIS more and more. How many more funerals will it take until we want to really see the truth of what’s going on here? Each one of us has to answer that question for himself.”

Father then walked over to the first pew where Ray and his family were sitting. He looked at Ray. Ray nodded his head slightly and grinned his approval as his chin quivered from the tremendous grief he was undergoing.

“Ray and Eva know what’s going on. They are ready to join me in this battle because they have other children, and they’re ready to fight to keep them. If we fail to join them, then

Elizabeth's death will be in vain. BUT, if we hear her speaking to us today, we will honor her and come together and stand tall as we tell this principality, 'NO MORE'!"

Father Macon walked back to his seat beside the altar and sat down. He could hear the back door softly slamming each time someone left the church. He prayed that God would help them to understand the reality of this situation and lead them into the truth. He finished the Mass and the funeral ceremony moved to the grave site near the church. It was a couple hundred yards to the prepared area so the hearse was pulled around to the side of the church and the girl's coffin loaded in the back. Father noticed that many people left right after the church service, and did not attend the grave site ceremony. He could not hold back the tears as he watched Elizabeth's parents and siblings sprinkle the coffin with holy water.

As each person followed the family and also sprinkled the coffin, Father noticed the sheriff's car pull into the church parking lot. He stopped by the trees that marked the beginning of the lane that led to the cemetery. He watched the sheriff get out of his car and look toward the grave site. He folded his arms and leaned against the front of his car.

Father hugged Ray and Eva then walked over and climbed back into the hearse. He kept his eye on the sheriff as they drove closer to where his car was parked.

"Let me off there by the sheriff's car," he told the funeral attendant, pointing to the sheriff.

Father got out, thanked the young attendant and walked over to where the sheriff was standing. The sheriff moved from his car, and walked over to meet the priest. He extended his hand. As Father took it the sheriff said softly, "Father, I've got some more bad news."

Father stiffened as he remembered Jamie had not picked up her car. "Has something happened to Jamie?" he asked nervously.

"Yes," the sheriff answered, "but she's okay. Mr. Bellows, I'm afraid, is not so fortunate."

"What happened?" Father asked quickly, remembering Phil's response about God when they had met at Mr. Bowman's farm.

"From what we can get from Jamie, she's pretty shook up, they were heading out here when Phil lost control of the car and they hit the bridge. The car rolled over and landed in the ditch. She remembers pulling him free from the car just as it caught on fire. He was DOA at the hospital. Two men passing by saw the flames. They called 911, and when we got there, we found her coming to and wanting to know about Phil."

"Where is she now?" Father asked, grabbing the sheriff's arm.

"She's okay. She's at the hospital. The doctors thought she might have a slight concussion so they want to keep her for a couple of days for observation. It's a miracle she came out of that car alive let alone with hardly any scratches. The car burned up completely, but it was only a mangled mess before the fire started. Someone was sure looking out after her."

"You are right, sheriff, and we both know who that Someone was."

"Amen to that, Father," the sheriff said, shaking his head. "She says she wants to see you as soon as possible. She wanted me to call you last night, but I knew how tied up you were with this funeral, and I knew she was all right so I decided to wait until this was over before telling you more bad news. Dr. Verney gave her a sedative, and he said she slept fairly well last night."

"Thank you, sheriff, for your concern, and thanks for being so supportive in this whole matter. I know these past few days have been trying for you, too."

"They sure have, Father," he replied, laughing nervously. "At first, I wasn't sure you knew what you were talking about. But after finding that girl's body and now this, your idea is looking more and more convincing."

"I hope my congregation thinks so," Father grinned. "If they don't, you may be a busy man."

"I don't like being busy with matters like this," he confided as they walked back to his car. The sheriff said he had asked Ray and Eva if he could come out and take a look at their house. He was supposed to meet Ray there later this afternoon. He told Father good-bye, got in his car and started to pull away. Suddenly, Father remembered something and flagged the sheriff down before he could get turned around.

"What's the matter?" he asked, after rolling down the window.

"Did you get a look at the autopsy report yet?"

"Yes, but it sure wasn't much after they took as long as they did on that poor girl," the sheriff replied, shaking his head in disgust.

"Sheriff," Father said calmly, "I promised I wouldn't say anything, but this is too important. Talk to Mike, the coroner, and let him tell you the real results. Tell him I'm sorry about sharing this with you, but this is vital information. Phil had the boys 'doctor' the results in fear it might cause him some problems with his superiors in Little Rock."

"What?" the sheriff exclaimed, then calming back down, "That doesn't surprise me one bit. I've never seen a more goof-ball operation. They're all good men, but every one of them walk on egg shells, afraid they're going to lose their jobs. They are the most brown-nosing organization I've ever seen."

"Well," Father replied, "if you can get them to put down the real results, now that Phil is dead, it would sure give me more credibility with my parishioners. It may help you a lot in the future, too."

"I'll see what I can do," the sheriff smiled as he started to roll up his window.

"Oh, by the way," Father said, turning and putting his hand on the window to prevent its closure, "let me know what you think about the Krouse home after you see it."

"Will do, Father," the sheriff said as he continued to roll the window closed, then turned the car and drove out of the driveway.

Father stood in the drive lane thinking. He looked back toward the cemetery and could still see the Krouse family gathered around their daughter's casket. They were alone now, except for the men who were responsible for covering the grave. They had arrived, and were respectfully waiting for the bereaved family to leave.

"Father God, please don't let there be any more," he prayed, as a tear made its way down his cheek.

He had not eaten anything this morning, so he thought he would make a sandwich in the rectory, then try to go see Jamie as soon as possible. He walked back to the rectory and passed Jamie's rental car. He knew something was up when they didn't show up last night. He rebuked himself for being too quick to theorize a resolution. He should have been more sensitive to the Spirit.

He walked into the rectory just in time to hear the phone start ringing. He reached the phone in the office and placed the receiver to his head. "St. Mark's Rectory, Father Rex Macon, may I help you?" he answered, trying to put some joy in his voice.

"Hello, Anthony," the voice replied on the other end, "this is Bishop Landers."

"Yes, bishop," Father Macon responded. "How are you doing?"

"Anthony, to be very honest, I'm very concerned about you."

Father Macon didn't say anything, but just waited for an explanation.

"I don't know what's going on up there, but I've had at least twenty calls since last night," the bishop continued, apparently very upset. "Some people are afraid to come out of their houses. Some say they're moving out of Engleton and two said they were leaving the Church because of nuts like you. I don't know what you're feeding these people, Anthony, but being the head of the flock, I have a responsibility to make sure all the bases in this diocese are covered. I can't have one of my priests scaring the heck out of his parishioners by telling them that they're all demon possessed and filled with darkness. Anthony, do you realize what would happen to that parish if these people leave? Some of these people are your best givers. Lose your financial support, Anthony, and we might as well close the doors."

"Bishop, with all due respect," Father Macon interrupted, "you don't have any idea what's going on here. These people are under severe attack by a very powerful principality. If they don't realize the spiritual ramifications of this problem, if they continue to just look at it with only the eyes of the flesh, you won't have to worry about the money from this parish. There won't be anyone left here to give it. This thing won't stop until it breaks up every family and turns every person, including the kids, into sexual deviates."

"Anthony," the bishop tried to interject, but Father Macon continued to talk.

"This thing only knows spiritual force and unless the people come together and pray, these people are..."

"Anthony," the bishop finally shouted, "that's enough. I've already arranged for Father Ashton to take your place there at Engleton."

Father Macon was shocked, "Bishop, Bill Ashton has only been ordained a year and he knows nothing about spiritual warfare. This thing will eat his lunch. You do not understand what we're dealing with here. I promise, you are killing this man by sending him here."

"Father Macon," the bishop shouted again, "I've already arranged everything. He'll be there before Mass on Sunday. I've arranged for you to be assigned to the monastery in central Arkansas for some rest and relaxation. You can go ahead and start to pack."

Father Macon was overwhelmed. He couldn't believe what he was hearing. There was no way in the world Bill Ashton could handle what was going on in Engleton. He knew what he had learned in the seminary. It wouldn't carry him two feet in this battle. "Bishop," Father Macon asked, "since you have me assigned for some R & R, does it make any difference to you where I do my sabbatical?"

"Anthony," the bishop replied, "I only want to get you out of Engleton ASAP. I don't feel like putting you in another assignment right now. Go ahead, take about three months and call me when you can. Anthony, realize I have to do what I think is best for the people."

"I know, bishop," Father replied, "but please include Father Ashton in prayer in your daily Masses. I promise you, he does not know what he is walking into."

"I will," the bishop answered, "and I'll also keep Anthony Macon in my prayers."

"I would appreciate that, bishop. Thank you."

After he hung up the phone, anger began to grab a hold of his mind. He immediately began to pray in the spirit and bind any evil influence trying to control him. "Father God," he prayed, "I don't know what's going on but I know You do. I praise You and thank You that You are in charge of every situation."

He knew where he had to go. It had given him refuge before,

and also provided the atmosphere he needed to hear the guidance of the Holy Spirit. "Lift up mine eyes to the hills from whence comes my help," he murmured as he began to reminisce, and plan for his departure.

CHAPTER TWELVE

THE ABDUCTION

His mind turned back to Jamie and her dilemma. He would have trouble telling her about having to leave. He knew she would be upset but there was nothing he could do. God would have to work things out. He could not figure how the people of Engleton could possibly win with him out of the way, but God knew, and in His own time He would bring in someone to defeat this principality.

He would miss Jamie, however. She had been a strong comfort and support, and he admired her hunger to know more of the truth. He praised God that she had been protected from the destruction of the wreck, and then he prayed for the soul of Phil.

He hurriedly fixed himself a sandwich, and as he ate it, he called Murphy's Auto and asked them to come out and pick up Jamie's car. He told them about Jamie's accident and assured them that they would be reimbursed for the rental. Before he hung up he found out that they also rented U-Haul trailers, and they agreed to bring one out for him to use when they picked up the car.

Father Macon locked the door to the rectory and climbed into his jeep. Driving toward the hospital in Bettis Bluff, he began to think about Jackson Hole. He would call ahead and see if the people who owned the Ski Lodge Motel in Jackson Hole would let him borrow their cabin on the lake again. He hoped they still owned it. Bob and Mary Owens had become good friends while he lived in Jackson Hole before, and they had allowed him to live in their cabin on a nearby lake while he was there. He had managed to write them a couple of times after being ordained, but he had not made contact with them for at least eight months.

It wouldn't take him long to pack, he thought. He didn't have a lot of possessions, but it would take him three or four days to tie up loose ends before he could leave. He hoped that Jamie might stick around until he left. He didn't know how long she would be in the hospital, but he figured she would head on back to Little Rock as soon as possible.

The hospital parking lot was not very crowded and no one was in emergency as Father pulled into the ministers' parking place. Barbara saw him walk in the door and greeted him with a big smile and a "Hello, Father."

"I believe you get better looking every time I see you," he kidded.

"I'll bet you say that to all your girl friends," she snapped back.

"Only the ones that smile as much as you do," he laughed.

"Well, I figure," she replied, "as much misery as this place sees, a smile is a ray of sunshine."

"It sure is to me," Father encouraged, as he walked over to the patient list on the counter. "What room is Miss Jamie McClain in?"

"She's in Room 168," Barbara answered without looking at the list, "last room on the East wing before the exit door."

Father Macon thanked her and encouraged her again to keep her smile shining. She laughed and said she would, especially for him. Walking down the hallway, he thought how he would miss Barbara and all the people of Bettis Bluff that he had come to know.

Reaching Jamie's room, Father stood at the door and peaked in.

She was sitting up in bed with her eyes closed. To him, it seemed as though she was praying in the spirit.

He rapped on the door and she slowly turned her head toward the sound. When she saw him she held out her arms to him, laughed at first, then began to weep. He walked over and leaned down and embraced her. They held each other for a long time as she continued to cry.

"I have so much to thank you for," she finally said, trying to stop crying. "I don't care who knows it. I love you." He felt her squeeze him even harder, and her crying increased as he drew back and looked into her eyes.

"You went though a pretty horrendous accident, according to Sheriff Martin," he said, thinking that her emotional state might be a result of the medication she was taking.

Jamie nodded her head, trying to stop the tears as she wiped her face with a tissue.

"I didn't tell the sheriff everything," she said, finally able to stop crying long enough to actually speak clearly.

"What do you mean?" he asked, looking at her and wondering what she had to hide.

"You remember when you were in the tomb in Iraq, and you saw the demon pull the soul out of the young man?"

"You mean Chad?"

She nodded her head yes. "I saw a huge demon do the same thing to Phil." She started to cry uncontrollably again, "It was horrible."

"What happened?" he asked, sitting down on the bed and hugging her again, trying to bring some comfort.

"We were right at one of the bridges. This huge thing stood in the middle of the road. Phil swerved to miss the thing, and in the heavy rain, he lost control of the car. I don't know how many times we rolled, but we finally stopped down an embankment. We had just gassed the car so it was full of fuel, and I could smell it really strong. I thought it might blow up any time so I tried to find Phil. When I found him, he was hanging halfway out of the car. The car did catch on fire, and I pulled him away from the car as far as I could. He was still alive, I could feel a heartbeat. I thought I had him out of the way when I heard this loud scream like a gorilla or something. I looked in the direction of the scream. The thing that had stood in the road was now coming toward us. I left Phil and began to struggle up the embankment. When he got to Phil, he reached down into his body and pulled out his soul." She again started to sob. "I didn't know what it was at first. It looked just like Phil but it was clear or smoke colored, and at first it appeared to be asleep or knocked out. Then he gradually seemed to wake up. And when he realized what had a hold of him, he began to scream violently. It was terrible. The thing would take him and shake him like a dog might shake a newspaper or a bone. I can still hear Phil's voice screaming at the top of his lungs. The thing then started coming up the embankment toward me. It talked to me and told me I was his. But I said no, I belonged to Jesus. I was so afraid that I could feel myself losing it. But, right before I passed out I saw the angel." She reached over and grabbed Father Macon's hand. "It was standing between me and the thing, and it was holding a sword. It looked at the thing. I could hear the thing yelling and cussing at the angel as it shook Phil's soul furiously. The demon then turned and walked into the flames of the burning car. I could see Phil's body still on the ground, but I knew he was dead. The angel then smiled and pointed his sword toward the road."

She sat dazed. She stared off in space as if she were seeing the whole thing all over again. "I know without a doubt, that if you had not shared your knowledge of Jesus with me and rekindled my awareness of my relationship with Him, I, too, would have died in that car crash. Those prayers of Psalms 91 that I have been saying every day kept that demon off of me, didn't they?" she asked, changing her stare and looking at Father.

"God's Word is true, Jamie," he replied, "and that angel was there because God promised it would be there, if you were a believer. When you said you belonged to Jesus, the Shepherd sent an angel to help one of His sheep."

"I know, without a doubt," she said again, staring off into space, "that this whole thing is true just like God said it was. We have to warn people," she exclaimed, again looking at him and grabbing his arm. "The people in Engleton, they have to know. Hell is for real." She paused, "Poor Phil." She again started crying. "If I had only known. I worked with him for sixteen months. I could have shared with him about Jesus, and the reality of the afterlife. Now it's too late."

Father patted her hand, trying to comfort her pain. He had been through the exact same thing. It had been the reason for his decision to become a priest. He could still shut his eyes and see the soul of Chad being carried off by that demon. Every time he needed a reason to overcome the obstacles of serving Jesus, he simply had to remember the look on Chad's face that last day in the tomb. Now Jamie had experienced the same thing.

"Father," she said, bringing his thoughts back to the present, "I want to help you fight Syrasohan. We have to let the people know. This thing is real, and it is as vicious as any animal we can know or imagine."

He dropped his head as she talked. He knew she was absolutely right and the people of Engleton were in tremendous danger, but he had been ordered out.

"What's wrong, Father?" Jamie asked, sensing his interior struggle.

Raising his head and looking into her eyes, he wondered how he could tell her.

"I've been ordered by the bishop to leave Engleton," he replied as tears began to form in his eyes.

"What!" she exclaimed. "Is the man crazy?"

"No," Father said softly, "he just doesn't understand spiritual warfare and he probably doesn't believe in demons."

"What if I talked to him?"

Father laughed, then leaned over and hugged her again, "He would probably listen more to you than he did to me. But I'm afraid, in the long run, it wouldn't do any good."

"What are you going to do?" she asked, anxiously waiting for a reply.

"I'm going to go back out to Jackson Hole, Wyoming," he sighed. "I have some friends there who own a cabin out on the lake, and I'm hoping they will let me use it for a little while. It's a great place to just get away, meditate and listen for the Voice of God.

Jamie started to cry again. "Would you like some company?" she asked, hoping for a miracle.

"I would love some," he replied looking deep into her eyes, "but I'm afraid it's impossible."

"I don't know what I'm going to do," she responded. "When I get out of here, I'm quitting my job with the state."

"How come?"

"I've been granted a giant favor, and I feel obligated to pay it back. I know now that I must tell others of the truth of Jesus Christ and of His victory over the powers of darkness."

Father smiled as he listened to her words. He knew exactly

how she felt. He had been in her shoes many years before, and he too, had realized that he could not do anything else but serve the living God.

"God has called you," he said confidently, "and He will show you the path that you must walk. You will need to learn many things pertaining to the realm of the Spirit and the Kingdom of God. It will be a wonderful journey, but it will not be easy."

"I know," she answered, smiling.

"What?" he asked, wondering what she was up to now.

"I received my prayer language this morning," she replied very excitedly.

"Really?" Father laughed as he clapped his two hands together.

"Yes," she answered with a glow of joy radiating from her face. "When I woke up this morning I was so glad to be saved by Jesus that I just began to tell Him how much I loved Him. When I told Him I loved Him more than I could express in words, suddenly these strange words began to flow out of my mouth. I knew instantly they were the mysterious words of the supernatural and the utterance of my gift from the Holy Spirit."

"Praised be the Lord Jesus Christ!" Father shouted again. "God is so good."

"What's going on in here?" a voice asked behind them. "I heard you two clear out in the hallway."

Father turned as Sheriff Martin walked up to the end of the bed.

"I'm glad to see you're feeling better, little lady," he added before either of them could speak.

"I feel fine," Jamie responded, "thank you."

Father had stood up from sitting on the edge of the bed and had turned to greet the sheriff as he spoke to Jamie.

"Good to see you, sheriff," Father Macon said as he extended his hand.

"I thought I would find you here," sheriff replied as he shook the priest's hand. "I went with Ray and Eva out to their house after I left you at the funeral. The inside of that house looked like a bomb had been thrown in there. I find this hard to believe, but Eva said every bit of that destruction was done by a demon?"

"Sheriff," Father paused, trying to collect his thoughts, "I know you've seen a lot of things in your years as a law officer. What's going on in Engleton is as real as anything you have ever experienced. But most of the time, this type of activity is not as blatant. Some of it I really don't understand myself, but I do know that no bullet or gun will stop what's going on." Father turned and looked at Jamie, "Jamie, why don't you tell the sheriff what you just told me about what happened at the wreck site."

The sheriff turned and looked at Jamie, thinking that she had withheld information about the accident. Father could read his eyes and he added, "Sheriff, why don't you sit down. She didn't tell you this part because, as you'll see, she didn't think you would believe her. Now that you've been out to the Krouse's and have seen the destruction, maybe now you will believe."

The sheriff pulled a chair up to the foot of the bed and listened intently as Jamie retold the details of the accident. Her remembrance of Phil each time brought more tears, but each time she would pause, gather strength, then continue. The sheriff would stop her at times to ask questions, then encourage her to continue.

"As hard as all this is to believe, I know that everything you are saying is true," the sheriff replied. "I don't know why, but I know that what is happening out at Engleton is supernatural in character. My wife belongs to a church where she talks about this sort of thing all the time. I thought some of the things she told me might be true, but I never challenged her on any of it. I just went along and let her do her own thing." He then turned to Father, "The other day at Carl Bowman's farm?"

Father shook his head, yes, waiting for the sheriff to continue.

"I knew you were right. Don't ask me how I knew, but I just did. I didn't even want to believe. Something inside of me knew. I guess I had heard my wife talk so much about what was going on at her church that demonic activity in an area wasn't as far-fetched as others might have thought. Looking back, I guess my wife's spiritual life has had more of an effect on me than I realized."

Father looked at Jamie and grinned.

"After seeing that house, I knew my hands were tied. If something in the supernatural realm did that to a house, I knew the only thing I could do was offer you, Father, my full assistance." He then looked Father Macon full in the face, "What do we do now?"

Father didn't know how to respond. He sat speechless, unable to answer. He could feel the tears starting to fill his eyes.

"He's been transferred," Jamie inserted, seeing that he was struggling with an answer.

"What do you mean?" the sheriff asked, suddenly feeling a greater sense of helplessness.

"The bishop received so many complaints about my talk at the funeral that he thought I was causing the people too much stress. When that happens, the only recourse is to give in to the people's wishes and remove the priest."

"What would have happened if he would have just said, 'Tough soup, you people need to hear what this man is teaching you.'"

Father laughed, wiping his eyes, "Sheriff, you don't understand. The church is in such a state of flux right now that any kind of wave is not good. Satan has done his job of keeping the people comfortable. He's not threatened by their powerless worship, so he leaves them alone. When someone threatens his domain, however, he reacts severely and uses the people's comfort zone as his instrument to shut down any activity that might bring enlightenment to the people."

"You mean," the sheriff paused, shaking his head, "the people are really their own worst enemy?"

"That's exactly right," Father nodded. "It's like a child taking medicine. If it doesn't taste good the child will kick and scream and refuse to take it, even though it may save his life."

"Why doesn't the bishop realize that, and press on, knowing that it will eventually prove to be the best thing for the people?"

"There are many reasons, but the greatest problems are time and money. In the Kingdom of God, actions bear fruit. Jesus said it was like a mustard seed, sown small but with time, capable of reaping a huge harvest. We live in such a 'drive-thru' society that we demand instant results and instant gratification. We don't want to wait, we want it now. That kind of mentality pretty much blocks the time necessary for spiritual growth of any magnitude."

"Can't the bishop teach people that?"

"Realize that the bishop wears many hats. He is our spiritual leader, but he is also an administrator. It's hard to do much administrating without money. When Catholics get upset about something, one of the first protest measures they use is to withhold their giving. It works well, and they know it works well. This puts the bishop in a very awkward position. In this case it probably wasn't a hard decision. We've got priests and deacons alike in the church right now that don't even believe in the devil or demons. They refuse to even allow the words to be used. How are the people going to learn if the ones who are supposed to lead and teach don't even know? And worse yet, don't want to know."

The sheriff couldn't believe what he was hearing. "Then what you're saying is that Engleton is hopeless?"

"Oh, no!" Father exclaimed excitedly. "It's never hopeless.

You see, God has a plan and He will prevail. I don't understand how, and I don't understand when, but some day Syrasohan and his entire demon hoard above Engleton will bite the dust. I don't know how bad it will have to get, but someday, the Lord will open someone's eyes. That person will understand what God's will is and run with it. That will be a great day for Engleton."

"What can I do?" the sheriff asked, realizing that Father's leadership would soon be lost.

"Sheriff," Father said, looking very seriously at him, "get to know Jesus personally and pray to Him every day. And get your wife to pray. It sounds like she knows exactly what's going on. Get involved in her church with her and come to know that the crime you are fighting in this physical world has its origin in the spiritual. Defeat it there, and you make your job much easier here in the natural. You can actually fight more crime on Sunday with a good group of believers than you can the rest of the week with all your deputies."

"It's funny," the sheriff responded, "but that's exactly what I've been feeling I should do. This whole thing has made me realize that I really don't know Jesus as well as I thought I did. I've been living my entire life not realizing that there is a whole other world out there. I thought that the spiritual world was only real to dead people. Now I know differently."

"I think that's great," Father smiled, "but realize that you may be the only one left here who really knows what's going on. Engleton will continue to crumble. I'm fairly positive about that. And each time something happens you will be called out. You will need to protect yourself with a lot of prayer and God's Word."

"Psalm 91 is great protection," Jamie added. "I believe with all my heart that quoting that every day, and having its truth in my heart, is what saved me last night."

"Do you know where you're going yet?" he asked as he looked back around at Father Macon.

"Yes," he replied, "I'm going to Jackson Hole, Wyoming, but I wish you would keep that quiet. I don't want anyone to know, and I think you can understand why."

"Perfectly," the sheriff nodded as he got up from the chair he had been sitting in. He pushed it back against the wall then turned back and extended his hand to Father. "Keep me in your prayers. I hope you are wrong about Engleton, but somehow, I know your words may be prophetical."

"I hope and pray I'm wrong, too," Father said as he took the sheriff's hand.

"Good-bye, Father and good luck." He then turned and looked at Jamie. "I'll be back tomorrow, and we'll finish the paper work on the wreck, if that's okay?"

Jamie nodded and the sheriff turned and walked out of the room. They waited for a few minutes, then Jamie broke the silence. "I wouldn't want his job for all the money in the world."

"It will be tough," Father agreed, "but I believe he will be all right. God is working on him in a great way and with our prayers, he will be fine."

"When will you be leaving?" she asked, remembering what he had told the sheriff about being the only one left.

"In about three days," he answered. "Father Bill Ashton will be taking my place, and the bishop said Bill would be here to say Mass on Sunday."

"Wow!" she exclaimed. "They want you out in a hurry."

"The bishop's afraid I might get another chance to talk to the people, and you know what that might mean."

"Another opportunity for the golden rule," she answered.

"What do you mean?" he asked, not understanding her

statement.

"It became the motto of the state investigation team," she laughed. "The one with all the gold, makes the rules."

"Isn't that the truth?" he laughed, glad to see her joking around and feeling better.

They were laughing as the floor nurse walked into the room. "Looks like you're feeling better, young lady," she said, removing a thermometer from its case on the night stand and then placing it into Jamie's mouth. She took Jamie's hand and checked her pulse, then placed the blood pressure cuff on her arm and grinned as she listened with the stethoscope. She replaced the meter and the stethoscope in its case on the wall, then removed the thermometer. "Everything looks very good, Miss McClain," she finally spoke again. "If everything looks as good tomorrow you may get to go home."

They watched as she excused herself, and then started to leave the room. She got to the doorway, turned and said, "If you need something Miss McClain, just call, but we're on short staff this week because we don't have very many patients in the hospital and it may take a few more minutes for us to get to you. You're apparently out of the woods, and I don't see any reason why the doctor won't release you tomorrow. Just take tonight and get a good night's sleep." She then turned and walked out the door.

"That sounds good," Father encouraged.

"Yes it does," she agreed, "but I really haven't decided yet what to do. I guess I'll go back to Little Rock and wait until I discern what God has for me."

Father Macon could see that she was trying to be strong, but after what she had been through, he knew she would need some guidance and instruction in living a life seeking the Kingdom of God. He knew also that Syrasohan would not just let her go. He saw her as a threat, and he would make sure she didn't give him any more trouble. He didn't want to tell her that, but he knew he had the responsibility to find someone to teach her and some place for her to stay.

"Jamie," he finally decided, "you get a good night's rest like the nurse suggested, and let me pray about this. I'll come back tomorrow with some suggestions. Does that sound okay?"

She nodded her head, and he walked over to the bed and hugged her again. She held on to him for a long time, and then she released him. As he pulled away, he could see the tears flowing down her cheeks.

"Remember," he said as he touched one of the tears on her cheek then brought it to his lips, "you will always be a special person to me. I know how you feel about me because I feel the same way about you, but I have given my life to God. You now know, more than anybody, why I must continue to serve the Lord Jesus Christ. If giving up my desires and wants can bring one soul into the Kingdom of God, it has been worth the sacrifice."

She nodded, then said through her tears, "I know."

He leaned over again and kissed her on the cheek then turned and walked out the door into the hallway. He could hear her crying as he walked away.

As he drove back to the rectory the midday sun was beating down heavy on his windshield. He hadn't realized that he had spent as much time with Jamie as he had, but he had enjoyed being with her. He truly had fallen in love with her, but time and distance would help his heart get over his feelings for her.

Suddenly, his concentration was broken by the sight up ahead. He could see the burned out remains of the car that Jamie and Phil Bellows had been riding in last night. He had been so busy before and worried about Jamie that he had failed to notice it on his trip to the hospital. From the other direction, the remains of the car were hidden by a small knoll. As he drew closer, he slowed his jeep to a crawl. He could see the guard rails of the bridge and the road sign still lying halfway knocked to the ground from the car's impact. He stopped and then pulled his jeep off the road. The burned body of the vehicle looked like a huge dinosaur lying partially submerged in the grass. Something about this whole scene looked familiar. It was almost like he had been in this exact same spot before. Tears welled up and poured down his face as he remembered. This looked like the exact scene from his brother's wreck. He turned and faced the bridge. That was the same. Then he looked down the embankment at the huge piece of metal charcoal. That, too, was very similar.

Suddenly he remembered. The same thing had happened to his brother. His tears turned to sobbing as he realized Satan had killed his brother. The EMT's that had found him said that just before he died, he had mumbled something about a creature in the road. Everyone had guessed that he swerved to miss a deer or a bobcat, but the creature he had seen that night was a demon. He had gotten too close to finding out the truth about the bull mutilations in the area, and they had killed him to protect their secrecy.

Anyone traveling at a high rate of speed who saw something highly unusual in the middle of the road would, by reflex action, swerve to miss the object. That might not propose too big of a problem unless the wheels of the car caught the guard rails of the bridge. That would almost certainly cause the driver to lose control of the vehicle. Add a steep embankment right after the bridge and that would make it almost impossible for the driver to correct any loss of control. There wouldn't be enough room. Couple all of this with a rain-slick highway and partial loss of vision, and it would mean certain death for anyone in the assigned vehicle. Only God's protective hand could possibly prevent tragedy, and for Jamie McClain, that's exactly what had happened.

He continued to sob as he pulled the jeep back onto the highway and headed for the rectory. If only he had taken more interest in the mutilations and listened to his brother, he might have prevented the accident. His anger began to increase within him as he realized he had failed then, and he had failed now.

"God, why?" he asked, still sobbing from the renewed grief he felt for his brother and the pity he felt for himself. "I'm doing my best. You know I would give my life for You, but right now I feel like a loser. A loser," he screamed with a loud voice. "Please, Father God," he continued to scream as if God was hard of hearing, "give me a crumb of a sign that I've made a difference. Somehow show me that we do win this struggle. Please, for the sake of my brother and Phil and Elizabeth, don't let this thing win."

He prayed in the spirit until he began to regain his composure. He dried his eyes and attempted to sing a familiar praise chorus, but he couldn't get his brother's death out of his mind. He pulled his jeep into the rectory driveway and as he did, he saw Ray and Eva Krouse sitting on the steps of the rectory.

He drove past them and waved as he parked his vehicle. They met him as he opened his driver's door.

"We hear you are leaving?" they asked, hoping that he had managed to change the terrible news.

"Well, that's what the bishop says," he replied as he shut the door to the jeep.

"Then Elizabeth did die for nothing, didn't she?" Ray asked, trying to keep his lower lip from quivering.

"No! Ray, don't buy into that lie. This thing isn't over because

I'm leaving. God could be making a strategic move by getting me out of the way."

"I don't see how," Ray countered.

"I don't either," Father Macon followed, "but we have to believe that He's in control and that He is faithful. We lose that and we might as well go back to being barbarians."

"We don't know what to do though, Father," Eva joined in. "Without you there is no way we can win."

Ray shook his head in agreement with his wife, waiting for a response from Father.

Father looked at them both and grinned. "You see, Elizabeth hasn't died in vain."

"What do you mean?" Ray asked, failing to understand where Father was going with this.

"How many others are here ready to do what you two are ready to do to help this community and to serve God?"

Eva looked at Ray as Father continued, "I want you two to do four things for me."

"Anything," Ray replied without any hesitation.

"I want you to stay here in Engleton and don't leave. I want you to pray together and with your kids every night. Thirdly, I want you to begin to read and study the Bible. And lastly, I want you both to read and learn everything you can about spiritual warfare." He paused and looked at them, waiting for a response. "Will you do that for me?"

"Father, we promise," Ray answered, raising his hand as if he was being sworn-in in a court room.

"Good," Father smiled, "then I know I'm leaving Engleton in good hands."

"We will never forget you, Father," Eva said as she walked over to him and hugged him.

As he pulled away, Ray also stepped forward and embraced him. His hands had been in his pockets while Eva had hugged Father and as he brought his hands up to hug him, small particles fell on Father's black shirt.

"Oh my gosh, Ray," Eva apologized, "you've got cookie crumbs all over him."

Ray reached up and began to brush off the small particles. "Sorry about that, Father. The kids put some cookies in my pockets at the dinner after the funeral and I forgot they were in there."

"That's okay, Ray," Father laughed. "Those are the most beautiful crumbs I have ever seen."

Father watched as they walked to their car, then he turned and walked up the steps. He waved as they pulled out of the driveway, and stood on the top step and surveyed the entire area. "Thanks, Father God, for the crumbs," he prayed quietly. "I needed that!"

Jamie had enjoyed a quiet afternoon. She spent a lot of the afternoon praying in the spirit and listening for an answer to what she was supposed to do after she left the hospital. There had been no other visitors after Father left, and no one had come to check on her until after the eleven o'clock shift change. The floor nurse had made her rounds about eleven twenty and once again confirmed that she was doing very well. She would certainly get to leave tomorrow. The nurse wished her good night and said she would not disturb her again until the next shift change but if she needed anything just ring. Jamie said she would be fine.

Sometime around twelve-thirty, she finally dozed off. Suddenly, she was awakened by someone pulling down her bed rail. She was groggy, but she heard a male voice say that he was the hospital orderly, and he needed to check her vital signs. The room was completely dark but she could feel someone take a hold of her right arm. She screamed as she felt something sharp pinch the skin of her upper arm. She started to say something but found that she could barely move her mouth. She could feel hands against her body as they picked her up from the bed and began to carry her. She tried to scream but nothing came out, and she had no energy to fight. She heard their mumbled conversation, then the sound of a metal door opening. She felt a cool breeze against her body as the flimsy hospital gown failed to offer much protection from the night air. She could hear them talking louder but their voices seemed so far away. She was still being carried but much faster than before. She heard a car door open, then she lost consciousness.

CHAPTER THIRTEEN

THE CEREMONY

Father Macon was sitting at the table drinking his morning coffee and reading his Bible when he heard the phone ring. He had not slept well and his spirit had been really unsettled. He had prayed in the spirit a lot during the night as he dozed in and out. He knew something was going on somewhere. The Lord had not revealed anything to his mind, so he had just praised God for using him as an intercessor. When he heard the phone ring, however, he knew whoever was on the other end was going to somehow reveal to him who it was that he had been interceding for.

Father picked up the receiver and sounded his usual greeting. "St. Mark's, Father Rex Macon, may I help you?"

"Father," a familiar voice started, "this is Sheriff Martin. Is Jamie out there with you?"

A cold chill went through him as he heard the sheriff's question. He knew immediately what had happened but he was hoping he was wrong. "No, what's the matter?"

"She's not in her hospital room. The floor nurse last night at eleven said she was doing great. But this morning, when the seven o'clock crew came on board, she wasn't in her room. They thought she might have gotten up and gone to the cafeteria, but we've searched the entire hospital and she is nowhere to be found."

"Did anybody see or hear anything last night?" Father asked, fighting the fear that was trying to enter his mind.

"Not a soul," the sheriff replied. "It was as quiet as a mouse all night, according to the nurse on duty."

There was silence on both ends of the phone. Both knew what had happened but neither man wanted to hear himself speak it. Finally Sheriff Martin broke the silence. "They took her, didn't they?" he asked, already knowing the answer to his question.

"I'm afraid so," Father agreed. "She knew too much and someone from the state could cause them a lot of trouble."

"What will they do with her?" the sheriff asked, remembering the small girl's body hanging from the tree.

"Unless God intervenes, we will probably never see or hear from Jamie again."

The sound of his own words almost broke his heart, but he knew now why he had been awake most of the night.

"I'll get the deputies together, and we'll see if we can put together a search team," the sheriff offered, again breaking the long silence.

"Sheriff, I don't want to sound negative, but you could deputize the entire city of Bettis Bluff and together they couldn't find these people. They are so well organized and secretive that it is impossible for them to be found. They hold their ceremonies and rituals in out-of-the-way places and then cover their tracks very well. We don't know how they took her or which direction they took. They could be in the next state by now. Our only hope is in the Lord. We have to pray and put Jamie in His hands."

"Father, I sure wish I had your faith," the sheriff replied, realizing that Father was right and that a random search would be futile.

"That's the only thing I know that can save her," Father answered, "so I'm hanging on to it with all my might. I believe my

God will come through."

"I will put my men on alert though, Father, and if anything the least bit suspicious shows up, we will check it out."

"I would appreciate that, sheriff. And if I hear anything you'll be the first person I notify."

Father took the cup of coffee as he came back into the kitchen and poured it down the sink. "Father God," he prayed, "I make a commitment to You today. I will fast and pray until I find Jamie. Please Lord let her be all right. Satan, I command that you release your hold on her in Jesus' Name."

Slowly Jamie began to awaken and become aware of her surroundings. She was sitting in a chair with her hands and feet bound to the chair which was tied to a pole behind her. She could feel the air on her body and she realized that someone had removed her hospital gown and had tied her to the chair without any clothes on. A strong wave of embarrassment came over her as she asked herself who would do such a thing. She began to look around the large room, trying to figure out where she was. She didn't like what she saw.

On the walls of the building were colorful murals depicting various scenes of sexual activity. Her mind immediately remembered Father Macon's description of the tomb walls in Iraq. As her eyes became more adjusted to the dim lighting, she noticed what appeared to be a large table to her right about twenty-five feet from her. On the table there were dozens of candles and directly behind the table on the wall was a large pentagram. An upside down crucifix was attached to the front of the table and she suddenly realized that the table was actually an altar. There was another large pentagram to the side of the altar painted on the floor of the room. Small candles were burning at different places along the walls. They were the only source of light except for some natural light coming from somewhere above her. She tried to see its origin but she couldn't bend her head far enough without the ropes cutting into her wrists. She could tell from the light that it was daylight outside even though the inside of the room was only dimly lit.

The more awake she became the more trouble she realized she was in. She vaguely remembered last night. But she remembered enough to know that she had been kidnapped by the group that had killed the young girl, Carl Bowman's bull, and Phil Bellows. A bolt of fear shot through her. What did they want with her? She tried to fight her imagination, but after remembering the young girl's nude body and seeing the explicit scenes on the wall, she could understand why they had her bound, nude, next to the altar. She was going to be a sacrificial offering to their demon god. She pulled at her bindings as she struggled to get free. The fear had increased the adrenaline level in her blood but not enough to overcome the power of the ropes which held her to the chair.

She struggled against the ropes until she exhausted herself, then she slumped back against the back of the chair. "Help me, Jesus" she prayed.

The room gradually became more dim as the light from above her head decreased in intensity. She knew the sun was close to setting. She noticed, as she continued to look around, that the room was actually a barn that had been turned into a ceremonial room. It was ornately decorated which indicated that this was not a group of beginners.

Suddenly, she heard something and looked up to see a door at the far side of the room open. For a moment it allowed more light into the room, and she saw two figures quietly enter. She could hear them talking softly between themselves, and as they approached her, she noticed they each wore robes which covered their entire body, including their faces.

"Well, well," one of them spoke, "our visitor seems to have awakened from her nap. Did you sleep well, my beautiful morsel?" He took her chin in his hand and gently stroked it. She quickly turned her head, trying to dislodge his hand. The man laughed, then began to move his hand lower down her neck. "I'm glad you're so feisty, my dear. You're going to need all the energy you can muster tonight."

"What are you going to do?" she asked, hoping to stop his hand from going any lower.

The other person had walked over to the altar while the man had been talking.

"Kodrone," he called, "bring the master over here so our pretty lady can get to know him."

The person picked up the statue again which he had just brought in and placed on the altar. He carried it over to where the man and Jamie were talking. "This will become your master," the man said as the other person held the statue in her face.

The statue was about sixteen inches high and looked to be made out of red clay or pottery. It appeared to be very old. It had a large muscular body resembling a man, but the head and face had the appearance of a horrible monster. It had a huge phallus protruding from its body, and it had a bow drawn as if it was getting ready to shoot an arrow. On its back was a quiver, and in the quiver were small white arrows that looked like bone slivers.

Jamie moved back away from the statue as she recognized the bone slivers as the fragments Father Macon had described both in the emergency room with Larry Geller and in Elizabeth Krouse's room.

The man laughed as he watched Jamie recoil from the hideous

object. "He desires you, missy, and he has chosen you to be his queen. Now that he's gotten that lousy priest out of the way, he plans to make this area a more suitable environment for himself, and he needs a high priestess to, shall we say, spread his message. You, my dear, have been chosen as the lucky lady."

"And what if I refuse?" Jamie spat.

"Refuse?" he laughed as he again began to fondle the side of her cheek. "How do you refuse the god of the universe? Once we prepare you for your position, you will be glad to serve," he mused as he opened the bottom part of his robe, exposing himself to her eyes. She turned away but he grabbed her head and forced her to look at his exposed flesh. "I don't know about you, but I can hardly wait," he hissed through his teeth.

"I thought your god already had a queen," she forced through the pressure of his hand.

"Too young," he recoiled, letting go of her chin and motioning for the other person to take the statue back to its place on the altar. "She couldn't handle the power," he confided, taking a step back and glaring at her nude body. "But I can see that you're much more experienced, and endowed with the features that will make the perfect concubine for our master."

Jamie squirmed as she felt his evil eyes studying her body. He then walked over to her and knelt in front of her, his hand coming to rest on her naked thigh and inching its way up. "Think of all those that this beautiful body will bring to the master. Your name will be written forever as the bride who most served the master. Your reward will be great."

"No," she said, trying to move her leg and dislodge his hand. "I belong to the Lord Jesus Christ."

"Jesus Christ," he snarled as he stood up and looked down at her. "What a joke. Who would want to belong to a pathetic, powerless loser like that? Our master defeated Him, and now you want to side with a loser like that. With a body and face like yours you could have thousands of men eating out of your hand, practically destroying themselves just to have the opportunity to sit at your feet. Think of the power." He raised his hand and made a fist. When he did, his sleeve fell down and in the dim light Jamie could see the tattoo, "Satan Rules." This was the man she had seen in the restaurant. They had been stalking her all this time, just waiting for the right moment.

"You will become our queen," he said forcibly. "We will see to that. In a couple of hours the ceremony will begin and it will culminate at midnight with you joining with our master. You will be ready by then, I promise."

The other person had come over to where they were and as the man finished speaking he motioned for them to go. "We are leaving now to prepare for tonight's celebration. I'm glad you could be our guest of honor. You might use these next few hours to thank our master for choosing you. I am thanking him already for being chosen as one of those who will prepare you. Tonight will be a night for all of us to remember."

The two figures turned and left through the same door they had entered but this time no light shown through the opened door. She knew the sun had set. They would soon return for the ceremony. She looked over at the altar and the grotesque figure standing in the center. She knew now what they had planned. They were going to have sex with her as preparation for something that would happen at midnight with their god. She began to cry. "Please, Father God," she said through the tears, "I don't mind them killing me, but please don't let them violate my body. I stand on Your word that You are my refuge and my shield. You make a way where there is no way. I yield myself to You. Your will be done."

After what seemed like a long time, the door opened again and a lone figure entered the room. The person also wore the same long robe. Jamie watched as the figure walked toward her then walked around behind her and untied the ropes which held her to the chair. "You may stand up," the voice said.

Jamie recognized that it was the voice of a woman. She was hoping the person was there to help her escape as she took Jamie's arm and led her slowly across the room. Jamie had to sort of hop because of her leg bindings but soon they reached a door off of the main room. The person opened the door and led Jamie into a small bathroom like facility.

"I must prepare you for tonight's ceremony," the female voice informed, as Jamie looked around the room.

The person then opened a door to a bathroom stall and told Jamie to go in and relieve herself. Jamie quickly entered and shut the door behind her. She sat down on the toilet and noticed a window about six feet above the floor behind where she sat. She saw, however, that it was bolted shut on two sides.

The female person finally opened the stall door and ordered Jamie to come out. Jamie hobbled up on her feet and managed to get back out to the main part of the bathroom. She noticed a large pan of water and some towels on the cabinet in front of her. The female dipped a wash rag in the basin and began to wash Jamie's body all over.

"What is your name?" Jamie asked.

The female paused in her work as she replied, "I am called Phezor."

"Well, Phezor, do you know what is planned for the ceremony tonight?" Jamie asked, hoping to get the female to talking.

"You will be highly honored tonight," she answered as if she had been programmed.

"By whom?" Jamie asked.

"The master means to possess you. That is the highest honor we may achieve," she repeated again like a robot.

"You mean the high priest of the coven?" Jamie asked, remembering the men in the robes.

"Oh no," the woman responded excitedly. "They will prepare you, but Syrasohan himself will become one with your spirit."

Fear shot through Jamie like a lightening bolt. How was that going to happen? What were they going to do to her? Was the demon Syrasohan going to appear there tonight? She began to tremble as Phezor finished her bath then wiped her entire body down with an oily perfume. Her body glistened in the pale light.

"You are a good choice," Phezor commented as she led Jamie back out into the big room. "You will bring many to our master."

Another person had entered the large room while they were away. That person came over and also took hold of Jamie, and both persons led her to the altar. She could never see the altar clearly from where she was tied, but now it was very visible. It was about six feet long and about two feet wide with an outcropping on one side which held the horrible looking statue. On the end above the pentagram, the table split like a "Y". In the middle of the "Y" was a small set of steps leading up to the center of the "Y". She noticed leather straps on all four corners of the altar. The two figures led her up the small steps and forced her to lie down on her back on the altar. She watched as they untied her hands but then bound them to the altar with the leather straps. She felt them do the same thing with her feet as they spread her legs apart and tied each one to each side of the "Y"-shaped altar.

She could raise her head off the table enough to see the statue staring at her from her right side. After the figures had finished binding her to the altar, she heard them leave. She felt so humiliated and so exposed lying naked and bound on an altar that had been dedicated to a perverted demon. She tried to pray but her imagination kept informing her of what was about to take place.

Her thinking was suddenly interrupted by the sound of chanting. To her right she could hear the sound of people coming into the room. The volume of their chanting increased until she began to see them circling the altar. To the best of her knowledge she could count six in the candle light. One held a staff with a pentagram on the end. Another held a staff with the two SS figures cast either in brass or gold. The rest of the group carried a staff with a flaming candle on the end.

"In the name of our lord, Satan, we dedicate this service and we invoke the god of the universe to come among us now," she heard one of the men say.

As he continued to talk, Jamie began to pray in the spirit under her breath and praise God for being her deliverer. Suddenly, she heard a siren coming in the distance.

"What is that?" she heard one of them ask.

"It sounds like a siren coming this way," another one answered.

"Hurry," the apparent leader commanded, "we must get outside and make sure this chamber is not discovered. Put a rag in the girl's mouth so that she can't scream and draw attention."

Jamie immediately felt a rag being stuffed in her mouth. She tried to push it out with her tongue but she felt a piece of tape stuck over it to hold it in place. She lay back quietly to keep from choking. The group quickly blew out their candles as the sirens seemed to be drawing nearer. She could hear them scrambling around as each one rapidly left the room.

In just a few minutes, everything was quiet except for the continuous sound of the ever approaching siren. She was lying there quietly, trying to listen when she felt the leather straps of her left hand being untied. She looked but could see no one responsible for the action. She felt it give and she pulled her hand free. She quickly reached over and untied the right hand then bent down and untied both of her feet. She slowly removed the tape from her face then spit out the rag. She could hear the siren getting closer as she jumped from the altar. She was free but she couldn't get out of the room. Like a flash, she heard the word "window" in her mind and she rushed to the small bathroom where Phezor had prepared her for the ceremony. She opened the stall door and looked at the window. Someone had removed both of the bolts which had previously secured the window. She quickly, but quietly, raised the window, climbed up on the back of the toilet and climbed through. She couldn't see what was below because of the darkness, but she jumped anyway. Her feet landed in soft soil. She stopped and listened for any sound. The impending siren was all she heard. She ran forward into the night. She could feel the weeds and vines rubbing against her legs and thighs as she ran. Her feet hurt from the rocks and stones on the ground but still she kept running as fast as she could. Suddenly the siren stopped. She stopped, too, and again listened. She thought she could hear some voices but they sounded pretty far away. It was very dark but she knew she had to keep moving. She moved slower than before as she listened for any sound. The sound of the voices increased as she looked back and saw flashlights coming in her direction. They were fairly far away but it caused her to run faster and with less caution. Without warning the ground gave way and she found herself rolling out of control down a dirt bank.

"Splash," she heard as she felt her body being swallowed up by the water. It was cold on her naked body, and she fought it at first until she realized that she had fallen into the river. She allowed the current to take her downstream as she tried to remember. Father had said that the river ran from Missouri down south so she was on the right side of the river. That meant that back the way she had come was the way to the road that led to the Church. Her muscles tightened as she thought of going back toward the barn knowing they were looking for her. She swam to the bank and quietly crawled up the shore. Jamie could see the flashlights away off in the distance. She started back toward the road, keeping the lights to her right when she felt her feet step on something that didn't feel like dirt. Reaching down in the dark, she picked up an old tee-shirt that someone had discarded while probably swimming in the river. Trying her best to be silent, she ripped the tee-shirt into two pieces and tied one around each foot.

The water caused her skin to become cold as the night air blew against it. The old shirt, however, made her feet feel much better against the ground as she again began to run. The lights slowly became faint dots and finally disappeared as she put more distance between herself and the river. Father had said that the river was about a mile and a half from the road but she had no idea how far she had come already. Pausing only briefly to rest, Jamie made her way through the tall grass and weeds, hoping any minute to hit the road that she knew had to be there. Finally, almost totally exhausted, she sat down on an old log. She could feel its dampness against her skin but she didn't care. She knew she had walked farther than a mile and a half and still had not come to the road. Maybe she wasn't even close to Engleton. What if the river was an entirely different river, and she was miles away from where she thought she was?

She wanted to scream, but was still afraid that her pursuers might be able to hear her, so she put her head in her hands and began to softly pray in the spirit. She rested for almost half an hour, listening intently for any sound around her. There had been a large limb crack nearby which caused her pulse to increase. After a while, nothing else was heard so she figured it was just some kind of animal messing around in the woods.

It was still very dark, and Jamie finally came to the conclusion that she didn't have the faintest idea where she was. She prayed and asked the Lord to be her guide, then continued on in the direction where she thought the road should be.

After about thirty minutes she suddenly felt something cold against her thigh. She jumped and screamed as she turned and found a large collie dog rubbing against her. He ran ahead of her then stopped and turned around and barked. She watched as he came back to her again then ran ahead, stopped, and barked. Jamie realized that this dog was wanting her to follow him so she motioned with her hand, "Go on boy, go home."

The dog led her through a small grove of woods, then through a plowed field, then though a freshly mowed field. If she fell behind, the dog would wait until she caught up, then continue on its journey. Jamie didn't have a clue where he was taking her until she came over a knoll and she could see lights off in the distance. As some of them moved she realized that they were cars and she was indeed moving toward the highway. A spark of excitement went through her as the collie barked, reminding her of his presence and their mission. She continued to follow the dog until she recognized that the lights were the lights around the church and the rectory at St. Mark's.

"Oh thank You, Lord, thank You," she began to repeat over and over as she began to run toward the lights. When she got to the road, she paused and waited. There was no sound so she quickly crossed the road into the church parking lot. It was then that she noticed the collie was nowhere around. She turned in all directions looking for him, but she neither saw nor heard any sign of him.

She whistled softly and called for him a couple of times but he never responded. She quickly gave up and looked toward the rectory. She was glad to see that Father's jeep was parked in its place, but she really didn't know how to approach the situation. The porch light was on. That would give her away if anyone was watching the rectory. She thought about going around to the bedroom window and knocking on it, but she was afraid it might startle Father and cause too much of a ruckus. She didn't care if he saw her naked. After what she had been through, modesty was the farthest thing from her mind. She waited for awhile, watching to see if anyone might be expecting her to show up here and try to recapture her before she could get Father's attention. She finally decided it was safe. So she slowly walked over to the rectory, up the steps and rang the doorbell.

Her heart picked up its beat as she saw the light in his bedroom go on. She became more excited as she heard his familiar voice yell, "Just a minute."

Father had looked at his clock when he was awakened by the doorbell. "Who in the world," he said to himself, "would be up and around at 4:00 in the morning?"

He had been tired and was in a deep sleep when he heard the ringing of the doorbell. He was still not fully awake when he opened the door.

"Ah," he screamed as he saw Jamie's nude figure standing before him. Assuming it was the succubus spirit trying to tempt him again, he jumped back and began to speak to it. "Satan, in Jesus' Name I will not be deceived by your filthy tricks. I cast you and all your foul spirits to the foot of the Cross, now!" He took his hand and made a motion for her to be gone, "in Jesus' Name."

Jamie sure didn't expect this type of reception so she began to sob. This surprised Father as he saw the tears. He took a step forward and said, "Jamie, is that really you?"

"Yes," she said softly through the tears, now feeling humiliated as well as embarrassed. "I escaped."

When he looked down and saw the rags wrapped around her feet, he knew it was the real Jamie. But just to be sure, he asked her, "Jamie, did Jesus our Lord come in the flesh?"

Not understanding why he asked this, but wanting him to let her in, she replied, "Yes, Jesus came in the flesh just like I am standing here in the flesh." She threw up her hands as she finished speaking as a gesture of her disgust for his rejection.

He grabbed her into the rectory and held her in his arms. "Jamie, I'm so glad to see you and I'm sorry for treating you like that. I'll explain later."

His apology made her cry even more. But his arms felt good around her, and she didn't want him to let her go. She felt so safe when she was with him. He tried to disregard her nudity, as he led her into the bedroom and made her sit on the edge of the bed. He walked over to his closet and pulled a bath robe off of a hanger and brought it back to her. He wrapped it around her, then sat down on the edge of the bed beside her.

"I have not been this happy in a long time," he said, looking into her eyes which were still filled with tears. "God is faithful, and right now I almost feel like dancing."

She looked at him and leaned over for him to hold her again. He took the silent message and took her again in his arms.

"I'm not sure I will ever feel safe again without these arms around me," she said boldly, not wanting to hide her feelings after what she had experienced.

He didn't say anything as he continued to hold her. He knew, however, that her life was in his hands. The coven would hunt her down and kill her for sure now. He knew what he had to do.

CHAPTER FOURTEEN

THE SABBATICAL

Father Macon released Jamie and stood up. He took her hand and pulled her up to him. "Let's get you a hot bath then let you get some rest. I've got some packing to do."

He led her down the hallway to the bathroom and she sat on the side of the tub as he prepared the bath water. After the tub was filled, he tested it with his hand. "Just right," he encouraged. "Jamie, just soak as long as you want. I'll find you a pair of pajamas and bring them to the door. There are towels and washcloths in the cabinet here," he finished, pointing to the door below the sink.

She waited until he had left the room, then removed the robe and stepped into the warm bath. "Ahhh," she said as her tattered body slid into the warm liquid. The fear had completely left. With the new found peace, she began to reflect on her experience.

Father Macon quickly dressed and began to move things out of his bedroom. He took Jamie a pair of his pajamas and laid them by the door then called to her and informed her they were there. He could tell from her voice as she answered that she was much more relaxed. He put everything from his bedroom into the dining area and office. As he was finishing the last load, Jamie emerged from the bathroom. She looked beautiful in his pajamas, but he could tell that even the hot bath had not taken the fatigue out of her eyes. She smiled back at him as he stared at her. "What?" she finally asked, unable to break his stare.

"I know what Adam thought the first time he saw Eve," he kidded.

"What did he think?" she asked, trying to see where he would go from here.

"He thought, Father God, you've done saved the best till last. T-h-a-n-k you!"

She laughed but blushed slightly. He was glad to see she could laugh so easily after her ordeal. He took her by the hand and walked her to the door of the bedroom. "You lie down and get some sleep. I've moved all my things out of the bedroom so I won't disturb you while I pack the U-Haul. Sleep as long as you want, you're safe now."

His last words were music to her ears. She never really knew before how important feeling safe was. She looked at him, then stood on her tip-toes and gave him a kiss on the cheek. "Thank you again," she said.

He watched as she turned and walked to the bed, then crawled under the covers. "Sleep tight," he said to her as he closed the bedroom door.

He spent most of the morning and well into mid afternoon loading the U-Haul and his jeep. He had unhooked the phone in the bedroom and had refused to answer any of the calls. He let it ring because he wanted whoever was calling to think that he had already left town. That way, anyone looking for Jamie would assume that she had not fled to him at the rectory and would look for her elsewhere. Only the sheriff knew where he was going and now he realized that Jamie had to go with him. She was his responsibility. If he left her here, she would be killed for certain.

He finished packing the trailer and was sitting at the dining table reading his breviary when Jamie emerged from the bedroom. "Good afternoon, sleeping beauty," he greeted as he watched her rub her eyes.

"What time is it?" she asked, walking toward him.

"Four twenty-five," he replied as he offered her a place at the dining table.

"I've got muscles I didn't even know I had," she laughed, twisting her body to try and ease the soreness.

"You went through one ordeal last night, I know, and I'm anxious to hear about it, but first, I've decided to take you to Wyoming with me."

"Yes," she yelled as she bounced excitedly up and down in her chair like a child on Christmas morning. "I knew it. I knew it. I asked God to give me a teacher that could guide me into the truth of the Spirit. I knew in my heart you would be the one. I didn't know how God was going to arrange it, but I knew you would teach me."

"Well, He has," Father agreed, "because I definitely feel like you're supposed to go with me.

"When are we leaving?" she asked, still excited about the opportunity.

"We're going to wait here until after nightfall," he explained, wanting her to understand the seriousness of their situation. "Then you're going to ride in the floorboard of the jeep until we get out of town. I've gotten you some of my clothes to wear until we can find a store, possibly in Oklahoma, where we can shop and not be recognized. I know the people who kidnapped you are looking everywhere for you and they'll keep a close eye on me until I'm out of town. I wouldn't doubt that someone is watching the rectory right now. That's why you need to stay inside and out of sight until we can sneak you into the jeep tonight under the cover of darkness."

Father had a few small chores to finish around the rectory. While he took care of them Jamie found a book in the rectory office library and sat down to read. He had sat down at the dining room table to write Father Ashton a note when he heard someone drive up. He quickly poked his head into the rectory office and told Jamie to be quiet and stay out of sight. She shut the door to the office and hid down behind the desk.

Father returned to the dining area just as the door bell sounded. He walked to the door, opened it, and was greeted by the smiling face of Walter Foust.

"Hello, Father," he said as he walked by Father and made his way into the rectory.

Father saw him looking around as he shut the door.

"What I can I do for you, Walter?"

"I just heard you were leaving, and I wanted to come by and apologize for blowing up at you the other day. I want you to know that there's no hard feelings." He extended his hand.

Father took his hand. "I understand. We all get up tight with our problems. Sometimes we just need to blow off steam."

"That's exactly right, Padre," he agreed as he let go of his hand and started walking back toward the bedroom. "Anything I can help you carry out before I take off?"

"No, thanks," Father replied as he followed him back to the doorway of the bedroom. "I'm out of here as soon as I write one more letter."

Father watched him as he carefully looked the place up and down. He noticed the closed office door and as he passed it he opened it and peeked in. "Not taking your books?" He closed the door back.

"No, they belong to the church and whoever takes my place."

"Well, Father," he said, obviously perturbed, "if I can't be of any help around here, I guess I'd better get on home. I sure hope you'll forgive me, and I wish you a lot of luck." He continued walking until he reached the door. As he opened it, he turned, "Whatever happened to that young lady that was in the car wreck down the road?"

Father was caught off-guard somewhat by the question but he quickly recovered and purposely scratched his head. "I don't know, Walter. Sheriff Martin says she ran away from the hospital. No one knows why, but after a wreck like that, she might have just lost it. I figure she'll show up one of these days. Sheriff Martin's pretty thorough. He'll find her."

"Sure was a shame," Walter grunted as he closed the door behind him.

Father watched Walter get in his car and drive out of the parking lot.

"What was that all about?" he heard Jamie ask from behind him.

"I don't know," he answered, still looking out the window. "If I didn't know better I'd say that Walter Foust was trying to find out if you were here." Now, certain that Walter had truly left, he turned around and looked at Jamie. "Isn't that interesting?"

Father went back to writing his letter to Father Ashton and Jamie went back to the rectory office to read. It was starting to get dark outside and he told her that they had just a couple more hours to wait before it would be dark enough to leave. Father sat at the table for a long time, praying and trying to discern what he should tell Father Ashton. Finally he wrote: *Dear Father Bill, I am excited about you taking over the role as pastor of St. Mark's.*

Please stay close to our Lord through prayer, the Word and the Eucharist. You will need our Lord's strength here. There is much evil here which means much grace abounds. Please stay rooted in His grace. Father Rex.

Father Macon was deep in concentration as Jamie walked back into the dining room. She knew that look so she waited for a few minutes before she spoke. "You're worried about him, aren't you?"

"Yes, I am. It's like sending a five year old to hunt a tiger. If I only knew how this thing would attack him, I could warn him. But as it is, I can only pray and hope that he will hear God's warnings when the attacks come."

Father left the note on the dining table where he was sure Father Ashton would find it and then finished loading his jeep with the small items he would need daily on their trip. When he thought it was dark enough, he turned off the porch light and all the lights in the rectory. He then had Jamie slump down and walk along side the garment bag that contained his vestments. She crouched down in the front floorboard as he hung the garment bag on the hook above the back window.

He checked the trailer hook-up after he had started the engine and turned on the lights. Everything looked fine so he said good-bye to St. Mark's Church and pointed the jeep and trailer toward Wyoming.

About a mile down the road from the church a car pulled out and followed his jeep very closely, sometimes getting very close to the back of his trailer. After following for about five miles the car went around and sped on down the road. As the car passed, Father Macon turned on the inside light, pretending to be fixing the rear-view mirror.

"What did you do that for?" Jamie asked, getting very cramped in her floor-board hideout.

"I wanted whoever that was to see plainly that I was the only one in here."

Nothing else unusual happened. When they were about twenty miles down the road he allowed her to sit in the seat but with her head below the back head rest. They drove for a long time without saying anything, as if their very conversation might give away their location. They finally felt safe enough and stopped just before leaving Arkansas to refuel and use the restroom. Each one of them was very cautious and made a point not to talk to anyone and to get back on the road as soon as possible. Because Jamie had slept so long during the day, Father asked her to take the wheel a while.

She watched him lay the seat back and pull his coat over him as she pulled the jeep and trailer back onto the interstate. In just a matter of minutes she heard him snoring lightly.

Both of them took turns sleeping and driving. He had her stop in a small town in Kansas so he could mail a letter to Sheriff Martin telling him that Jamie was safe and with him. The sheriff was the only person who knew where they were going and if anyone read the letter and then checked the postmark, they would only be able to trace them to a small town in Kansas. He had been afraid to call the sheriff before they left for fear that even the phone lines might be tapped.

They stopped in Colorado long enough to buy Jamie some clothes and other needed items. They decided they would get the bulk of their supplies in Jackson Hole before heading on out to the cabin. He had called Bob and Mary Owens. They not only still owned the cabin but said that Father could use it for as long as he needed it. They told him it would be cleaned, and the key would be in its usual place.

They arrived in Jackson Hole around noon and bought enough supplies to fill the last vacant space in the jeep. Before going to the cabin, Father Macon wanted to take Jamie out to the little chapel in front of the Grand Tetons.

"This is a special place," he shared as they walked into the small area and looked at the mountains through the large picture window behind the altar. "I used to come here every day when I lived here before." She could tell he was reminiscing from the excitement she could see in his eyes. She continued to look around as he knelt and prayed. She was standing outside, still admiring the view when he walked up beside her and took her by the arm.

"We need to enjoy our stay while we are here because the Lord just told me that we will be going back to Engleton."

"When?" she asked, hoping it would be later rather than sooner.

"I don't know," he answered, looking in the direction of the mountains, "but we must not take this time of rest lightly. I feel God has pulled us away only long enough to get the people ready."

"What people?"

Father Macon turned and looked Jamie in the face, "Me, you, and the people of Engleton."

The cabin was as beautiful as Father had described it. It rested about fifty yards from a beautiful blue lake. Father found the key on top of the crossbeam that supported the front porch and unlocked the door. Inside, the cabin looked as neat as a pin. It had been recently cleaned just as the Owens had promised. Jamie was quick to claim the bedroom overlooking the lake, and Father moved into the other one. They worked hard together moving everything from the trailer into the cabin. As they carried in the last item, the sun was just starting to set over the trees.

"Let's quit for today and go sit down by the lake," Father suggested as the clouds began to turn red and orange above the lake. Jamie agreed. So he picked up his Bible from the table and they walked down to a group of rocks that stuck out over the water. They sat down on a flat area together. Father opened his Bible and began to read. "*I will bless the Lord at all times. His praise shall forever be in my mouth. I sought the Lord and He heard me and delivered me from all my fears.*"

He closed the Bible and sat it down beside them. They watched the sky grow darker as the sun's light slowly faded. Neither of them said anything for a long time. Jamie finally broke the silence. "He really is more than most people realize, isn't He?

"Jamie," Father responded, inspired by her question, "if people would only give Him a chance. Most people know more about their favorite baseball player than they do about the God who created them. He is so wonderful, but few of us know that."

"I never knew He wanted us to know," Jamie replied. "I was taught that life was a game of random drawings with the luckiest person winning more times than average, resulting in a group of people who never won and whose lot in life was to always be on the bottom. I thought God just never got involved." She paused, picked up a small rock and threw it into the water. "It has been only since I've known you that I've come to realize how much God really loves me and wants to be a part of my life."

Both of them sat quietly until it became too dark to even see the tree-line. "It's about my bedtime," Father yawned, as he put his hand against the rock and slowly pushed himself upright. He then gave a hand to Jamie and helped pull her to a standing position. Together they walked back to the cabin. He said his night prayers while she made use of the bathroom then after she retired, he took his turn. Lying in his bed he could hear the crickets outside. A lone hoot-owl called from across the lake. It caused a sense of peace to rush over him, and he thanked God for this time of rest. But in truth, his heart was with the people of Engleton.

The next morning Father was awakened by the smell of fresh coffee mixed with the aroma of fried bacon. He quickly dressed, made his way to the bathroom, then went out into the kitchen where Jamie was just finishing the toast.

"Just in time," she smiled as she saw him walk into the room.

He walked over and put his arms around her. "Do you think the bishop would approve you as my housekeeper, when I'm reassigned?"

"That would be one smart bishop," she laughed as she returned the hug.

He said grace after they sat down and as they ate, he kept complimenting Jamie on her great cooking. Both cleaned their plates and after breakfast, they both washed dishes then finished unloading what was left in the jeep. Jamie worked on her room and Father went out and sat in the large swing that hung from two chains on the front porch. He shut his eyes and began to pray in the spirit. After a while he heard the screen door and felt the swing move as Jamie sat down beside him.

"What happened after they took you from the hospital room?" he asked without opening his eyes.

Jamie paused then began to relate her story. "They must have used some kind of drug because I was out for most of the day. When I woke up, I was in a large room that I finally realized was actually the inside of a large barn. They had removed my clothing and had tied me to a chair which they then tied to a pole in the center of the room. The room was very dimly lit by candles all along the interior of the room. On the walls were large paintings or posters of men and women engaged in all forms of sex. It reminded me of your description of the grave tomb in Iraq.

"I was still very much out of it when two people came into the room. One was a man. The other one I'm not sure because both wore long reddish brown robes which hid every part of their bodies, including their faces. One of them talked, and I recognized his voice as a man. In fact, he opened his robe and exposed himself to me so I know he was a man. And you know what?" She leaned up and turned to Father very excited. Her pause caused him to open his eyes and look at her. "The one that exposed himself was the man in the restaurant with the tattoo."

"Are you sure?" Father asked as he, too, leaned forward.

"Absolutely, it was the same 'Satan Rules' tattoo that I saw on the arm of the man in the restaurant. The other man brought in this statue and set it down on the altar. The tattooed man then ordered him to bring it over to where we were. They called it their master, and they stuck the thing right in my face."

"What did it look like?"

"It was about this tall." Jamie held her hands about sixteen inches apart, "and it was made out of red pottery that looked really old. It had the body of a real muscular man but its head was hideous looking. It also had a real big, you know, thing, between its legs." Father grinned to himself as she continued. "It had a bow drawn like it was getting ready to shoot something. A quiver on its back was filled with those white bone spears or fragments you talked about with the Geller boy and the girl that hanged herself."

"Holy smoke," Father jumped up and turned to face her. "That statue was one of the ones we found in the tomb. I didn't remember until you mentioned the quiver. It was empty when we found it, and I remember Chad commenting about making it a condom dispenser at his fraternity parties." Jamie laughed which made Father realize what he had just said. “Oh, I’m sorry Jamie. I didn’t mean to offend you, I was just remembering out loud.”

“That’s all right,” she smiled. “I went to college, too.”

“How did that statue end up in Engleton?” he continued, getting back to the important discovery. “If we can figure that out…” he paused.

“Then we can point our finger at the person responsible for inviting Syrasohan into the area,” she finished.

“Exactly. Without that statue, Syrasohan has nothing to hold him to the area. Unless…”

“Unless what?” she repeated, wanting to know what else could be a reason for holding the principality.

“Unless those spears in the quiver also offer him the opportunity,” he replied, remembering the one in the Geller boy’s hand in the emergency room and the one taped to the headboard in Elizabeth’s room. “If new spears or darts were placed in the quiver before each sacrifice was offered to the god, that would give the demon the freedom to be where any of those consecrated spears were placed.”

“Oh, my gosh,” Jamie exclaimed. “Do you understand the consequences of what you just said?” Father looked at her as she continued, “One of the members of the coven could plant one of those spears in anyone’s house, car, or whatever, and give that darn demon the right to show up in that place.”

“That’s right, and that’s just what happened at Elizabeth’s house. She wasn’t there, but she had left the anchor taped to her bed, and there were enough demons in that house to host a soccer game. When I destroyed that spear with the Blood of Jesus, they took a fast train to hell’s gate.”

“You know what?” Jamie asked, looking up at him from the swing.

Father shook his head no, not knowing where she was leading.

"I'll bet someone planted one of those spears in our car the night of the wreck. Phil was acting really strange that night, kidding me about taking my clothes off and joking that he was possessed. I remember him even saying that Engleton gave him the creeps. Phil never ever talked that way before, and I had worked with him for a good while. I thought that night he was just nervous about the girl's autopsy."

"Isn't it handy that any evidence went up in smoke?"

"If that's what's going on, then no one is safe in Engleton."

"It certainly doesn't look good for the home team," Father agreed, "but I know that God has a plan, and I believe that good will overcome evil."

It was getting past noon and they had agreed that they needed to run back into Jackson Hole and pick up some things that they had forgotten the day before. They stopped off at the little chapel again as they headed in and spent some time in prayer for the people of Engleton. They both praised God that there was no distance in the spiritual realm so they could easily pray for the people there who, they knew, needed God's help.

They drove into Jackson Hole and decided to walk around town for a while before they picked up their supplies. They stopped off at the Lodge and met Bob and Mary Owens. Father thanked them again for the cabin. Bob wanted to know if priests could now have girl friends. Father carefully tried to explain the situation but Bob laughed and said he didn't believe a word of it. When Father tried to get Jamie to tell Bob the truth she shrugged her shoulders and said she thought they had come out here to run away with each other. Father finally realized that he was being ganged-up on and that it was useless to explain anything else to these people.

Throwing up his hands he told Mary she might as well go find him the nearest justice of the peace.

After joking and visiting with the Owens they decided that they needed to get back to the lake. They said good-bye and walked to the store to get their supplies. By the time they returned to the cabin, it was already getting late. The sun was again just above the trees. Both of them helped carry the supplies into the cabin, then after putting things away, they decided to go back down to the rock ledge by the lake.

The lake was so still that it looked like a sheet of glass. They sat quietly at first. The only sound was an occasional trout breaking the surface of the lake.

"Look there," Father whispered, pointing to the end of the lake.

Jamie squinted her eyes and watched as a cow moose and its calf walked from the edge of the woods and waded into the shallows of the lake.

"Oh, how beautiful," she cooed.

As they continued to watch nature's show, Father Macon began to read: "*O Lord our Lord how excellent is your name in all the earth! Who has set your glory above the heavens. When I consider your heavens, the work of your fingers, the moon and the stars, which you have ordained. What is man, that you are mindful of him*?"

The words he read went through her mind and she reflected again on her ordeal.

"Why do people get involved with junk like those people that kidnapped me?"

"I've wondered that myself," Father replied after a short pause. "I think it starts out from many different reasons but somewhere hidden within each reason is the thirst for power; power to get out of a circumstance or problem, power to control another person or group of people, power for revenge or just to satisfy the cravings of the flesh."

She turned away from the lake and looked at him as he finished talking. "Do the demons, then, provide that power?"

"Absolutely," he replied quickly. "Some people may not even realize that demons are the source. However, the more involved they become, the more demonic power they obtain because they attract more and stronger demons to themselves."

"How could anyone in their right mind ever subscribe to giving themselves to a demon? If demons are real then hell is real. How could anyone not understand that their eternal destiny was being decided by their association with the demon?"

"Most people never start out thinking that way, Jamie. Satan is very subtle. He makes it look very appealing at first until you get sucked into the trap, then he begins to slowly change your mind, your attitude, and your morals. For example, an Ouija board is a doorway for Satan to come into a person's life, but it is one of the most popular board games on the market! Kids play the game every day. Of course, not one of those kids would, by choice, invite a demon into his life."

"I know a lot of people who have played with Ouija boards and they seem to be all right," she challenged.

"The game is merely a door. The demon may not use the door for a long time, until the right opportunity presents itself, then the demon uses the door as a way to attack the individual. Once the door is opened it stays open until it is closed with repentance and confession."

"Why don't the churches teach this stuff?" Jamie exclaimed, revealing her disgust.

"That's simple. Most ministers don't believe it themselves. We have become so sophisticated and intellectual with all of our electronics and gadgetry that anything demonic is seen as medieval idiocy. I was not taught one thing about spiritual warfare in four years of seminary. The Church has adopted the idea that all of man's problems have been created by man. If we can feed enough of the poor, or counsel enough young, pregnant unwed girls, or simply go to church, everything will eventually work out. That idea hasn't worked for centuries, and it will never work. Pope John XXIII tried to tell the people what was wrong with the world but few listened or believed."

"What did he say?"

"He basically said, 'Folks, the devil and his demon hoard are real and if we don't come to grips with that truth, then we as a Church are in deep trouble.'"

"He sounded like a wise man."

"Yea, so wise that they thought he had lost his mind and charged him with trying to take the Church back four centuries."

They both sat with their heads down. The sun had set and the critters of the night had started their opera.

"What's going to happen, Father?" Jamie asked, raising her head to look at him.

He waited a long time to answer then turned his head to look out where the darkness covered the lake. "I don't know. People have to be taught the truth, but we've become so carnal in our thinking that we don't want to hear the truth. For this thing to change, there has to be a huge paradigm shift in our thinking and how that's going to come about, I don't have a clue."

The night air began to cool down enough to where Jamie became uncomfortable with the chill. "Why don't we go back to the cabin?" she finally suggested.

Father agreed. They got up and walked back to the cabin, listening to the songs of the night.

Jamie lay in bed that night realizing that what he had said was true. She had gone to church as a small girl and had been baptized later after accepting Jesus as her personal Savior, but never had she heard about demons and spiritual warfare. She had heard about the devil and that he was bad, but never that he was purposely out to destroy her. She listened to the sounds outside as she remembered being strapped to the altar in the barn. Having them violate her would have definitely destroyed her. Tears filled her eyes as she thanked God for rescuing her.

The next morning Jamie was up and had breakfast ready again as Father Macon sleepily walked into the kitchen.

"You're going to spoil me," he greeted her, then walked over and gave her his morning hug.

He could tell something was wrong from her response. She smiled as he hugged her but quickly went back to her preparation. He said grace. Then they sat and ate breakfast without saying a word. Jamie got up and put her dishes into the sink and began to fill the sink with water.

"Want to share what's going on?" he finally ventured.

Jamie turned away from the sink and came back over and sat down across the table from him. Tears were running down her cheeks.

"I didn't sleep very well last night." She took a napkin from the table and blew her nose and wiped her eyes.

"When I was tied up in that barn," she started, "the man with the tattoo let me know, very emphatically, that they were going to have sex with me and they were going to enjoy it. He kept saying that they were preparing me for their god. His god had chosen me to be a high priestess and that I would bring many to the master. I asked him what if I refused and he said when they got through with me, I would be glad to serve. Every time he looked at me and every time he touched me I felt like I did the day in the church when the statue fell and we first encountered Syrasohan. He was having sex with me in his mind, and I could feel it. It made me feel filthy on the inside." She started to cry again.

Father reached across the table, took her hand in his and began to softly pray for her in the spirit. "Jamie," he said as he finished praying, "what I am going to share with you now, very few Christians understand. But every demon in hell knows this with full certainty."

CHAPTER FIFTEEN

THE RETURN

"When God created us," Father explained, "He made us a spiritual being and then covered us with flesh from the earth. Our true nature is spiritual, not carnal or worldly. Our energy, or power to live and move, comes from our spirit. That power is placed in the soul which then magnifies that input. The soul amplifies or enlarges whatever it receives, regardless of the source. Our Blessed Mother, when she received the knowledge about her conception from the Holy Spirit, said, 'My soul MAGNIFIES the greatness of the Lord.' That is God's wish for each of us. Without the Holy Spirit, however, our soul magnifies whatever spiritual input we force it to receive. That's why there's power in any of the supernatural avenues we expose our soul to."

"Like the Ouija board," Jamie added.

"Yes, there are only two sources of spiritual power: The power of Light available only through the Holy Spirit and the power of darkness, available through demonic intervention. The soul, being neutral, will magnify any supernatural input. Our mind must discern what we place into the soul. If our mind is clouded and we do not have access to the Holy Spirit, then our mind is controlled by the nature of the flesh, which is Satan's kingdom."

"But where does sexual intercourse fit into the plan?" she asked, anxious to return to her original question.

"When God created man, He said it was not good for man to be alone. So He created man a helpmeet. Now Adam and Eve were created with sexual organs and were not ashamed of their sexuality until after Satan caused them to fall. Sex was wholesome and wonderful for both of them because when they were united physically in intercourse they were spiritually intimate with each other also. God describes it as 'knowing' her, not 'having sex' or 'making love', but 'knowing'. The word in Hebrew is 'yada' and it denotes the most intimate and closest possible union between two people. The people, during the sex act, actually pass blessings back and forth from one soul to another. When you think of it, the plan is brilliant. What better way to get every soul empowered with blessings which then in turn keep being magnified and added to daily? It's God's idea of multi-level marketing. A married couple, under the Sacrament of Marriage, grows and passes blessings back and forth, each one's soul magnifying and enlarging the input, then exchanging that input every time they have sex. The couple then passes those blessings on to their children, who in turn add to it with their respective spouses who then pass the magnified blessings on to their children. That was God's plan for an earth that would never stay static but ever change and grow in the blessings of the infinite Spirit. Man was given the opportunity to be co-creator with the Father."

"What happened? How come it's so bad now?"

"One thing," Father expounded. "The power of darkness entered the picture and man thought more of the darkness than he did the Light. When man chose, of his own free-will, to follow the devil, God withdrew His Spirit and man's spirit was left without any spiritual input that was good. Satan then began to instruct man to use his flesh to teach and control his mind. Man in turn fed that to his soul, and it magnified the input. Satan, however, didn't stop there. He knew the potential that sexual intercourse held for the passing of blessings. He began to work on the mind of man to cause man to develop a sexual appetite that was fueled by his senses. Man threw marriage to the wind and began to act like an animal, having sex wherever and whenever he wanted. Outside the marriage bed, the soul was unprotected. So now, cursings, or darkness, began to be passed from one soul to another during sexual intercourse. Satan is very aware of this. That is why orgies and perverted sex are a major part of every Satanic ritual."

Jamie leaned back in her chair. "That explains so much. The man with the tattoo meant that he would prepare me for their god by having sex with me, and by that, pass demons from his soul to mine."

"Yes, and the more coven members you had sex with the more demons you would receive and the more demonic power you would possess. The more demonic power your mind had to contend with, the less power you would have to reason in a sensible frame. After a while you would actually enjoy having sex with anyone and everyone. The more the better."

"Then I would go out and have sex with other men and pass the demons on to them which would in turn draw them, and anyone else they had sex with, slowly into the web."

"That's exactly right. Do you see now, Jamie, why Satan has trained our youth to be so sexually oriented? Free sex was started back in the sixties and now the children of that generation have inherited the sins of the fathers. That's why so many of the kids are killing themselves. They're having sex with everybody and passing all of that spiritual garbage around. Then suddenly, it becomes too powerful and overwhelming. When they hear a voice inside their head that says 'kill yourself', they don't have enough Godly power or sense to say no."

"Oh, my gosh," Jamie cried, suddenly remembering, "that's what happened to Elizabeth."

"The minute I saw that note, I knew what had happened," Father revealed. "The autopsy, or the true autopsy report, confirmed it."

"When the man told me I had been chosen to be a queen, I told him I thought his god already had a queen. I meant Elizabeth, and he knew who I meant because he said she was too young to handle the power."

"Jamie, do you remember from the Bible the story of the man in the country of the Gadarenes? He was the one dwelling among the tombs that no chains or fetters could hold because he was too strong and always broke the chains?" She looked puzzled so Father continued. "You know," he encouraged, "Jesus asked him what his name was, and the demon said 'Legion, because we are many'?"

"Oh yes," she replied shaking her head, "now I remember."

"Well," Father explained, "that was human flesh that was breaking those chains, but it was demonic power using that flesh. The demon even told Jesus that there were many demons attached to the man. So many, in fact, that the mind of the man was really controlled by the wishes of the chief demon. The very same thing happened to Elizabeth. She had so many demons attached to her that her mind couldn't handle the input."

"But I don't see how a young girl like that could allow herself to be used by that many men," Jamie stated with a look of disgust.

"She was probably already to the point where her mind didn't think it was a big deal at all. Haven't you read where some kids have killed their mom, or kid brother, and not had one ounce of remorse? That seems impossible until you understand the mind and the power that darkness can have over it. What's really frightening is that one, good looking girl can infect a lot of innocent people. That was the whole idea behind the temple prostitutes in the old pagan rituals. One prostitute could transfer a lot of demonic power, and in the process, wreck a lot of lives."

Jamie looked down at the table and Father could tell that something else was bothering her. "The light's beginning to come on, isn't it?" he asked, watching her struggle.

"Yes," she said. "I know, now, why I started using the same vulgarity as my boy friend when I dated him a few years back. We had frequent sex and I really didn't think there was anything wrong with it." She turned her head back up and looked at Father. "I was being deceived, wasn't I? I was really doing a lot of damage to my soul, wasn't I?"

"Without a doubt. Your soul was being influenced by the same spirits of profanity that were on your boyfriend's soul. Your soul magnified that junk, then sent it to the flesh by way of your mouth."

"It makes me mad that I was never taught this," Jamie cried, hitting her fist against the top of the table.

"Jesus taught a lot about it in His ministry because He knew the damage it could do to the soul. In the Old Testament, a woman caught in adultery, or fornication, was stoned to death. That's pretty serious. God has not changed His mind on the subject today, regardless of what people think.

"Sex is something that is powerful in the realm of the spirit. Satan knows it and uses it to destroy as many people as possible. Some of my most difficult counseling cases have been people that were sexually abused as children. I'm not really sure what it does, but to a child's soul, illicit sexual abuse can be devastating. And what makes it even worse is that in our society today, it's rampant."

"What can people do?"

"They need to repent and change and allow the Blood of Jesus to wash their soul clean of the sin. Then they need to renew their mind to the Word of God so that Satan can't continue to use the effects of the darkness against them."

"What do you mean 'the effects of the darkness'?" Jamie asked, wanting to understand the wisdom of this man.

"Even after the sin has been confessed and washed with the Blood, Satan will still try to convince the person that he's guilty. The guilt and shame can be as horrible on the mind as the sin was on the soul. If the mind does not receive the truth, it may find some other means to remove or cover up the guilt."

"Like what?"

"Like alcohol or drugs or work, anything that keeps the mind occupied and away from dealing with the pain of the guilt or shame."

"You know, this is heavy stuff."

"The truth usually is," he smiled as she got up, went to the sink and started cleaning the dishes.

He helped her finish cleaning up the kitchen, then after his prayer time, he rejoined her on the front porch. She was already swinging lazily in the porch swing when he sat down. She stopped the swing as he sat down.

"You know, there's one other thing that really puzzles me about what the man with the tattoo said. He said that the ceremony would culminate with the master joining me at midnight. I didn't think too much about that until one of them, a female, was cleaning me up and preparing me for the ceremony. She said the demon would possess me and join with my spirit. What did she mean by that?"

Father Macon listened very intently then leaned back in the

porch swing. "About two years ago I had a call from a man who lived close to Memphis. He was really upset. He told me that his wife had been going to some New Age health food store, and, suddenly, she had developed a breathing difficulty. The doctors couldn't find any reason for the problem. They had run every test in the book on her and had come up empty. They put her on medication but she didn't show any improvement. While he was talking, I heard the Holy Spirit say, 'Incubus'. I asked the man if the owner of the health food store had seduced his wife and had sex with her. After a long pause he told me, yes, and that it was all he could do to keep from 'killing the son-of-a-blank'. I asked him if his wife was showing any other signs of odd sexual behavior. He said he didn't know how I knew all this stuff, but he was going to tell me. He said his wife was having sex with a spirit. An angel, he called it. He said she allowed him to watch, and it was the weirdest thing he had ever seen. He said that his wife looked like she was having sex with somebody, but nobody was there. He said she exhibited all the movements and sounds of someone having sex, but he couldn't see anything with her. As you can guess, it was a real strain on their relationship. He said that she told him that he could no longer satisfy her. He was about to end the relationship because he said there was no way he could compete with an angel. Before he did, however, he met a priest friend of mine that knew I had dealt with some of this kind of 'stuff' before, so he called me."

"What ever happened?" Jamie asked, trying to force herself to believe his story.

"I don't know. I set him up with an acquaintance who was a Christian counselor and that's the last I heard of them."

"That's the craziest thing I've ever heard," she responded, halfway laughing, hoping that he would confess that he was joking.

"Remember, I told you that we first ran into this sort of thing while excavating the tomb in Iraq. Some of the men told stories of women appearing to them at night and forcing them to have sex. I thought they were crazy then, too, or that they were getting high and just imagining things, until the first year after my ordination. Some friends of a young girl called me to a rock quarry one night where their friend was trying to attempt suicide. I finally convinced her to climb down from the rocks and talk to me. She told me that she had been dedicated to Satan as a child and that she was a priestess. We talked and one of the things she told me was that she had been having sex with demons. I thought she was loony until the Holy Spirit reminded me of the stories of the men during the expedition. I began to do some research. It was unbelievable the amount of information I found by different authors throughout history who talked about this same thing. I still wasn't convinced, so I asked the Lord to show me. He took me to Genesis Chapter Six where it says the Sons of God saw the daughters of men and had children by them, and they were giants and mighty men in the earth. Now they can no longer produce children. God did something to fix that, but somehow, some spirits are able to simulate copulation. A male spirit is called an incubus and a female spirit is called a succubus."

Father put his head down and tried to hide his laugh as he finished speaking, remembering his own encounter with the succubus spirit.

"What's the matter?" Jamie asked, not understanding anything humorous about demonic spirits having sex.

"I wasn't going to tell you," he explained, "but I had a succubus spirit visit me the other night after your car wouldn't start, and it looked just like you."

"Oh, come on," she laughed, again thinking he was trying to

pull one over on her.

"No, I'm serious. It was in bed waiting on me when I got back from the encounter at the Krouses."

"And you turned it down?" she exclaimed, still not believing his story. "Thanks a lot!"

"Jamie, I am dead serious," he laughed, trying to overcome her doubt. "It was trying to seduce me so that it could attack my soul and my mind because it knew that was the fastest way to gain my control."

"You are serious, aren't you?" she replied, finally believing him. "How could it look like me?"

"I believe they can look like anything or anybody. The men during the expedition said the women that seduced them were beautiful women. The Bible says they can even imitate an angel of light."

"So what you're saying is that Syrasohan was going to unite with me, sexually, during the ritual? That's really disgusting!"

"I have talked with a few people who were saved out of Satanism and each one shared a common story. Sex with demonic spirits happened very frequently in their rituals, especially when human sacrifice was involved."

"Could they see the demons, you know, doing it?" she asked, blushing a little.

"They said some could and some couldn't, it depended on each one's level of possession."

"How did you know it wasn't me the other night?" she smiled, wanting to get back to his personal experience.

"I thought it was you at first until I noticed you wouldn't come out into the light. Then I caught a glimpse of your eyes and you had none, or appeared to have none."

"Do demons not have eyes?" Jamie asked, leaning forward in

the porch swing.

"Because eyes receive and operate through the use of light and demons are pure darkness, they appear not to have any eyes. That's what gave her away."

"What did you do then?"

"I asked her if Jesus Christ came in the flesh."

"Oh yes, I remember you asking me the same question the night I escaped," she pouted. "That made me so mad. I'm standing there nude, cold, hurting, and scared and you're asking me religious Jeopardy."

"You really frightened me. I thought it was that darn spirit again. When I saw your feet wrapped in those rags, I thought it was you for real, but I just couldn't take the chance. I'm sorry I hurt you."

"I forgive you," she said, patting his hand, "but how come you ask a demon if Jesus came in the flesh?"

"If they admit Jesus came in the flesh, then they admit defeat. They will never admit defeat to a human. They're liars, they're full of pride, and they hate all humans with a passion. Anything they can do to destroy or abuse God's children, they will do."

The day was moving on fast and they decided to use the canoe down by the lake to go fishing that afternoon. They made a sack lunch and put some sodas in a small cooler, then loaded their gear in the canoe and pushed it out into the lake. They fished for a fairly good while but failed to catch even a single fish. Jamie said she was getting hungry, so they pulled the canoe up on a gravel bar across from the cabin and fixed their picnic lunch. Father Macon said grace, and they ate the lunches they had prepared.

"We need to get you another Bible, Jamie," Father said, putting his trash into a paper sack.

"I was thinking of that last night," she replied. "I sure could have used it. I miss not having the one you gave me."

"We'll get you one next time we go into Jackson Hole."

They lay back on the shore, enjoying the afternoon sun and just relaxing after their lunch. Neither one said anything for a while until Father asked, "Jamie, how did you escape? I've never heard of anyone really escaping a ritual service."

"The Lord set me free," she replied without hesitation. "I know without a doubt God sent His angels into that barn, and they rescued me."

"What happened?" Father pressed, wanting to know the specifics.

"After they prepared me for the ritual, two of them strapped me to the altar which forced me to lay spread out in an obviously vulnerable position. Then they left the room. About fifteen minutes later six or seven of them came in, chanting and dedicating the service to their master, Satan. Suddenly, we all began to hear a siren coming in the distance."

"A siren?" Father asked.

"Yes," she laughed, "and it kept getting louder and louder. They thought it was the sheriff coming, and they panicked. They were afraid I would yell and give them away, so they stuck this rag in my mouth and put some tape over it. Then they left me. I was just lying there listening to the siren get closer when someone started untying the strap on my hand. I couldn't see anybody, but it loosened up enough where I could get my hand out. So I undid the rest of the straps, took the rag out of my mouth and got off of that altar. I didn't have a clue what to do, but then I heard the word 'window' in my mind, and I remembered a window in the bathroom where they had cleansed me in preparation for the ritual. Before, however, when I saw the window, it was bolted shut with two huge bolts. But when I got there, the bolts were out and the window was ajar. I climbed up on the toilet and jumped out the window. I ran as fast as I could go and I could still hear the siren coming closer."

"Did no one see you?" Father asked, amazed at her story.

"I think they were so busy with the siren coming and they knew I was strapped down securely, so every one of them left to deal with what was coming."

"What did finally show up?" he asked, wanting her to continue.

"Nothing, I think. I had run for about five minutes when suddenly the siren stopped. I don't think the coven knew what was going on either because it didn't take them long to discover I was gone. I could see their flashlights in the dark as they searched for me."

"The old 'sound of the approaching army' trick," Father laughed.

"What?" she asked, not seeing any correlation.

"Oh, in the Bible, Second Kings, Chapter Seven, there is a story about four lepers who are starving to death. They decide to go beg from the Syrian army camped over in the next valley. As they set out, God caused their footsteps to sound like an approaching army. The Syrian army heard the sound and, thinking that Israel had hired mercenaries, they fled in mad haste. When the lepers got to the camp, the army was gone but the food and booty were still there. Those four lepers made out very well that day because of God's trick with sound. I believe He did the same thing for you, Jamie. That siren was not real but an angelic decoy. It gave you the time you needed to escape."

"I now realize God's hand was on me all night," she said, as tears filled her eyes. "I ran so fast that I fell into the river, but I remembered what you had said about the river and which direction it ran. I knew that to get back to the road, I would have to run in the direction I had just come. I floated down the river for a while, then crawled out and ran back the way I had come. I could still see the flashlights over in the distance." She took her hand and pointed over to her right side. "As I climbed up the bank, that's where I found the tee shirt. Boy, I needed that, too. The ground was really taking its toll on my bare feet. I tore the shirt and then tied each piece on my feet. I really ran then. I ran until I became exhausted. I had not yet found the road, and I realized that I was lost. I knew I was lost and despair really began to get a hold on me. That's when the dog showed up."

"A dog?" Father laughed, leaning up into a sitting position.

"Yes. There was this big collie dog, and he came up to me and put his cold nose against my leg. I about had a heart attack. Then he would run ahead of me and bark, then run back to me, then run ahead and bark. I finally figured out he wanted me to follow him. I did and after a while, he led me straight to the church. When I crossed the road to your driveway, however, he was nowhere to be found. I looked and even called for him but he was not there." She paused, then sat up and looked at Father Macon. "That dog was an angel too, wasn't he?"

"It had to be, Jamie," he rejoiced. "God honored your prayers and your faith in His word. 'I will say of the Lord He is my refuge and my fortress. Surely He shall deliver me from the snare of the fowler'."

"Psalm 91," she smiled.

"Psalm 91," he repeated, shaking his head up and down. "Is God awesome or what?"

The sun was beginning to sink beyond the tree-line around the lake when they put the canoe back on its dry dock below the cabin.

They decided one good thing about not catching any fish was that they didn't have any to clean. They decided on hamburgers for supper and as Father Macon placed the hamburger meat on the grill, he watched the last rays of light dissolve from the surface of the lake.

That night Jamie prayed in the spirit for a long time in gratitude for God's goodness. She couldn't wait to get another Bible and learn more about her wonderful Lord. Maybe they would go into town tomorrow.

They did go into town the next day and Father purchased Jamie two Bibles. He told her some translations were easier to understand than others and she could kind of cross-reference between the two.

In the days and weeks that followed, Father taught her much about the Scriptures, about God's Kingdom and about spiritual warfare. She was constantly amazed at his wisdom and his understanding of spiritual things. He made it simple to understand and she wished that every person could have the opportunity she had.

They also enjoyed the area and absorbed as much of the beauty as they could. They went on a camping trip for a week up to Yellowstone and Father showed her how to enjoy God in His creation and how to use nature to grow in the knowledge of God's Kingdom. They traveled many times to just sit in the small chapel in front of the Tetons. It was a very special place for Father and he was happy to just spend hours there with the Lord. Jamie had grown also to the point where she could spend time with the Lord, listening for His voice. If a year ago someone would have told her that she would be able to sit still for one or two hours and do nothing but pray, she would have told them they were crazy. But,

Father Macon had taught her so much and she was beginning to understand and love her wonderful Lord. Spending time with Him now was a thrill, not something boring or something that she had to force herself to do. She had never experienced the peace in her life that she was enjoying now. She still thought every once in a while about her experience in Engleton but it had lost its power to instill the fear in her that it once did. She prayed every night for the people of Engleton and hoped that everything there was going all right. She could tell in her spirit, however, that the struggle there was still going on because the Lord brought the people there to her mind often. Each time she was obedient to pray and intercede for their welfare. From what she had sensed from Father Macon, he too, was deeply concerned about the situation there. She had gotten up one late night about two weeks ago to get a drink and found him on his knees in the den praying. She did not disturb him but she had learned enough to know that he was fighting in the spiritual realm for the people of Engleton.

Three and a half months had passed since they had left Engleton. The cold weather had moved in and the tourist trade had really picked up around the area. There were so many people in and out of Jackson Hole that they tried to avoid it as much as they could. Father enjoyed skiing but his days were mainly spent in prayer and scripture study. They had not had any company at the cabin except for the man that filled the propane tank. He was an older man and apparently he thought that Jamie and Father were married. Jamie laughed to herself the first time the man referred to Father Macon as her husband.

They still stopped and visited with the Owens every time they were in town, but, with ski season at the lodge being so hectic, their visits were short. Father had bought an old chain saw at a yard sale which he used to cut up old trees around the cabin for firewood. Many a night they sat and talked in front of the fireplace as they watched the different colored flames jump from the logs. One night his concentration was so strong that he sat and stared at the fire for an hour without moving a muscle. She had to know what was going on.

"You're sensing in your spirit the trouble in Engleton, aren't you?" she finally asked, wanting to know what he was feeling.

It took him a few seconds to respond and when he finally spoke he continued to look deep into the fire. "I have felt the tremendous urge from the Spirit to pray for those people. I don't know what's going on but whatever it is, it is of a very strong magnitude."

"Do you think we should call and find out?" she asked, curious about what was happening back in the small community.

"No," he replied, still gazing into the fire. "If God wants us involved, He'll make a way and let us know when it's time."

About two weeks later, they decided to spend the day in Jackson Hole. The town was sponsoring a winter festival and offered the opportunity for them to do something different. There would be different types of music offered by different groups and one of the jazz bands on the flier had caught his eye. *El Buho* was the band and Father Macon knew that the leader was from somewhere in Arkansas.

They had begun the day early, and after breakfast and prayer, they started on the trip to Jackson Hole.

"You know what I realized this morning?" she said, happy that they were spending the day in Jackson Hole.

Father didn't say anything but looked over at her, waiting for her to continue.

"I've been in love with you since almost day one," she smiled. "I had never met anyone like you before and immediately I sensed your gentleness and the peace around you and I fell in love with that peace, not with Father Macon."

"Thanks a lot," Father laughed, slapping the steering wheel as he drove.

"Oh, I didn't mean it that way, Father," she apologized.

"I know, Jamie," he smiled. "That happens in my job a lot of times. Women long for love, tenderness and gentleness and when they find it in a priest they immediately fall in love, thinking it's the man. It's called transference, and it has caused many in the priesthood to fail. Being celibate is tough. We have hormones, too, and when a nice looking woman starts making advances, it's a tremendous struggle."

Jamie blushed, then smiled sheepishly. "I apologize for those advances I made. You could have had me in a New York minute, and I praise God for your obedience."

"To be honest with you, Jamie," he confessed, "you have been the hardest struggle of my life. If I could marry I'd grab you up in a heartbeat because I love being with you."

His compliment and words caused tears to flow down her cheeks. "How do you find the strength to overcome the temptation?" she cried, wiping her tears with her sleeve.

"I understand the magnitude of eternity," he replied, sensing her struggle, "and every time I am faced with a temptation I ask my self how many souls may suffer hell for eternity because of my failure to be strong in the Lord." He turned and smiled at her, then reached across the seat and took her hand. "It doesn't take me long to overcome the obstacle once I understand the price."

He had just finished speaking when he saw a set of blue lights in his rear-view mirror. "I wonder what I've done?" he said, as he looked down at his speedometer then pulled the jeep off the road.

Jamie didn't know what he was talking about until she turned around and saw the blue lights of the state trooper's car blaring behind them. She watched as the officer stopped his car, got out, and walked up to where Father was waiting.

"Good morning, sir," the officer greeted. "Are you Father Rex Macon?"

"Why yes," Father replied, startled as to how the trooper knew his name.

"May I see your driver's license, please?" the officer asked, extending his hand up to the glass.

Father reached into his back pocket and pulled out his wallet. He thumbed through it for a few seconds then handed the officer his driver's license. The officer looked at it for a moment then handed it back to Father.

"I have a message for you," he said, "from a Sheriff Martin in Bettis Bluff, Arkansas. He wants you to call him as soon as possible. He called us yesterday and told us to keep an eye out for your jeep. It must be pretty important. I was there when the call came in and he sounded pretty stressed. I'd call him as soon you can."

Father thanked the officer then rolled the window back up. He watched in his side mirror as the trooper got back in his car, turned off the blue lights, then pulled out and went on around them. He then turned to Jamie. "I believe God's ready."

CHAPTER SIXTEEN

THE ANSWER

Father made sure it was clear, then pulled the jeep back onto the highway. He was in one of his concentration modes where his eyes were on the road but his mind was already talking with the sheriff.

"I'm afraid to even hear what the sheriff wants," Jamie offered, wanting to hear what he was thinking.

"We both knew when we left that the situation was serious," he answered. "Now, almost four months later, I hate to even think what could be going on without anyone there to combat the principality. He could be very well entrenched by now, which means everyone in the community should be feeling the effects."

"What kind of effects?" she asked eagerly.

"Well, we know the principality is one of sexual perversion and death so if something is going on, somehow those two things can be expected to be in the forefront."

"We could not call them," she found herself saying because of the fear that was trying to take hold of her.

"I know it is scary," he reassured her, "but everything I've been taught by God and everything that I have shared with you, I feel is for right now. To run from this thing would be like saying no to my destiny."

She knew he was right. Still, she dreaded his making that

phone call. They drove on into Jackson Hole and found a payphone at a gas station just inside the town. It was crowded and hard to find a place to park because of the festival so they decided to put some fuel in the jeep and as she was pumping the gas, he made the phone call. She pulled the trigger on the gas nozzle slowly to give him time to talk. She watched as he dialed and then as someone on the other end apparently answered. He waited for a few seconds, then his bodily movements showed that he was talking to the sheriff. Slowly his countenance changed. She could tell by his facial expressions that whatever he was hearing was not good news. She finished pumping the gas and went in to pay the attendant. As she walked out of the station, he was just hanging up the phone. She had never seen him so pale. He looked like a ghost as he walked over to the jeep.

"You drive," he said as he walked around to the passenger side and got in.

She opened the door of the jeep and crawled into the driver's seat. She started the engine, then looked over at him. He was still very pale as he looked at her and said, "Let's go back to the cabin."

She pulled out of the station and headed the jeep back the way they had come. She kept looking at him, waiting for him to let her know what was going on.

"Father Ashton is dead," he said as he burst out sobbing.

"What?" Jamie screamed as she too began to cry just from witnessing his pain.

They both sobbed as she tried to drive the vehicle. Finally, she pulled over to the side of the road, waiting to gain her composure.

"What happened?" she finally asked.

Father Macon took a while to answer. He took a deep breath and said, "Sheriff Martin said that Father Ashton had been sexually abusing some of the young boys in the parish and one of the boy's fathers found out. He caught his son and Father Ashton in the rectory nude together, and the father of the boy shot Father Ashton right there. Right there in the rectory." Father Macon began to sob again. "I knew he didn't stand a chance against Syrasohan. I tried to warn the bishop but he wouldn't listen. Now Father Ashton's dead."

Jamie again eased the jeep back onto the road and continued driving to the lake. Father continued to sob and pray in the spirit until they had almost arrived at the lake. He then turned to Jamie. "That's not all," he said. "Three more children have been killed."

Jamie couldn't believe what she was hearing. Three more like Elizabeth Krouse had now been killed, all because a community was too proud and too hard-headed to listen.

"Do you know what happened?" she asked, still stewing from her anger for the people of Engleton.

"The sheriff didn't tell me a lot but something about one of the young girls getting pregnant and not wanting to put up with the shame and ridicule. The other two were boys. One of them was the father of the baby and together they were running a small prostitution ring using the young girls. They killed themselves together when the sheriff found out what they were doing." He paused, then shook his head. "Things have certainly gone to hell in Engleton."

They arrived back at the cabin, and she could tell by his actions that they were going back to Engleton. "Who's asking you to come back," she asked, as she watched him obviously taking mental note of his packing agenda, "the sheriff, the people of Engleton or the bishop?"

"Right now just the sheriff," he replied, "but he said that the bishop had called his office looking for me a couple days after Father Ashton was killed. As for the people, he said it was getting really bad in Engleton, and if something wasn't done in a hurry, the entire community was going to implode on itself."

"What are you going to do?" she asked. "Do you think the people will be any more receptive to the truth now than they were before?"

"I don't know, Jamie," he replied, walking over to her and taking her hands, "but I do know I can't stand around and just watch when I know what the problem is and what the people need. I'm hoping the bishop will at least listen to me now."

She took his hands and pushed them behind her as she let go and embraced him. They held each other for a long while, each wondering what they could do to put a stop to this madness.

"I guess we need to get packing, huh?" she asked with her head squeezed against his chest.

"I think we need to get back as soon as possible," he agreed. "I'm just hoping that the Lord gives me the answer as to how to put an end to Syrasohan and the demonic depression over Engleton before we get back."

She prayed for him in the spirit as they continued to hold each other. She knew he would need all the spiritual assistance he could muster.

It took them three days to get everything packed and ready to go. They had to find a U-haul again in Jackson Hole and then find time to tell Mary and Bob Owens thanks for the use of the cabin. The Owens hated to see them go. They had become good friends again, and now Father was leaving once more. Bob kidded Father about writing the Pope and seeing if he couldn't make one exception in Father's case about priests getting married. Father told him he didn't know how in the world he was going to get along without Bob's concern for his love life.

Both Jamie and Father had grown to love their new home. They agreed that they would miss the cabin, the lake, and especially the little chapel in front of the Tetons. On their way out of town, they stopped one more time and prayed together for a safe and victorious trip back to Engleton.

They took their time driving back to Arkansas. Father had been putting off talking to the bishop, but he knew he had to, sooner or later. He finally decided to stop and call from a payphone on the interstate. He would need a place to stay, and he was hoping he could stay in the rectory. Jamie had decided to stay at the motel again until she found an apartment. And this time, she would make sure that the sheriff kept an eye on her, especially if someone started stalking her again.

"There's one," Jamie yelled, pointing to a telephone booth next to a super-mart store.

Father pulled the jeep and trailer into the space in front of the phone booth. He laughed about whether the bishop would receive a collect call from him, but he declared he would take a chance. She watched him as he dialed the phone and began talking. She kept her eyes glued to his face again as it went from being very sober to a slight grin. She was relieved that he wasn't as white as a ghost and about to faint this time. He had an even larger smile on his face as he hung the phone up and walked back to the jeep.

"Well, praise God," he said as he climbed back into the seat, "I've got my old job back."

"Hallelujah!" Jamie exclaimed.

"I think he must be pretty shook up about the whole thing. He said he would support me in anything I needed to do at St. Mark's. He said he didn't fully understand what was going on but apparently I did. And he gave me the freedom to do whatever needs to be done. I told him that it might get dirty before it was over."

"What did he say?"

"He said that it didn't get any dirtier than having a dead priest on his hands. After that he could handle about anything. He said he would pray for me, and he wanted me to keep him updated as to how things were going, and if I needed anything."

"What you need is a plan," she grinned. "It's going to be like Daniel in the Lion's den."

"Remember, though," Father replied as he started the jeep, "God shut the mouths of the lions."

They arrived at the rectory early in the morning. They had stayed the night before in a motel about two hours away because they wanted a full day to get unloaded and settled. The church looked bleak and barren as they drove into the parking lot and parked the jeep in front of the rectory. He still had his key so he unlocked the door and they both went in. It smelled musty even in the chilly weather. The heat had been left on but the thermostat had been turned as low as possible. It looked the same except for new carpet in the bedroom. His thoughts returned to Father Ashton and why the carpet had probably been replaced. He would say a Mass in the building soon and offer the Mass for Father Ashton. Jamie had also been looking around and noticed that the carpet was different.

"You know, having something as vile as that to happen in a parish should be enough of an eye-opener to anyone," she said, expressing her thoughts.

"I don't know, Jamie," Father replied. "Spiritual blindness is something that is so simple to those who can see and yet such a prison to those who can't. Sometimes I think that Syrasohan could appear and give the homily at Mass and most of the people sitting in the pew wouldn't believe, and those who did wouldn't care."

"What causes that?" she asked, not understanding such apathy and unbelief.

"It's called rule-book Christianity," Father explained. "When the Church first started, it was mostly dealing with people who couldn't read. So in wisdom, the Church set down guidelines for the people to simply memorize and follow, hoping that the minimum would instill in each person the desire for more of our Lord. What happened was the people saw the minimum as a maximum and used it as a totality of their spiritual life. The obligation of the church turned into a set of rules that people thought they had to follow to get to heaven. Dedication to the rules became so strong that even after people learned to read and write, the minimum was as far as anybody saw the need to go. Their parents and grandparents had never grown any farther, so the next generation kept the same spiritual mentality as their forefathers. Everyone was bored stiff with the ritual but no one was willing to challenge the tradition. That type of a mentality just invites a principality of some kind. The people think they can hate each other, steal from each other, lie to each other and even kill each other, and, as long as they go to Mass, they're okay because they're following the rules. They wouldn't think a thing about stealing another man's cow or committing adultery with a next door neighbor, but they'd drive a thousand miles to make sure they didn't miss Mass."

"That's pretty sick," Jamie replied. "I don't understand a mentality like that."

"People seem to lose all sanity when their religious tradition is threatened. In one parish, we had a group of kids who were interested in receiving the gifts of the Holy Spirit and learning more about their relationship with Jesus. We formed a weekly study group for those kids. The parents became so threatened by their children's religious fervor that they organized a pizza and movie night for the kids on the same night as the study group." He laughed and shook his head. "Regardless of what has happened here to these people, many of them will not be glad to see me back."

They spent the rest of the morning carrying things in from the trailer and unloading the jeep. They stopped long enough to fix some sandwiches for lunch, then sat out on the porch and let their food settle before going back to the unpacking.

"I still don't understand something," Jamie offered after sitting quietly for a long while. "Nearly every person that belongs to this parish was at Elizabeth's funeral, and they heard you tell them that if they refused to become involved there would be more deaths. It happened! Just like you said it would, and yet the same people still don't want to get involved?"

"Change is the key, Jamie," Father replied, leaning back against the rectory wall. "No one likes change, and if they admit I'm right, then that means they must change. That takes too much effort. They might have to miss a card game, or bowling night or a football game, and that's asking too much."

"Then how do we fight this thing?" she asked. "There's no way me and you, even together, can defeat this thing."

"You're right, we can't, and I know it looks hopeless but God has a plan and at the proper time, He'll let us know."

She was laughing and telling Father that she wished she had his faith when they heard a horn sound from the highway. They looked up to see Ray and Eva pulling into the parking lot and driving toward them. They both got up as the car came to a halt.

Ray and Eva were all smiles as they got out of the car and walked to the steps. Each one of them hugged Father and Jamie. Ray was the first to speak. "Man, are we glad to see you two. Sheriff Martin told me you were coming back, and that was music to my ears. Father you were right. This place has turned into a hell-hole."

"And you said they wouldn't be glad to see you," Jamie chimed in quickly.

"Well, I guess I was wrong," he smiled, glad to see some friendly faces.

"Not all the way, Father," Ray quickly added. "Some of the people had a fit when they heard you were coming back."

Father Macon turned to Jamie and winked. She responded by shaking her head side to side and pulling her finger across her throat. "Let's all go inside," he suggested, motioning to Ray and Eva.

They all went inside and sat down at the dining room table. "Tell us everything that's been going on, Ray," Father said as he sat down.

"You don't have that long, Father," Ray laughed. "After you left, things started going down fast. Father Ashton came in and was a good man, but he was so inexperienced that the people didn't give him much respect. He was good at saying Mass, but no one offered him much support. He quickly got involved leading the kids in the choir and with training the altar servers. Parents would drop their kids off and then, thinking they were safe, they would pick them up when the meeting was over. After a while rumors started flying around, but no one wanted to believe it until Roland Franks caught his son and Father Ashton here in the rectory. He blew him away, right over there." Ray pointed to the spot by the bed that they could see from where they were sitting. "It was pretty bad," he continued. "Folks were upset, but not one person mentioned what Father Macon had predicted. Then just a couple days later, Jessica Rugers was found dead in her bed. She had taken an overdose of some pills that no one knew she had. The sheriff had an autopsy done and found out she was pregnant. Twelve years old, can you imagine that? Well, the sheriff kept digging and found that Eddie Long and Mike Carson were running a prostitution ring with these little girls. They were taking them down to the truck stop and selling them to the truckers coming through. Before the sheriff could arrest them, however, they hooked a hose up to their exhaust and placed it inside the car. Someone found them both down by the river with the car still running. They were both dead when they got them to the hospital."

"Is there any good news?" Jamie asked, unable to stand any more information of this type.

"Not much, I'm afraid to say, Jamie," Ray continued. "I quit my job on the boats and moved back here to be with my family. I found a job in town. It doesn't pay near as much, but we decided after we lost Elizabeth, that our lives and our family were more important than the money I was working for. He grabbed Father's hand and tears came to his eyes as he spoke. "We pray together as a family every night now, and it is the best thing that has ever happened to us. Elizabeth's death helped us all to understand that our eternal lives are much more important than anything else. My whole family now tries to live for the Lord every day. It has cost us some things, but it has only made our family stronger."

"What kind of things, Ray?" Father asked.

"Well, we don't have many friends any more. People think we're all Jesus freaks. And it got to be such a hassle at school that we had to take the kids out and home school them. But, you know, that's been a blessing, too. We've grown close to each other, and we really enjoy each other's company."

"I'd say that's some pretty good news," Jamie complimented. "In fact, that's the best news I've heard in a long time."

"Amen to that," Father added.

They all laughed. Eva reminded Ray that she had groceries out in the car, and she needed to get them home.

"We were on our way home," Ray explained, "when we saw your jeep. It was certainly a sight for sore eyes. We're really glad to see you back, Father, and we want you to know that we're ready to fight this thing with you. Whatever you want us to do we'll do. And so will Pat Geller. Those prayers you gave her? She said Billy would be dead along with Eddie and Mike if it hadn't been for those prayers. She says them every night over her kids, and she swears by them. She thinks you hung the moon, so count her in also."

They exchanged hugs, then Ray and Eva walked out and got in their car. Father and Jamie watched as they drove out of the driveway.

"Well, that's five of us," Jamie smiled as she turned to face Father.

"I'll gladly take all I can get," Father laughed as he turned to walk back into the rectory. As he turned he saw another car pull into the driveway. It was Sheriff Martin.

"This has been quite a welcoming committee," he said as he pointed to the Sheriff's car pulling in the driveway.

Jamie turned and watched as the sheriff's car pulled almost into the same spot where the Krouse's car had been. The sheriff stopped his car then got out and walked to the steps where they were standing. He was smiling but he didn't say anything until he shook Father's hand.

"I don't know when I've ever missed anyone as much as I've

missed you, Father," he said as he dropped his hand, then greeted Jamie.

"I never thought I'd hear that from a sheriff," he laughed.

"You were as right as rain about this community. Since you left this place has gone to hell in a hand basket."

"That's what I hear," he shared. "The Krouses just left and they told us what has been going on here. Some pretty bad stuff."

"Real bad," the sheriff agreed. "My office has answered 218 disturbances of various kinds since you left. Everything from kids skinny dipping down at the river to, you know, the death of Father Ashton. Some of it was just plain crazy, too, like those boys selling the young girls to the truckers. Man, I about lost it on that one. Some of those little girls were ten and eleven years old. The boys knew they were in deep trouble. I guess that's why they killed themselves. If you hadn't let me know what was really going on out here, I'd have lost all hope for humanity. This thing is big and it is affecting everything in this area."

"Sounds like you're convinced, sheriff," Father stated.

"I'm not only convinced, I'm completely convinced. In fact, I owe you my salvation."

Father looked at him with a questioning look on his face. The sheriff continued. "I started going to church with my wife after you left. I wanted to know if this spirit stuff was true. What I found out shocked me. I realized I had been fighting crime for twenty-two years when I should have been fighting the source of that crime. I got saved, baptized, and now I even teach Sunday school. I know what we're up against out here, but I know the people are not convinced, and without their help this principality will continue to use and destroy these people."

"I praise God for what He has revealed to you, sheriff," Father replied. "And I praise Him that you have been open to His revelation."

"You had a lot to do with that, Father, and I'm thankful. But, when I saw Carl's bull and the inside of the Krouse's home, it brought back things that my wife had shared with me. Between her and you, God was able to convert this old sinner and put his feet on the right track. Now we're ready to help you in any way we can. If you need us for anything, my wife said she, too, was ready to help. She's thankful also for what you did for me." He turned and walked back to his car. "I'll let you all get back in the house. It's getting colder. But if I can help in any way, let me know. I mean it, Father."

"Thanks, sheriff," Father responded. "You've been a great support through this whole thing. Thanks for being a friend."

The sheriff nodded his head and started to get into his car. "Oh, by the way, I almost forgot. The autopsy team, after Phil was killed, changed the report. They blamed it all on Phil, and, since they could use him as the scapegoat, they revealed everything. It was just like Mike Broadway said it was. If you need to use that information now, we can back it up with documentation."

"That's great news," exclaimed Father. "The truth is coming to light. God is faithful and we will beat this thing."

"Amen," the sheriff yelled, and Jamie agreed.

They all rejoiced, then the sheriff told them to take care. He waved as he backed out, then they again watched as he pulled onto the highway.

"Well, that's seven," Jamie shouted. "This army is growing. Now all we need is a bugler to lead the cavalry charge."

"What?" Father exclaimed.

Jamie looked at him puzzled as to his response.

"What did you say?" he shouted as he grabbed her by the shoulders.

"I said this army is growing and all we need is a bugler to lead the cavalry charge. Why?"

"That's it!" Father shouted. "That's the answer."

"What?" Jamie questioned. "What answer?"

"Quick, help me find my notebook that contains my dream-work."

They went back into the rectory and began to go through the boxes, trying to find the notebook.

"God gave me the answer a long time ago, and I didn't realize it. It's in that notebook. He gave me two dreams. One I didn't write down, but He was faithful, and He gave it to me again."

"Is this it?" Jamie asked, holding up a notebook.

"Yes, that's it," he yelled. "Quick, let me see it."

He grabbed the notebook and rapidly turned the pages until he found the right page. Jamie listened excitedly as he began to read.

CHAPTER SEVENTEEN

THE RECKONING

"I am fighting a group of renegade Indians. I am a Union soldier and I am completely surrounded by the band of attacking Indians on horses. You are there reloading my guns for me as I empty each one in the heat of battle. The chief charges my position, jumps off his horse and begins to fight with me hand to hand. I recognize the chief as Walter Foust. We fight for a while and the chief begins to wear me down and push me to the ground." Father turns to Jamie who is listening intently and smiles. She grins, then motions with her hand for him to keep going. "You slap at the Indian but he uses his foot and kicks you to the ground. You hit your head on a rock and it knocks you out. The Indian begins to yell and chant as he realizes he is going to win. Suddenly I start praying in tongues and just as he is about to kill me, I hear a bugle blow and it startles the Indian. We both look in the direction of the bugle and a group of cavalry soldiers on flying horses come to the rescue. The soldier leading the charge is the woman from Rogers who taught me about spiritual warfare. They attack the Indians and drive them away. The chief is knocked to the ground and disappears."

"Wow, what a dream! What does it mean?"

"I thought a little about it at first but forgot about it until you said what you did about the bugle. In the dream, I am the Union soldier. That symbolizes the battle we are in right now with the presence of evil. The Indians symbolize the enemy and Walter Foust is a symbol for the attitude of the people in Engleton. It almost allowed the enemy to do me in. You represent the people like Eva, Ray and the sheriff who have tried to help support me in this fight, but have also been overwhelmed and taken out of the fight. The bugle is the sound that means help is on the way, and the help is…." He paused and grinned, adding to the suspense.

"Come on, Father, this is no time to keep me in suspense," Jamie encouraged.

"The help is the people from the Rogers area," he exclaimed excitedly.

Jamie didn't share his excitement because she still didn't understand. "I guess I'm not following you."

"Don't you see?" he asked, still overjoyed with the revelation. "The Body of Christ involves more than just the people of Engleton. These people need help because they don't understand the battle they are in, so we call the cavalry. The people from Rogers can come here and help us fight this principality. I'll call Sheila Reany and tell her what's going on. I'll ask her to round up as many people as she can who can come and help us defeat this thing. I know that's God's plan."

"Where would they stay?" Jamie questioned, still not really following the whole idea.

"Most of them have motor homes or travel trailers that they could stay in, and we could turn the parish hall into a cafeteria. We could set up twenty-four hour prayer in the church until we bring this thing down."

"How long will that take?" she asked, amazed at his dedication.

"As powerful as this thing is and as much control as he has

already exerted, it won't take long for him to realize he's being challenged. He will then begin to come against us. That may be enough to finally convince the people of Engleton what's going on."

"He had better come after us with a sledge hammer," she replied, "because that's what it's going to take to wake these people up."

"I promise you," he said smiling, "when he comes after us, it will make a sledge hammer look like a toothpick."

"You make it sound like World War Three," she said, laughing to hide her fear.

"The dream said it would be a battle," he reminded her. "That much we know. It also revealed that it would look like we were about to lose the battle. Our trip to Wyoming was that part fulfilled. We thought we were through, finished, defeated. Now God is telling us to bring in the cavalry. It may take a while, and the battle may be severe, but we will win. I know that for sure now. The Walter Foust mentality in this parish will, I repeat, will be defeated."

"I sure want to believe that," Jamie smiled.

"Then do, because I'll bet you that when I call Sheila and ask her to come she will have already known something is up. She's that sensitive to the Holy Spirit. That will be my confirmation that I'm right in my discernment."

"Well, let's call her," Jamie prompted. "I'll blow the bugle."

"Help me find my rolodex, and I'll call her right now," he replied as he began to once more dig through the boxes.

They searched for a few minutes until once again Jamie came up with the hidden item. As she held it up, Father said, "Look under R's and find James and Sheila Reany."

Jamie began to flip through the pages of the rolodex until she came to the R's. Father Macon had managed to find a pen and piece of paper and was waiting patiently for her to find the number. "Here it is," she finally said. She read him the number and then he went over to the phone and dialed. She was close enough to hear the phone as it rang and then the click which indicated that someone had picked it up. She heard a woman's voice say, "Hello."

"Hello, Sheila. This is Father Rex."

"Father, how are you doing?"

"I'm doing fine."

"Where have you been? James and I have had you on our hearts for a long time. We tried to call but no one knew where you were."

"I've been in Wyoming for the last few months."

"Have you been on retreat?"

"No, the bishop thought it best for me to take a sabbatical."

"Why would he do that?

"Well, we've been having some very serious spiritual warfare here. That's why you've probably been praying for me. It got so sticky that the bishop thought I needed a rest."

"Sounds like you made old Beelzebub pretty angry."

Jamie listened to them talk for a long time. Father Macon told Sheila most of what had happened and what he thought God's plan was for the community. She laughed and told him that last week the Lord had told her to tell James to get the motor home ready. They would be on the road for the Lord.

Father Macon turned and grinned at Jamie. He momentarily put his hand over the receiver. "I told you so," he laughed.

Sheila told Father that she would try to round up as many of the people there that could come at a moment's notice and put in the time needed to pull down the stronghold of the principality. She said that she could probably be in Engleton by the next afternoon but she wasn't sure about any of the others. She said she would call him back that afternoon and tell him how many were coming. They continued to talk for a few more minutes, and then Father hung up the phone.

"What did I tell you?" he beamed. "She knew we were battling and she was already making preparations to go somewhere. She didn't know where, but she was obedient to the word of the Spirit and now they are ready to travel. They'll be here tomorrow afternoon."

"What do you plan to do?" Jamie asked, glad to see him so excited.

"Jamie, I know that the only thing that will bring this thing to its knees is enough prayer, praise, and fasting in this area. We will take as many people as Sheila can bring and put them in the church, praying and interceding along with anyone in this community that wishes to join. I realize some people may have to work but anyone and everyone who can, we will take shifts praying until we know that Syrasohan is gone."

"How will we know that?"

"I don't know," Father answered. "God will show us."

"Where will the food come from to feed everyone?"

"When we see how many of us there are, we will go into Bettis Bluff and get supplies. I have a special fund that can pay for them, but many of us who can will need to fast while we are battling this thing."

"What if it lasts for weeks?" she wondered out loud.

"For some reason," he replied, "I feel in my spirit that the principality will try to confront us very quickly and try to put a stop to the threat."

They worked the rest of the afternoon getting the parish hall ready and preparing the church for the battle. They called Ray and Eva to let them know what was going on and they quickly left what they were doing and came to the church to help Jamie and Father Macon with the preparations.

Sheila had called back and was very excited. They had rounded up seven more couples from their surrounding area who had agreed to come and be a part of the spiritual army. Sheila stated that many of them had been preparing for something that they knew in their spirit was coming. One couple was already fasting. Father just knew that this was more confirmation from God that now was the time to strike.

The four of them finished the preparations about dark and decided to go out and eat together for tomorrow the battle would begin. They drove to Bettis Bluff together and enjoyed dinner in one of the restaurants. They shared their concerns about the coming trial, but each one knew in their hearts that it had to be done if Engleton was to ever survive. Ray said he would never rest until the thing that had killed his daughter was gone forever from the community. Father encouraged them but also warned them that this would not be a cake walk. Each one of them had to stay in a constant state of prayer and not allow their emotions or their flesh to control them. If they did, he warned, they would be ineffective in the heat of battle. Father could tell by how quiet everyone was on the way home that they understood the seriousness of what was getting ready to happen.

Ray and Eva invited Jamie to stay with them. They could tell that Father didn't want her staying alone in a motel after what the coven had attempted, so they told her they had plenty of room and she was welcome. Jamie could tell by the look on Father's face that he wanted her to accept so she said yes and accepted the Krouses' offer.

Ray dropped Father off at the rectory, and they prayed together before the others went home. Father Macon told them to get a good night's sleep, and he would see them sometime before noon the next day. He suggested that they have a lunch ready for the people when they arrived, and those that wanted to, could eat before they set up the prayer teams and assigned shifts.

Father was up early the next morning working on strategy. He had spent a lot of the night in prayer attempting to discern God's battle plan. He had decided to start with a Mass and invite everyone. Then all would stay in church and pray for the first five hours. After that they would pray in teams of five unless someone wanted to join them. Each team would pray for five hours and then be relieved. Father based the entire set-up on the number five. In ancient Hebrew the number five stood for grace. When David fought Goliath in the Old Testament, he took five stones from the earth. God's grace prevailed then. It would prevail this time. He sat at his desk and drew up enough sheets with five lines in each group. He would wait and talk with Sheila before he filled in the lines and assigned each team.

Jamie and the Krouses showed up a little before noon. They had gone into town and picked up some supplies and Eva and Jamie had spent the morning baking in anticipation of feeding a large number of people. Ray and Father rounded up extension cords and water hoses for the people's motor homes and trailers that would be coming. Father decided a small field next to the parish hall would be the best place for the visitors to park their temporary homes. They were just finishing the last of the preparations when they heard a loud horn from the direction of the highway. Both Ray and Father looked up to see James and Sheila waving at them through the windshield of the large motor craft. Following them in convoy fashion were seven more vehicles. Father waved and directed them to the large field that he and Ray had just prepared. As he watched each one pull into position, he praised God for the Body of Christ and for the people who were so dedicated to seeing His Kingdom come to this earth.

James and Sheila were the first to emerge from their motor home and Father was waiting for them when Sheila's foot hit the ground.

He gave her a hug as James walked around the front of the motor home and joined them.

"I am so glad to see you two," Father said as he also hugged James.

"You've really got a strong one here, don't you, Father?" she answered quickly, brushing aside his greeting. "James and I started feeling the oppression about eight miles away from the church." She then turned and looked at James. "The principality knows we are here."

"It is unbelievable how much damage it has done in such a short period of time. The people here, however, still refuse to believe or get involved. To them it's just bad luck that everything is happening."

"Have they never been taught anything about spiritual warfare or demonic spirits?" Sheila asked, not understanding how Christians could let it get so bad.

"You know as well as I do, tradition is a very hard shell to break and these people are so deep in tradition that they refuse to embrace anything that sounds new," Father replied, trying to explain the vastness of the problem.

"Have you not taught them what Jesus said about putting new wine in old skins?" Sheila persisted.

"I have tried for over a year to teach them a lot of things, but I might as well have been talking to a brick wall. They come to Mass, fulfill their obligation and that's it. Nothing more, nothing less."

"I know it is tough," she continued. "I was just as bad until I had my bout with cancer. After I worked through my anger at God, I began to realize that it was Satan that had put that mess on me and not God. I began to seek and search for every piece of knowledge I could find that might help me fight this stuff. When I realized it was demonic, I fought that thing like a pit bulldog, and in the fullness of time, I was healed. By His stripes I was healed."

"Amen," Father replied as the others from the other motor homes and trailers began to form a circle around him, James, and Sheila. James introduced the travelers to Father and Father introduced Ray to every one of them. After introductions, Father informed them that Eva and Jamie had lunch ready for the group in the parish hall. James stated that the travelers would need just a little time to level their motor homes and trailers and to get everything settled in. Father said that was fine. They agreed to meet in the parish hall in one hour.

Father and Ray were helping Jamie and Eva get things ready for the meal when the couples began to enter the parish hall. Father waited until they had all arrived then he introduced Jamie and Eva to everyone. Jamie was glad to see such an energetic crew. Every couple was retired and in their sixties but they each seemed so youthful and full of life. Father gave each couple time to meet Jamie and Eva. Then he told them all to take their seats. He said the blessing over the food then invited those who wanted to eat to go ahead and form a line for the meal.

After lunch, while Jamie and Eva served coffee, Father stood up and began to inform them of the situation. The audience sat very captive as he told them of everything that had taken place since the day Mr. Bowman's bull was found dead. He then had Ray and Eva tell their story. Ray held Eva and encouraged her as she broke into tears as she told of her daughter's death. Father could see the determination building in the people as they listened to Ray and Eva share their story. After they finished, Father had Jamie relate the story of her abduction and how the Lord had helped her escape. The people laughed and applauded as she related how the collie dog had led her to Father's doorstep. After she shared about her escape, the room began to break out in spontaneous praise to the Lord Jesus

Christ and His infinite power and mercy. Soon the entire room was filled with their songs and shouts.

"Honor and glory to the Lamb that sits upon the throne!" one of the men shouted, as the others continued to sing and praise. Suddenly the entire group began to sing in tongues. Jamie joined in as she rejoiced in the zeal and fervor of these people. As she sang and listened, tears began to run down her face. She knew that this is what loving Jesus was all about.

The group continued in praise for over an hour and as it became quieter, suddenly one of the men spoke forth in prophesy. "I am the Lord your God and this battle that stands before you is not yours but Mine. I have called each of you here to be My hands, My feet, My ears and My mouth. Stand firm in the power of My might and know that I will never leave you nor desert you. Encourage each other with My words and put on My full armor that you may be able to stand. Do not allow the words or the deeds of the enemy to cause you any fear. Do not be afraid. I am your source and I am your strength. Stand still, be not afraid and each of you shall witness the power of My glorious right hand. Thus says the Lord."

The group again began to break forth in praise as the man finished speaking. Father Macon began to dance as each person laughed and clapped. Sheila, too, began to dance and joined Father at the head of the tables. Soon everyone in the room was dancing and singing praises to the Lord for the victory.

The praise continued for another ten or fifteen minutes, then Father suggested that they adjourn to the Church. A few wanted to freshen up before Mass so he told them that they would take a thirty minute break then meet in the Church ready to continue the battle. As Jamie and Father Macon walked to the church, she was aglow with what she had just witnessed.

"That's what heaven will be like, won't it?" she asked.

Father laughed, "God inhabits the praises of His people. He is not an old fogy who wants us to be sad. Heaven is a happy place, but we can experience a piece of it here on earth. It's up to us."

"The man who spoke," she continued. "While he was speaking I could hardly stand up. I felt like I was drunk and about to fall over."

"That was the anointing of God," Father explained. "When that word came from God, the anointing that came along with it was enough to have a profound effect on our flesh. It's not uncommon for some people to simply fall to the floor under the power of that anointing. They call it being slain in the Spirit."

"All I can say," she smiled, "is that this is wonderful, and I want to learn all I can."

"Jamie," Father encouraged, "that's the kind of attitude that pleases the Father. He calls it a contrite spirit."

Jamie followed Father in through the side door of the church. She knelt down and began to pray as she watched him through the sacristy door preparing for the Mass. One by one the people began to filter into the church and when everyone was accounted for, Father began the Mass. During the consecration, he had the urge to consecrate more hosts than they would need for the people present. He was obedient and after distributing communion to the people he retired the extra hosts into the tabernacle behind the altar.

After the Mass the people continued to pray and praise as they had done in the parish hall. After removing his vestments, Father Macon joined them and they continued for hours. They sang every praise song anyone could think of, then they spent time in prayer. After the first five hours, Father and Sheila filled in the work sheets Father had prepared and decided who would take the first visit. Jamie, Eva, Ray and two of the visitors took the first round. Father, James, and Sheila stayed for a couple more hours then retired to the rectory to discuss possible obstacles that might arise. At midnight they went to bed.

The next morning, there was a strange and heavy overcast over the whole area. It had even made the news. Father had gotten up early and gone into Bettis Bluff to get supplies. As soon as he hit the outskirts of the city the overcast lifted. The weather bureau said that it was some strange phenomenon caused by the air along the river bottom. It was really strange to stand on the sidewalk in front of the supermarket and look back toward Engleton. The clouds looked like a large dark garbage can lid just sitting over the area. He wondered about it, but the weather bureau seemed to know what they were talking about. He ignored the heavy cloud cover as he drove into it on his way back to Engleton.

When he arrived back at the church, Jamie said that Walter Foust had been by. He hadn't gotten out of his truck or said anything to anyone, but she could tell that he was looking the entire situation over and trying to figure out what was going on. Mrs. Geller was also in the church. She had come this morning with her daughter, Patty, who had stayed out most of the night. Mrs. Geller said that Patty had come home this morning acting really weird. She wouldn't eat or hardly talk and she would just sit and stare into space. It had scared Mrs. Geller and she wanted Father to talk to Patty and see if he could figure out what was going on.

Father immediately thought of Elizabeth's behavior before her sacrificial suicide. He didn't like the sound of Jamie's description of Patty. He knew Patty had been involved before they had gone to Wyoming but he figured that somehow Patty had been able to get free from the group she had been running with. He knew Mrs. Geller was praying for her children. Ray had told him so. She had been excited to receive the prayers he had given her before his sabbatical.

As he walked into the church and looked at Patty he could tell that the source of her problem was demonic. She had that lost in space stare and he could feel in his spirit the evil around her. As he walked over toward her, Sheila approached him and grabbed his arm. Father stopped and turned to face her. "She's got so much demonic baggage she is out of it," Sheila related.

"I know, but now is not the time to do a deliverance," Father replied quietly.

"She doesn't seem to be causing any problem," Sheila observed. "I would let her sit here in the presence of the Lord, and allow the praise and the prayers of the team to just soak her. I would caution her mother, however, to not take her out of this place but keep her close where we can watch her. They can stay in our motor home when we're not using it."

"Have you noticed the temperature starting to drop in here since she came in?" Father asked, looking at the other team members still praying around the church.

"Yes," Sheila replied, "and if I am right, this principality has planted her here for a reason. She's much too calm to be carrying around the baggage she has."

"I'll talk to her mom outside," Father suggested, "and you keep an eye on the girl. Any problems, call."

Sheila nodded her head as Father went over to where Mrs. Geller and Patty were. Mrs. Geller was kneeling and Patty was just sitting in the pew, staring. She didn't even acknowledge Father's presence. Father tapped Mrs. Geller on the shoulder and she smiled as she opened her eyes, then turned and faced Father Macon. Father put his finger to his lips to tell her to be quiet and motioned for her to follow him. She got up, looked at Patty, and then followed Father out the back of church. When they walked outside, Father turned and asked, "How long has she been like that?"

"Just since this morning," Mrs. Geller replied. "When I came home from work last night she was not in the house and she didn't show up until this morning. When she did, she seemed agitated and angry then she just slumped into a blank stare. She's been like that ever since. What do you think is wrong?"

"I think she is under very heavy demonic oppression," he replied, which caused Mrs. Geller to gasp and grab her mouth. Tears formed in her eyes as she remembered Elizabeth and her own Larry.

Father told her what he and Sheila had decided and Mrs. Geller agreed. He told her to leave Patty in church with the team as much as possible.

Much of the day was spent in prayer and listening for God's direction. The overcast seemed to get darker as the day wore on. By late afternoon, it already looked like midnight. Sheila walked up to Father as he finished his shift and walked out of the church.

"This is not natural," she said, pointing up with her finger. "I can feel the evil getting more pronounced over us."

"You're right," Father agreed. "I can feel something is in the works. We need to inform everyone to be on guard and not to be by themselves for any long period of time."

"These are veteran spiritual fighters," Sheila related, "but I don't know that any of them have been up against anything of this caliber. I'll talk to each one and encourage them separately."

"I would appreciate that," Father grinned. "I would also warn them to watch Patty's actions and inform either me or you if they notice anything strange. I'll take an early trip in the morning into Bettis Bluff and see if the weather bureau is sticking to their guns about this strange weather."

"It's coming to a head quickly, isn't it?" she asked.

"This principality is so arrogant that he is not going to wait for us to put a lot of pressure on him. He is already feeling the pinch and he doesn't like it. The next twenty-four to thirty-six hours should be very interesting."

He patted Sheila's hand as he smiled, then turned and walked toward the rectory.

The next morning the darkness was still overwhelming. As Father crawled into his jeep and turned the lights on, he knew things were starting to boil. He had a few supplies to get at the store. He would also check on the weather while he was in town. The sky gradually became lighter as he distanced himself from the church. When he reached the city limits of Bettis Bluff it was dramatic as to the change in the amount of light penetrating the clouds. He picked up the supplies quickly then asked one of the managers in the store about the cloud formation over Engleton. The man said that the weather bureau had released a special report saying that the condition had been worsened because of a fire that had broken out in the wildlife refuge up river from Engleton. The smoke combined with the condition along the river had caused the weird cloud coverage. Coming out of the store Father could see that the formation had gotten much darker and much more pronounced since the day before. It was an eerie feeling as he drove back into the haze and watched as it got darker and darker the closer he got to the church.

When he pulled into the parking lot, he knew something was up. He could see Walter Foust's truck and another car parked in front of the church and about eight men arguing with James and Jamie. The men had guns and they were yelling and holding their guns up in the air. As Father stopped his jeep near the men and got out, he recognized every one of the men including Walter as parishioners of St. Mark's.

As Father walked toward the group, Walter turned and started walking toward Father. "You're the problem," he yelled, pointing his finger at Father Macon. "This community was fine until you showed up and brought this bunch of devil worshipers into Engleton."

"What are you talking about, Walter?" Father asked, trying to calm him down.

"I'm saying that the people of Engleton were doing fine until you came among us and started your false religion around here, this speaking in tongues crap and talk of demons and death. We're good Catholics and damn good ones, too."

"Tell him, Walt," one man behind him encouraged.

"The boys want to drink a little and play a little cards and you shut the whole damn thing down," he continued, spurred on by the man's comment. "We thought we had gotten rid of you and your crazy ideas and here you are again. We're here to tell you that this is our church, and we want you all off our property."

"That's right, get the hell out of here," the mob agreed.

Father put up his hands to silence the crowd, then he said calmly, "This property does not belong to you, it belongs to the diocese of Little Rock and I don't work for you, I work for the bishop. Only he can run me off, so you boys need to take yourselves and your guns and go back home before I call the sheriff."

"Looks like someone already has," James revealed, pointing to the driveway entrance.

The men began to mumble and talk among themselves as the sheriff drove into the crowd of people and stopped his car.

"Father, have you decided to have an all day meeting on the grounds?" he kidded, getting out of his car and eyeing the mob.

"Just some of the men with some weird ideas, sheriff," Father replied.

"He's holding devil worship ceremonies in our church, sheriff, and we the people of Engleton want him out of here," Walter Foust cried.

"Walter, I advise you men to take your guns and get out of here or I'm going to arrest every one of you for assault," the sheriff exclaimed as he walked toward the mob.

"Sheriff, it's not fair. This is our community and these people are trespassing on our property," Walter continued, refusing to give up.

"I would advise you to take this up with the leaders of your church in Little Rock," the sheriff advised, "because I'm serious about arresting every one of you. In fact, I'm going back to my car. And if you all haven't made an effort to leave by the time I get my pen and book, I'm writing you all up and hauling you in."

As the sheriff finished, he turned and started back toward his car. The men behind Walter began to get into the car and two got into Walter's truck. When he turned and saw that he had been deserted, he gave Father a hard look then walked to his truck. He slammed the door, then both vehicles turned on their lights and sped out of the parking lot.

The people watched them leave, then Father turned to the sheriff. "I don't know who called you, but I'm mighty thankful."

"No one called me," the sheriff replied. "It was kind of odd. I just had the feeling I needed to come out here and check on you. This darkness really looks weird from Bettis Bluff and I wanted to make sure you were all right."

The sheriff looked around as he spoke and noticed all the strange faces. "Looks like you've brought in some reserves," he said, grinning and shaking hands with James.

"That's the American way, isn't it, sheriff?" Father asked as he introduced the people to Sheriff Martin.

"It's the only way," the sheriff agreed as he continued to shake the hands of the visitors.

"Let's go over to the parish hall and I'll bring you up to date," Father suggested as he motioned for the sheriff to follow him.

They all walked over to the cafeteria except for the team in the church. Father told the sheriff about the dream and how he knew this was God's way to win this thing. He told him they had been active in prayer for two days and how he thought the cloud was a direct result of their threat to the principality.

They were all drinking their coffee and discussing the situation when one of the men came running in and yelled at Father. "Father, come quick! You need to see this."

Everyone jumped up and ran outside. The wind was beginning to blow but instead of in a straight line, it seemed to be blowing in a circle with the church as the vortex.

"Quick," Father yelled, "get everyone into the church."

CHAPTER EIGHTEEN

THE TABERNACLE

Lightning began to pop and crackle as the people scrambled to get everyone into the church. Some of those who had been asleep were awakened and told to get to the church immediately. The wind was becoming gale force as the last few people made their way into the church. The lightning and thunder were almost constant and rain began to beat against the stained-glass windows above their heads. Father looked around at the people and told them to pray because this looked as if it might be the attack they had been expecting. He noticed a new couple over in the back pew and he walked over to them. He recognized them as some of his parishioners and he knelt down on one knee to facilitate an eye to eye conversation.

"I'm glad to see you folks," Father said gently. "I know this is scary but it is necessary to rid our community of this evil."

"We know, Father," the man replied. "We didn't believe any of it until we saw the cloud. Then we thought it was the end of the world. We thought the safest place would be here in church."

"Keep your eyes closed in prayer, and keep your ears focused to your prayers," Father warned. "If you have to, lie down on the floor, but don't go outside. Understand?"

They both shook their heads but Father Macon could tell that they were scared to death. The man's wife was holding on to him for dear life, and he could see her rosary hanging between her fingers. She had been praying the entire time Father had been talking to them.

As Father started to get up the lights went out. Only the lights of the votive candles kept the inside of the church from being really dark. Father could feel the fear coming into the room so he started praying the Lord's Prayer. The people quickly joined in as the cold began to increase inside the church.

"Remember who we are in Christ," Father yelled as he felt the cold getting deeper. "Greater is He that is in us than he that is in the world."

The people began to pray in the spirit as they sensed the presence of evil increasing around them. Suddenly, a wild scream came from the back of the church as demon spirits began to manifest. All over the church song books and papers began to fly through the air around the people. Terrible looking demons appeared and began to fly around the room, stopping in front of the faces of some of the people.

"Keep your eyes shut and listen only to our prayers," Father yelled above the racket the demons were making.

"Ah," the man screamed from the back of the church, "I can't take it, I can't take it," he yelled as he jumped up and slapped at his body as if he were being attacked by a swarm of wasps. His wife tried to help him, but he pushed her back into the pew and ran out of the church. Everyone heard him yell a horrible scream as he came in contact with the outside storm.

More and more demons were manifesting in the church until the air was thick with their presence. The air smelled of sulfur and the roar had increased to the point where it sounded like interference on TV. As Father listened closely, the interference sound was actually the voices of the demons talking and cursing the people in the church.

His concentration was broken by the spine chilling cry of Patty Geller. Suddenly, the quiet little girl had come to life in a big way.

"You're all dead," she screamed. "Syrasohan is god. He is the ruler of this community and none of you will prevail."

She jumped up, pushed her mother aside and began to run for the door. "Don't let her get out the door," Father cried. "Quick, sheriff, grab her."

The sheriff made a lunge for the small girl as she ran past him for the door. He managed to just grab her ankle which caused her to trip. James then ran over and laid himself down over her body.

"Let me go, you son-of-a-bitch," she yelled in a deep masculine voice. "I'll kill you."

She rolled over on her back and threw James off of her like a piece of styrofoam. The sheriff grabbed her leg as she attempted to get back on her feet. She kicked at him, trying to dislodge his hand but he held on. James again grabbed onto her as she fought the two men trying to get free.

"Help them, men," Father yelled as he ran to the back of the church in an attempt to add his assistance. The girl had once more overpowered James and thrown him to the floor. She was about to get to her feet when three of the other men got to her and pulled her back down to the floor. She began to cuss and rant as the men held tight to their captive.

Father was praying in the spirit along with the other men as the demons swarmed around them and began to scream and yell at the men holding the girl. In the spirit, he heard the word, "dart".

"Jamie," he yelled, looking around for her. "Come here quick."

Jamie made her way back to the pile of bodies as the demons swirled around her, yelling and trying to break her mind's concentration. As Father caught sight of her he yelled, "Jamie, she's got one of the bone darts on her somewhere. We've got to find it. We'll keep her held down while you look for it. You know what they look like and there's no telling where it's at. Find it. Don't worry about modesty. This is no time is worry about that."

Jamie began to feel of the girl's hair, trying to feel for the small bone spears that she had seen in the quiver of the statue on the Satanic altar. Convinced that it wasn't on her head she began to feel under the girl's blouse and around the front of her bra. The girl tried to fight the men but they held fast. Not finding the spear there, Jamie checked the pockets of the girl's jeans.

"Are you sure it's here?" she yelled to Father Macon over the sound of the demons screaming in their ears.

"It has to be, keep looking. If we have to, we'll take her jeans down but let's roll her over first and check down her back."

She fought them and continued to scream obscenities as they rolled her over and Jamie put her hand under the girl's blouse. As her hand felt along the girl's bra strap she felt the tip of the dart. She grabbed a hold of it and pulled it out.

"Here it is," she yelled as she held it up, exposing it to the eyes of everyone.

"No!" the girl screamed as Father took the dart out of Jamie's hand. She fought furiously for a few minutes then fell back against the floor. She lay there quietly, breathing very heavily, then relaxed in the grip of the men.

Father knew he couldn't get outside with the dart and he knew there was no way he could say Mass. Then it hit him. The tabernacle. The Body of Jesus. He had consecrated enough hosts at Mass so that the Body of Jesus was in the tabernacle. He would put the dart in the tabernacle with Jesus.

He could feel the evil radiating from the small dart at the tips of his fingers. He got up from his position around the young girl who was now lying lifelessly on the floor. As he started toward the front of the church, suddenly a tremendous wind began to resist his efforts. He turned around backwards, trying to overcome the force but it was just too much of a struggle. The wind was as bitter cold as any he had ever felt. Even in the dead of winter in Wyoming, he had not felt such cold. It was as if the entire demon hoard inside the church had figured out his plan and they were trying with all their power to keep him from making his way to the front of the church.

It was the sheriff who first noticed the priest's dilemma. He pulled himself along pew by pew as he, too, fought the power of the ice cold wind. Father was trying to pull himself along as he felt the hand of the sheriff touch his back, then began to shove him along against the force. "Everyone pray in the spirit," Father commanded as he continued to pull himself and allow himself to be pushed along from pew to pew. All of the others except for Jamie, who was still with Patty, began to pray earnestly in the spirit and focus their attention on Father and the sheriff. The demons were still trying to distract those who were praying by getting right in their faces and screaming and yelling and changing into grotesque forms and shapes. The team had realized, however, that fear was the only weapon the demons could use against them. As long as they stayed in the church, they would be all right. This added to their confidence so they kept their concentration on helping Father and the sheriff.

Father's hair had grown frost colored from the cold. It was like being in Antarctica. Still he inched along trying to make his way to the altar. He could feel the evil power of the dart trying to make its way down his arm.

"Father God, please help me," he prayed as he fought to even stay upright along the sides of the pew.

Suddenly he felt his feet leave the floor slightly and a tremendous force began to push him forward. The sheriff saw what was happening, and just fell away and clung to the pew. Slowly the force propelling Father Macon was now causing him to gain ground. The wind was just as fierce but somehow it was no longer as penetrating.

The demonic activity had been so strong that it had obscured his vision of the altar, but now he could barely make it out.

He stalled as he came to where the altar railing used to be. It felt like an invisible wall holding him back as he struggled to overcome the obstructing power. His body felt like it was being squeezed in a huge vise, the unseen hand behind him pushing forward and the force field before him resisting him.

"Jesus," he screamed as he felt his body being pressured beyond his ability to endure. "Help me."

With a sudden rush, he found himself being propelled forward with such force that his body hit the altar like a runaway truck. The pain racked his body as he fell to the floor. The evil in the dart had managed to work its way to his elbow and he fought with everything he had, trying to hang on to the small bony spear. He could see the hands of the demons trying to use every amount of their power to somehow dislodge the dart from his hand. They snarled and growled at him like dogs as they saw him watching their efforts. He grabbed a hold of the altar cloth in an attempt to pull himself up into an upright position. His rib cage on the left side felt like he had been kicked by a bull.

He somehow managed to get up off the floor. He could see the tabernacle clearly now. He placed his foot on the first of three marble steps that led up to the area of the tabernacle. Again his body seemed to be squeezed between two pieces of concrete. With one quick lunge he fell against the marble shelf that held the tabernacle. He groped for the key that lay in front and finally his hand connected with the familiar chain which housed the key to the tabernacle. He inched his fingers along the chain until he found the key. As he grabbed the key he screamed with excruciating pain. The key felt like white hot metal. He knew he must hang on but the hot metal felt like it was burning his fingers all the way to the bone. With every last bit of energy he could muster he jabbed at the key hole of the tabernacle until suddenly it hit its mark. He turned the key and the door to the tabernacle sprang open. As it did, something hit him across the face with such force that it knocked him down the steps back into the altar.

He lay against the altar not able to go any more. Looking up he saw the huge eight foot demon standing on the steps between him and the altar.

"I told you, you couldn't win, priest," he taunted. "Your puny power is no match for the mighty Syrasohan. I will kill you and this community will be mine."

Father's body would not respond as he commanded it to get up. It was just too worn out.

"You are a liar, demon," Father responded. "I know the power of the word of God and you have not prevailed. You are defeated."

As he spoke he felt energy coming back into his body. "Jesus defeated your raunchy carcass, and I'm going to kick the crap out of you and your entire operation." The more he talked the stronger he felt. When he climbed back to his feet, he saw a tall being dressed in light suddenly hit the huge demon from the side, knocking it seven or eight feet to the side. As it attempted to regain its position, Father quickly bounded forward and tossed the dart into the chalice with the Body of Jesus.

Father fell to the floor as the huge demon screamed so loud that the two stained-glass windows behind the altar blew out. Father could hear the broken glass hitting the ground outside as he watched the demon writhing in apparent pain. The huge demon began to struggle toward the back of the church. He stopped about midway and screamed again. This time two of the side windows blew out as the other members of the team crouched behind the pews. With one last cry of despair the huge spirit threw back his head and yelled,

"PRIEST, DAMN YOU!" With that he fell to his knees and disappeared.

Father sat on the steps and breathed heavily. His body hurt as he turned and looked at the tall being dressed in light. The being smiled then turned and genuflected toward the tabernacle. Father watched as the angel then slowly disappeared.

Father turned and looked toward the back of the church. No one moved or said anything. Slowly the darkness began to give way to the light that came in through the broken windows. After a few minutes, the sun began to shine. The people slowly began to move around and suddenly someone broke out in praise. Soon everyone joined in and began to clap and sing. Patty woke up from the floor and Jamie helped her to her feet. She shook her head and wanted to know why she was in the church. Jamie gave her a hug and walked her over to her mom. The sheriff walked up to Father as the people continued to praise.

"You all right, Father?" he asked as he grabbed him and hugged him.

"I'm fine," Father laughed as he returned the hug and noticed that the soreness was almost gone and that he had gotten most of his energy back.

"Let's go check on the man that ran out," the sheriff suggested as they broke their embrace. The other people were hugging each other in victory as Father and the sheriff walked to the outside of the church. At the foot of the steps lay the body of the man with a huge tree limb protruding from his chest. Father knelt down and prayed for the man as he made the sign of the Cross on his forehead.

"We're fortunate that this is the only casualty after what we have just experienced," the sheriff remarked as Father rose to his feet. "Do you think it's over?"

"I don't think so," Father said sadly. "It won't be over until we destroy the statue that keeps the principality anchored here."

Father and the sheriff removed the limb from the man's chest, then carried his limp body over to the grass beside the sheriff's car. The sheriff took a blanket out of the trunk of his car and covered the corpse.

They turned and started back toward the church as Sheila came out on the steps and yelled, "Father, come here quick. Patty has something to tell you that seems very important."

Both men ran to the church and up the steps. Entering the church again, they found Patty surrounded by Jamie and the other team members. As Father walked up to the group, Jamie smiled and said, "Patty knows where the coven has been holding their rituals."

CHAPTER NINETEEN

THE BARN

"I am free," the girl cried. "I am free. I have been in such torment since Billy got me involved four months ago. It was fun at first, the power that the spirits gave me, but then I couldn't get rid of them. They talked to my mind and caused me to desire to do things that were bad."

"What kind of things?" Father asked.

"The boys got involved because of the sex and drugs. We got involved because of the stories the boys were telling about the spirits and how powerful they were. We were just curious. But once we got involved in the rituals, the power was so strong that everything became a game. I remember the night Elizabeth killed herself. The ceremony became so wild that everyone was having sex with everyone. It was a wild orgy. She kept telling everyone she was going to be made queen. Before I passed out that night, I saw two of the men strap her to the altar and have sex with her. She invited everyone to, because she wanted to be their queen."

"Did the demons ever manifest during the ceremony?" Father asked, enthralled by her story.

"All the time," she replied. "I couldn't see them at first, but the more I had sex with the others and the more I became involved, the clearer they became. Many of them appeared as great looking guys and had sex with us. Others appeared as beautiful women and had sex with the guys. Many nights it was pandemonium, but that seemed to please the spirits even more." She turned and looked into Father Macon's eyes. "Father, the day of Elizabeth's funeral, what you said opened my eyes to what was really going on, but as hard as I tried I couldn't get away. A major part of my mind wanted to be with the others who were having all the fun."

"Patty, where are the meetings going on?" the sheriff asked.

"The ceremonies take place in a hidden room in Walter Foust's barn," she replied.

"Walter Foust!" Father and the sheriff repeated together. "That's why he's been so upset about our goings on here at the church," Father continued.

"How about a man with a tattoo on his arm, Patty, that says, 'Satan rules'?" Jamie asked.

"That's Phozral. His real name is Albert and he's from some where up in Missouri," Patty explained. "I think he's kind of second in command after Walter."

"What makes Walter the head honcho?" the sheriff asked.

"He's the one that is responsible for the principality being here. While he was in service in the Gulf War and fighting Iraq in Desert Storm, he bought this statue from some old Iraqi peddler who told him it had magical powers. He brought it back to Engleton with him when he was discharged, and it began to converse with him. It promised him women, money, and power if he would just worship the god, Syrasohan. It told him how to get the ceremonies started and what was needed to bring more power into his life."

"How many people are involved, Patty?" Father asked, looking up at the sheriff.

I've been at some of the ceremonies when there have been as many as a hundred and twenty-five people," she replied.

"All of them from around here?" Father asked, again amazed at her answer.

"No," she continued. "Most of them I didn't even know. I met one nice looking guy from St. Louis, so I figured they came from all over."

"How about the small bone spears that we found on you and around at different times?" Father questioned.

"In the group, those are called anchors. They are carved from the bones of animals that have been sacrificed to the spirits. It allows the spirits to anchor to a person or place where the bone fragment has been placed. All of us wore them because it gave us more power and enabled us to hear the spirits much easier. They are placed in a special container on the statue and during each ceremony they are empowered by the spirits."

"I saw that the night I was there," Jamie offered, remembering her ordeal.

"Syrasohan was one mad spirit the night you escaped," Patty related. "I thought he was going to destroy Walter for allowing you to escape until they realized that the angels had been responsible for your rescue. They were sure mad about the siren. That was the night I knew I had to get out, but I just couldn't." She started to cry and her mother held her close and comforted her. "Mom," she said as she wiped her eyes, "it was only your prayers every night that kept me and Billy from being killed. When Eddie and Mike killed themselves, Billy had been involved with pimping the girls earlier, too, but he said something told him to drop out of the 'business' and he did. A short time later the boys killed themselves. We both knew then it was your prayers that had protected him." Mrs. Geller looked at Father Macon and nodded her head in thanks. Father grinned as he patted her hand.

Everyone around the girl had heard her explanation and knew what had been accomplished there today. Father stood up and looked at the people.

"Ray, would you and James mind going into town and getting some plywood to fix the windows until we can get someone to repair the glass?"

"We'll be glad to, Father," Ray answered, looking at James and nodding.

"Sheila," Father continued, "why don't you and Jamie go with Mrs. Schratz after the sheriff calls the coroner. I'm afraid her husband was not equipped well enough to be here. The demons got him to run, and when he got outside a tree limb fell on him. Mrs. Schratz will need your support."

As he spoke, Father looked to the back of the church where the woman still sat, obviously shaken by what she had witnessed.

"I'll go too, Father," Eva spoke up as she too saw the poor lady sitting by herself in the back of church.

"Sheriff," Father said as he took a deep breath and turned back to face the law officer, "we know what we must do."

"I'll call in my deputies and tell them where we're going and to meet us there," the sheriff replied.

"I wouldn't do that, Father," Patty exclaimed as she realized that they were going to Walter Foust's place. "They have someone monitoring the scanners all the time."

"Father, I guess it's just me and you," the sheriff smiled as he turned to Ray. "Ray," he continued, "when you get in town, stop by the office and tell the boys where I'm at, and tell them I said to bring both cars."

Ray nodded as the group began to disperse and take up their

assignments. Father watched as Sheila, Eva, and Jamie went and sat down by Mrs. Schratz.

As he passed Jamie he tapped her on the shoulder. As she looked up, he said, "Have the rest of the people stay in the church and pray. This thing is not over yet."

She shook her head okay and then grabbed his hand. "You be careful," she warned.

He grinned, then winked as he walked out the back door with the sheriff. They walked to the sheriff's car and both men got in. The sheriff immediately picked up the radio and called the coroner's office. Mike answered. He told Mike to come out to St. Mark's and pick up a body. There had been an accident and a Mr. Schratz had been killed by a falling tree limb in the storm. Mike acknowledged the message, and said he would send the ambulance immediately.

The sheriff hung the radio back in its place and started the car. He put it in gear and headed out of the driveway. He knew the way to Walter Foust's farm and this was one trip he was not looking forward to.

"This may be dangerous, Father," he said, turning and looking at the priest. "Let's not take any chances."

"I don't intend to, sheriff," Father replied, "but I want to make sure we destroy that statue. We can always find Walter and his gang."

"What about the demons?" the sheriff asked.

"We've dealt them a pretty hard blow. Now is the time to go after their puppets. If the people in the church will continue to pray we should have the definite advantage."

They drove until they arrived at the gravel road that led to Walter's farm. It was still a mile to the actual home site.

"Turn on your siren," Father ordered.

"They'll hear us coming," the sheriff countered.

"They're going to hear us coming if we don't make some kind of distraction," Father Macon explained. "I'm hoping they'll think it's a false siren again, and write it off as another angelic trick."

"I hope you're right," the sheriff breathed as he flipped the button which turned on the siren. Immediately it began to blare.

"Let's go after them," Father smiled, pointing his finger down the road toward the farm.

The distraction worked. As they pulled into the yard the sheriff saw four men run into the house.

"Remember what I said, Father," the sheriff warned. "Watch yourself."

The sheriff turned off the siren and the car and both of the men got out of the car. The sheriff took the latch strap off of his weapon but kept it in its holster. Cautiously they approached the front door of the house and knocked on the door. No one answered so the sheriff slowly opened it. As he did he pulled his revolver. The house was quiet as they entered. Father followed close behind the sheriff but also kept watching behind them. They started into the kitchen when they heard the back door slam. Sheriff Martin ran to the window in time to see one of the men run to the barn and the other three hurriedly get into a car. He watched as the men backed the car around and sped off down the road they had just arrived on. He turned to Father Macon. "Father," he exclaimed, "one of them ran to the barn, the other three are getting away. You go after the one in the barn and I'll go after the three in the car."

Father nodded as they both hurriedly ran back out the front door. Father Macon ran toward the barn door as he watched the sheriff climb in his car and take out after the three men. He could still see the dust in the air stirred up by the wheels of the men's speeding car. When he got to the barn door, he carefully opened it. It opened into what appeared to be nothing more than a barn. There was hay equipment stored in the room in front of him and there appeared to be no doors anywhere that he could see. He remembered what Patty had said about the barn and he began to look for a hidden door. He quietly checked each board plank but nothing seemed to be movable. He made it around the entire circumference of the room and found nothing. Then he noticed an area of hay on the floor of the barn that was caught under some of the boards. He wondered how the hay could have been shoved up under the planks unless it had been drug under there when the door opened. He walked over to the boards and to his surprise found a place that looked like it didn't quite fit together with the other boards. He pulled on the board and it moved enough for him to realize that it was the door. He pulled it open enough for him to enter.

The sheriff had chased the car until he was right on their bumper. He could tell by the way the driver was handling the car that he was not very skilled in fast car driving. He had nearly lost control on two of the curves. The sheriff called the other deputies who had already started toward Engleton. Ray had come by and informed them about what was going on.

"Get the state boys on the line," he spoke into the radio, "and have them set up a road block just back this side of the state line. I'm not sure which way these boys are headed but right now they're driving north on the old Dombacker Road. If we keep going this way they'll have to cross the river over the old steel bridge."

The sheriff watched the driver once more almost lose control of the car. He thought about trying to shoot the tires out on the vehicle but decided against maybe losing control of his own car. He knew he had them if he would just be patient. They really had no place to run.

"Sheriff," the radio said, "Deputy Forester here. I'm coming around by the highway and will set up a block across the east end of the steel bridge. My ETA is approximately four minutes. Will that be enough time?"

The sheriff listened and then picked up the radio. "Forester, this is the sheriff. We are still on old Dombacker road. We are approximately two miles from the intersection that leads to either the Engleton highway or the steel bridge. I'm almost certain they will take the road east and come your way. Get in position and wait. I'll let you know when we get to the intersection."

The car continued to swerve all over the gravel road. After a few minutes the sheriff saw the brake lights come on indicating that they had reached the intersection. "Please go right," the sheriff prayed as he knew they should decide any second.

"Yes," he exclaimed as he saw the car in front of him turn right and increase its speed as it again headed down the gravel road.

"Forester," the sheriff calmly spoke into the radio, "they're heading your way. Block the east end of the bridge and stand clear. We've got them. They'll be on you in about three minutes."

The road was fairly straight as it headed almost parallel to the river until it got to within two hundred yards of the bridge. Then it made a sharp turn and came up over a levee just before it came to the bridge. This meant that the men would not see the deputy's car until right before they got to the bridge.

The sheriff started to put a little pressure on them by nudging their bumper. This caused the driver to speed up in an attempt to outrun the nuisance. The sheriff backed off a little as the men made the sharp bend in the road then again increased their speed. He backed off even more as they approached the bridge, in anticipation of the men seeing the deputy's car and trying to turn around and come back at him. Instead, they charged the bridge full speed. The sheriff came to a stop and watched as the car got to the bridge. Suddenly it whipped right, caught the loose gravel then grazed the side of the bridge and flew off into the air like a stunt car. It sailed through the air, then went out of sight as it dropped below the brush-line on the banks of the river. The sheriff could see the deputy running on the bridge. He gunned his car and drove to the edge of the bridge. He jumped out and ran to the railing of the bridge just in time to see the top of the car go under water.

"Think I ought to go in, sheriff?" the deputy asked, starting to unbutton his shirt.

"I don't think it's any use," the sheriff replied, "the water's too swift here, and I don't want to take a chance on losing you." They watched as air bubbles continued to surface in the current, but no sign of life appeared.

"You call the state boys and have them get the diving team up here," the sheriff ordered. "I'm going back to the Foust farm. Father Macon is there alone."

The young deputy nodded his head and ran back to his car as the sheriff turned and ran back to his vehicle. He quickly turned it around in the road and headed back toward the farm. "Please, Lord Jesus," he prayed, "let Father be okay."

As Father Macon eased his way into the hidden room, the hair stood up on the back of his neck. He could feel the evil in the room. The candles that lined the walls were the only source of light except for the ray of sunlight that was coming from the loft above the room. He carefully surveyed the room and his eyes stopped as they found the altar. It was just as Jamie had described it and in its center stood the statue.

He started to make his way toward the altar when he heard something move in the loft above him. He saw the ladder leading to the loft over in the corner and he slowly made his way over to it. As he climbed it, he listened and watched above him. When he reached the top, he waited before he looked over into the loft area. Finally, and with a deep breath he peered over into the loft. He saw nothing but hay bales and piles of household junk. Old bottles and furniture lined the walls. Things hung from the rafters. He watched for any movement as he climbed onto the floor of the loft. The light was coming from the hole in the side where bales of hay were elevated and pushed into the hay loft. He walked toward the opening. Suddenly his ribs ripped with pain as someone blind-sided him and pulled him to the floor. He wrestled with the individual, slugging and hitting the person with his hand. He could feel the pain as the other person also slugged Father with his fist and kicked with his knees. They wrestled around on the floor until they rolled into the wall. The sudden jolt enabled Father to break away and get to his feet. As he watched, the other person quickly stood up. He recognized him as Walter Foust.

"This is one time when there's no one to help you, Father Dead Man," Walter snorted as he ran toward Father, butting him to the floor, then once again slugging him with his fist. Father put his feet to the chest of the man and pushed him back. Walter flew through the air and fell backwards against one of the pole supports. Father stood up, dazed and shaken. He noticed that his feet were only a foot or so from the hay opening. He tried to move but his feet felt like lead. His head began to swim and he knew he was about to pass out.

Walter scrambled to his feet and saw the priest standing in front of the hay opening. "Say hello to your defeated God, Jesus, when you see Him," Walter screamed as he charged the silhouetted form of the priest, intending to knock him through the opening to the ground below.

Father Macon watched the blurred form of Walter Foust charging toward him. He again tried with all his might to move, but his body would not cooperate. He heard the fiendish laugh of the madman as he charged headlong toward him with his arms extended in front of him. Just as his hands reached Father's chest, Father felt something grab his arm and pull him down to the side. "Ahhhh," he heard Walter cry as he watched the man's momentum carry him over himself and out of the hole of the barn loft. Father lay there as he heard Walter's scream end with a heavy thump on the ground below.

His head continued to spin as he lay on his back breathing heavily. Slowly, after several minutes, his strength began to return, and he carefully climbed to his feet. He steadied himself on the side of the barn, then walked over to the opening and looked down. He made the sign of the Cross as he saw the crumpled and lifeless body of Walter Foust on the ground below.

He took his time slowly climbing back down the ladder to the room below. He looked around the room to make sure no one else was around and then walked to the altar. The statue was as hideous as Jamie had described it. And it was, indeed, the statue that they had carried out of the tomb in Iraq. He scanned the room until he found a piece of loose two-by-four lying against the wall. He picked it up and walked back over to the altar. He stood before the statue and raised the piece of wood high in the air.

"In the Name of Jesus," he yelled as he brought the two by four down against the clay statue. The impact sent pieces of the false god flying through the air in all directions. Suddenly, the barn began to shake as he continued to pulverize the clay statue. The fire from the candles began to increase. Many exploded like Roman candles. Fragments of the fire hit the floor, setting fire to the scattered hay. The fire quickly spread, and the flames were growing in intensity as Father finished crushing the last piece of the clay god to dust.

He took his handkerchief and placed it over his mouth as he attempted to find the hidden door through all the smoke. At last, he found the section of boards, pushed it opened and walked out into the area that led to the outside. He followed along the wall until he found the barn door. He pushed it opened and staggered out into the sunlight. Flames were already coming out of the sides and roof of the barn as he made his way over to Foust's body, grabbed the lifeless form and began to drag it away from the heat of the burning building. He was standing over the man's body, watching the barn go up in flames, when the sheriff pulled his car in behind him.

"You all right, Father?" he asked as he opened the door and leaned over it with his radio in hand.

"I'm fine," he answered. "I think it's finally over."

CHAPTER TWENTY

THE RESURRECTION

The sheriff notified the state police and the coroner's office and within thirty minutes the farm was crawling with law officers. Father Macon told his story to the sheriff, and the sheriff informed Father of the results of the chase. When Father got to the part where he was suddenly jerked out of the path of the charging lunatic, the sheriff grinned and clapped his hands in praise of such a protecting God.

"I began to worry about you when I started back to the farm," he revealed, "but then, a sense of peace came over me, and I knew you were all right."

"I'm just sorry that all the evidence is gone," Father replied as he watched the barn still burning but now just smoldering flames and smoke.

"There's plenty of evidence for those who want to see," the sheriff responded, "The killings, the weird cloud, the church, the car in the river, this farm. How much does anyone need before they believe?"

"I wish I knew," Father replied as they watched the coroner's assistant load the body of Walter Foust into the ambulance and then, with lights blaring, speed down the gravel road back toward town.

"How will we really know if it's over?" the sheriff asked, finally breaking the silence as they continued to stare down the road at the retreating cloud of dust.

"Only time will tell us that," Father answered. "Things should, however, begin to improve around here."

"I certainly hope so," the sheriff agreed. He watched the state investigation team coming in and out of the house with their equipment, then slapped Father on the back. "Why don't we head back to the church and check on everyone there. It looks as if the state boys have everything pretty well in hand here."

Father agreed and they walked back to the sheriff's car.

It was getting late by the time they arrived back at the church. The men of the team had temporarily repaired the church windows and the women had cleaned up the interior. Many of the song books were destroyed and some of the carpet was ruined, but except for the windows, the church had survived a pretty awesome attack. It would take a few days to clean up all the debris outside. A few of the larger trees were down, and there were tree limbs everywhere. They would need some chain saws and trucks to clear all the brush and fallen debris from the area. It looked as if a tornado had hit just within a perimeter of a few hundred feet around the church.

Ray and James stopped their clean up and walked toward the sheriff's car as it pulled to a stop in the church parking lot. The others slowly made their way there also as Ray and James greeted Father Macon and the sheriff. The ladies that had gone with Mrs. Schratz had not made it back yet, but everyone else gathered around the two men in order to hear them share what had happened at the Foust farm.

"Let's all go over to the parish hall," Father encouraged, "and we'll tell you what happened. I will say this now, however, Jesus Christ is Lord of all!"

The crowd broke forth in cheers and praise as they all turned and headed for the parish hall, anxious to hear the details.

Once in the hall, everyone took a seat and Father began to tell the story of the barn. Everyone applauded and cheered when Father shared the part where some unseen force had pulled him out of harm's way. He told them that it was only through their prayers that he had been saved and thanked them all for responding to the call of God and giving of their time and talents. They applauded again as he finished. He then asked the sheriff to relate the story of the chase and give the details surrounding the car crashing into the river. The sheriff was just finishing his account when Sheila, Jamie and Eva walked into the room. They stood together in the corner as they listened to the sheriff finish his story then as everyone got up to prepare for supper, Father quickly filled the three women in on what they had missed. Jamie was glad that the barn had burned. No one would ever have to undergo what she had gone through in that place.

After supper Father announced that they should all get a good night's sleep, then in the morning they would have a Mass of celebration in praise and honor for what God had done for the community of Engleton. As he finished, the room again broke forth in spontaneous singing and praise. Father loved being with these people.

He left the parish hall and walked the sheriff back to his car. Neither of them spoke until they reached the vehicle and the sheriff opened the door. He turned and looked at Father. "I'll let you know the report on the car in the river when I get it from the state. I'm guessing that we'll find Walter's brother and the man Patty called Phozral as two of the three men I saw get into the automobile."

"I sure appreciate your help and support through all of this, sheriff," Father Macon confided. "You were one of the few I could trust and count on."

The sheriff grinned, then laid his hand on Father's hand. "My eyes were opened more than they have ever been." He paused as his voice wavered from his emotions, then he continued. "God allowed me to experience something here that few people are allowed to witness. I saw things in that church that make some of today's horror movies look like Mr. Rogers' Neighborhood. I figure that, in itself, is quite a blessing, and I don't intend to take it lightly. I don't know what I'm going to do, but the rest of my life will be devoted to serving the Lord."

Tears came to Father's eyes as he pulled the sheriff to himself and they embraced.

"Take care, sheriff, and thanks again," Father spoke as they broke and the sheriff climbed into his car.

Sheriff Martin nodded and waved as Father watched him pull out of the parking lot and onto the highway.

He was still standing there when he felt someone gently grab his hand. He turned and found Jamie standing next to him.

"God is good, Father Rex Macon," she said as she saw the tears still in his eyes.

"All the time," Father laughed as he pulled her to himself and hugged her.

"What's going to happen now?" she asked as she enjoyed the feeling of being next to him.

"We'll just have to see what God has planned," he replied. "I'm hoping on Sunday that we can all share with the people of Engleton and let them know what really went on here. Faith, you know, comes by hearing. Maybe now they'll realize that they have been blessed by God to have been chosen to receive so much grace. Hopefully they will see the light and put that light to good use."

"I've decided," she said as she pulled away from him, "to go with James and Sheila. She's invited me to stay with them for a while and maybe check out some of the Bible colleges over in Oklahoma."

"I think that's wonderful," Father said encouragingly. "Sheila and James are both very well versed in the anointing of God. They will be able to teach you a lot. You can see how dedicated to the Lord they, and all the people with them, are."

She nodded her head and began to cry. "I'm going to miss you so much," she sobbed.

Father again took her in his arms. "I know and I'm going to miss you, too. You're the only reason I have ever questioned my role as a priest, but you know that we all have so much work to do, and I can best do mine while wearing this collar."

"I know," she replied, still crying, "but I'm going to pray everyday that your church changes its rules about priests getting married."

"You'll be the first one to know," he laughed as he gently squeezed her.

"Promise?" she asked, wiping her eyes.

"Scout's honor," he responded, pulling away and holding up a scout's salute.

She laughed, then unexpectedly raised up and kissed him on the lips. It caught him off guard, but she quickly turned and ran back toward the parish hall.

The Mass the next day was wonderful. Even some of the people from the community came. It was a true celebration. The excitement was catching, and soon everyone in the church was raising their hands and praising God for His wondrous deeds.

Sheriff Martin called and informed Father that he had been right about the men in the car. One of them was Walter's brother, the other one was indeed Phozral, who was, in reality, a Larry Bentley from Kansas City, Missouri. The third man was identified as Glen Crandle, a man from Baton Rouge, Louisiana. He also said that the state investigation team had found a hidden room in the basement of Walter's home. It contained thousands of pornographic video tapes including some that had been made of the rituals and ceremonies there at the barn. They had also found enough evidence to prove that they were also dealing drugs from the farm. He said the farm would be confiscated by the state and sold at auction. Father again thanked him for his help, and asked him if he would come and talk to the people on Sunday. He said he would be honored to speak.

By the time Sunday came, word had gotten around in the community, and the church was packed. They used all of the folding chairs from the parish hall and there were still people standing along the walls. After Mass, Father told them everything that had happened with the principality. The church was as quiet as a morgue while he talked. He then asked the sheriff to share his story about the barn, the men involved, Elizabeth's autopsy, and how the entire episode had touched his life and made him understand how much he needed Jesus in his life. Some of the visitors shared their experience with the storm and the demons in the church, and how they were blessed to be a part of the ordeal.

Father had Patty Geller tell of how she had been lured into the whole thing, and how it had slowly turned her into a zombie with no conscience. She encouraged all of the young people involved to repent, go to confession, and get rid of everything that was associated with the coven. Finally, Ray and Eva shared how they had been affected by the battle, and how they now knew what living a life for Christ was all about.

The people of Engleton sat spellbound by each speaker, and as

Ray and Eva finished they began to applaud, first one, then many. They began to rise as they stood together and continued to applaud. As the noise died down, Father led the people in singing, "Amazing Grace."

He could tell, as the people left, that there was a new vigor in them. He rejoiced as he stood at the door of the church and greeted each family. The team from Rogers had prepared a lunch in the parish hall for everyone who had attended the meeting. Many people came up to Father and thanked him for what he had done for their community. Several of them even wanted to know how they could learn more about spiritual warfare.

After everyone had left, the team finished cleaning up the hall and made preparations to head back to Rogers. He thanked each couple individually and gave them a blessing. He told them that the people of Engleton would always remember their fellow saints from the west who had helped them conquer the darkness. As each couple climbed aboard their vehicle to leave, Father made his way to James and Sheila's motor-home. They, along with Jamie, were waiting for him.

"I don't know how I'll ever repay you all," he said as he approached them.

"God will do the repaying, Father," Sheila was quick to respond. "In reality, this is what every one of us is called to do. Remember the kingdom of God suffers violence, and the violent take it by force!"

"If only every one of us knew that," he laughed as he hugged each one of them, pausing as he hugged Jamie.

"Somehow," Sheila continued, "I think we're going to learn before this whole thing ends. How many more communities across this world are held in bondage by a principality like Syrasohan? When people finally get their can full, maybe they'll realize that we battle not against flesh and blood but against powers and principalities in the heavenlies."

"I hope you're right, Sheila," Father agreed, as he watched each one of them climb into the cab of the big motor home. He could see the tears on Jamie's face as he helped her up the step into the cab. Sheila stood back as she allowed Jamie to sit in the passenger's seat. As James fired up the engine, Jamie rolled down the window and stuck her head out. With tears still flowing down her cheeks she looked down at Father Macon. As the big wheels began to roll she cried, "I love you."

"I know," he replied as the tears came to his eyes, too.

It was a sad sight as each big motor home or trailer fell into single file and pulled out of the parking lot onto the highway. God's Cavalry was heading back home. As he watched the last big vehicle roll out of sight he wondered, what has God wrought?

Father Macon stayed on at St. Mark's and things did change. The people began to realize that all their efforts had been directed toward this short period of time we call life, and they had failed to understand the importance of eternity.

Jamie stayed with James and Sheila for about six months, then enrolled in a Bible college in Oklahoma. She still stayed in contact with Father Macon by letter and sometimes by phone. There was not a day that went by that she didn't pray for him and for the rules of the church. He always enjoyed hearing about what she was learning and always encouraged her to share her knowledge of Jesus with others.

Toward the end of her second semester she received a letter from him. She couldn't wait to get back to her room and read it. As she unfolded it, she read:

Dear Jamie,

May our Lord and Savior Jesus Christ be with you and bless you abundantly. I hope your studies are progressing well. I thought I would write and share some of the good news that's happening in Engleton.

Ray and Eva have been accepted into the diaconate program in the church. They are so excited. Mrs. Geller and some of the other divorced women have started a support group for single and divorced women, and they have started a day care in the parish hall for working mothers.

Patty and Billy Geller have started a prayer group for the teens. It has really grown. Even some young people from Bettis Bluff are attending. Billy says that when he graduates this summer he plans to go into the seminary and study to become a priest.

Sheriff Martin resigned as sheriff, and he and his wife are preparing with some others in their church for missionary work in Central America.

Mike, the coroner, is in our adult education program and will join the church this Easter.

Two other couples have started a program for those who have trouble with alcohol, and we have a great charismatic prayer group that meets every Tuesday night. There are more young people there than adults and it is growing each week.

Something is going on in the parish hall or church every night. People are coming to understand the power of prayer and community.

The bishop has been so impressed with the community's turn around that he wants to talk to me about giving some spiritual warfare seminars around the diocese. God has certainly turned the awful ordeal into a wondrous and glorious testimony to His faithfulness and to His power.

I know you will always be blessed and honored by God for what you went through to help bring this wonderful change into being. God has magnificent plans for you. Just be obedient to His voice.

I miss your beautiful smile and if you can see yourself clear this summer, I might see if Bob and Mary might let us borrow the cabin again. What do you think?

I'd better run, it's time for confessions and I'm late. Take care and I'll talk to you later.

Love,
Father Rex

P.S. The stained glass is all fixed in the church and the O'Learys purchased a new statue of Archangel Michael to replace the one that fell. It looks fantastic.

As Jamie closed the letter, she wiped her eyes and quickly pulled out the calendar in her top dresser drawer. "What day does school end this summer?" she said out loud.

The Last Word:

Some readers may think that no one can be as spiritually strong as Father Rex Macon. I personally believe there are many. I have seen numerous individuals who understand the value of eternal life.

There is a life after death and those who really understand have made the decision to opt for eternity rather than the seventy odd years we may enjoy on this physical plane.

Where will you spend eternity? The decision is yours and yours alone.

There is One who waits for you to make that decision. His name is Jesus. He suffered and died two thousand years ago so that you might enjoy the splendor of His heavenly Kingdom. Just as in the novel, He overcame sin and darkness and now empowers anyone who will ask with His precious Holy Spirit.

If you would like to know Him better, just ask. He wants the best for you not only now but for all eternity. Pray this prayer:

Lord Jesus, something is missing in my life and my heart is telling me that it is You. I repent of my sins, the things I have been involved with, and now I ask You to be my Savior. Come into my life and become my Lord. I renounce Satan and all his evil works. I give You my life, Jesus. Amen.

If you prayed this prayer and meant it, then you have sealed your fate for eternity. The Kingdom of God is yours. All that remains is learning how the Kingdom functions. That is the job of the Holy Spirit. He is a faithful Guide and Teacher. Learn to yield to His voice and to His prompting. If you're not already going to church, find one that can assist you in your growth and be diligent in your study.

I'll see you in eternity somewhere around the Throne.

Other Books by Dennis Holt

Presented by
CORNELIUS' HOUSE MINISTRIES
Available online at: www.corneliushouse.com

Handbook To Heaven – Reclaiming The Kingdom

The Kingdom of God

The Covenant

Living a Life in the Spirit
(Manual: A seven week course)

The Principality – A Novel

The Manitou – A Novel

The Anakim – A Novel

All books are available from: Cornelius' House Ministries
3115 Pyburn Extended
Pocahontas, Arkansas 72455
www. corneliushouse.com

THE WARFARE CONTINUES...

THE MANITOU
A NOVEL

An old relic is discovered while clearing the way for a new state road. It causes the local sheriff to become involved with the supernatural as he attempts to determine the source and the purpose of the old relic. His investigation points to the lost treasure of DeSoto, but something very strange seems to be guarding the treasure's resting place. With the help of Dr. Marion James, a beautiful archaeologist, and Chief Walking Cloud, an old Indian medicine man, he tries to solve the mystery and recover the treasure.

In their search, they encounter the awesome power of a strong evil presence. Each one of them is forced to face the turmoil that lies hidden within their own soul. Drawn into its evil snare, they realize that they must find someone who can provide an answer.

Responding to their plea, Father Rex Macon helps them to discern that only through sacrifice can the evil be defeated. Will they choose to make that sacrifice or will they become victims of the MANITOU?